A Crown in Time

Jennifer Macaire

ACCENT

First published in 2020 by Headline Accent
An imprint of HEADLINE PUBLISHING GROUP

1

Cataloguing in Publication Data is available from the British Library

ISBN 978 1 7861 5776 8

Typeset in 10.5/13pt Bembo Std by Jouve (UK), Milton Keynes

Printed and bound in Great Britain by Clays Ltd, Elcograf S.p.A.

HEADLINE PUBLISHING GROUP
An Hachette UK Company
Carmelite House
50 Victoria Embankment
London
EC4Y 0DZ

www.headline.co.uk
www.hachette.co.uk

I'd like to dedicate *A Crown In Time*
to my father, Robert Berroyer.
I miss you, Dad.

Chapter One

Pax in nomine Domini

Peace in the name of the Lord

The nurse in charge of freezing my molecules inserted a glowing needle into my arm and had me count backwards from ten. I got to zero and stared at her, perplexed.

'Now what?'

'Again.'

I obeyed without question. Years of prison had left their mark.

Then a cold wave washed through me. I felt my blood freeze. No one had told me it would be so painful. My teeth chattered and the place where the needle was inserted into my arm ached and ached. The pain grew. Frost bloomed in silver flowers on my hands and face.

The pain was so intense I passed out. My last thought before I fainted was that despite all the work and planning, the program would now lose its Corrector.

I was dying.

I didn't die. I woke up lying on my back in the middle of a large mud puddle. Rain pelted my face, and my body convulsed with painful tremors. Groaning, I rolled over and propped myself up on my forearms. I retched and gagged, waves of nausea rolling through me. I tried to stand, but my legs wouldn't hold me. I crawled off the road and collapsed on the verge. I had no idea why I'd been beamed into the middle of a road. I could have been killed.

I looked closer at the road and sighed. If anything was going to come down it, it would probably be an ox plodding before a heavy farm cart. The farmer would have been able to stop in time. Unlike me. I hadn't been able to stop my car in time. I'd killed a child, and I'd been punished with life in a reproduction prison. For four years, I lay on a metal table once a month and donated an ovule, and in between, I worked at the prison library, copying ancient books and disks onto gel matrix for safekeeping.

Then one day, I'd been given a choice. Go back in time and change a mistake, or continue to live in solitude, where my only jobs had been to produce eggs and reproduce books. I'd been twenty years old when I went to prison. Twenty-four when I entered the Corrector Program at Tempus University, and now I was twenty-five, though I knew nothing of life. I felt both ancient and absurdly young. I'd barely had time to start living my own life when it ended. Now, I had the chance at a new beginning. If only I could remember what that was.

My mission now lay before me. I closed my eyes and tried to remember exactly what I had to do. Unfortunately, there seemed to be an empty space in my brain where that information was supposed to be. I couldn't remember the first thing about it. I shivered with panic and cold. If my mission failed, the Time Correctors Facility from Tempus U would erase this portion of time, and I'd be erased along with it. I would never have existed past the day I entered the Tempus University Time Corrector Program. In the far future, it would be as if I stepped inside the doors of that building and simply vanished. The part of the past that was out of sync would be erased as well, and history rewritten to fit what had originally happened. At least, that's what I had been told. I honestly had no idea what really happened, and I had no wish to find out.

I closed my eyes, took several deep breaths, and saw the image of a crown. It was coming back to me. I had to meet someone. I had to save the future crown of France by befriending a young boy and convincing him not to join the ill-fated Eighth Crusade. I knew his name: Jean. I even knew what he looked like, thanks to a time-travelling journalist's holograms. I knew where he'd be on a certain date. I wasn't sure where *I* was, though.

I sat up and looked around. The squall had blown over and the sun peeked from behind the clouds. The road stretched to my right and left, bordered by fields and dark copses. I wiped the mud off my dress as best I could and thought of my mission. It had all happened because of a mistake.

Time travel was reserved for a select few – mostly highly trained journalists chosen to go back in time and interview famous people. The journalist who'd caused the error I'd been sent to correct had spoken of the crusade in front of a boy who should never have heard about it. The man had taken holograms, as per regulation, but carelessly, he hadn't checked to make sure nobody else listened to his interview with Queen Marguerite.

Jean de Bourbon-Dampierre had been near enough to hear. On the hologram, he cocked his head as the journalist began to speak. Because of what he'd overheard, the boy had slipped out of his bedroom one night and run away to join a ragtag gaggle of youngsters on their way to fight the infidel.

Jean would not do anything of note during his life, but his descendants would eventually rule France. By running away, he'd changed the course of history dramatically.

I was supposed to find him and bring him back. If I succeeded, I'd be allowed to live the rest of my life in the thirteenth century. If not, I'd be erased, along with all the mistakes the journalist had wrought in only two sentences. Just two little sentences which had been approved for the queen, but not for Jean de Bourbon-Dampierre, who had been visiting the court that day.

'*My Queen Marguerite, what have you heard of the crusade your husband, the King of France, has embarked upon? What about the group of youths calling themselves crusaders who have nearly reached Chartres?*'

The words had echoed weirdly around the room, and that evening, Jean packed a few belongings in a leather bag and clambered nimbly down a castle wall in search of adventure and a way to get out of his Latin studies.

3

My mission was simple – get time back on track.

Time travel was invented in 2300 and used for short trips into the past. At first, trips were only possible with inanimate objects, primarily those made of quartz crystal.

When it was perfected in 2900, Tempus University, already an elite institution, started their reporting program. Because their time in the past was limited, researchers and historians had to make the most of it. It was decided that specially trained journalists would concentrate on interviewing famous people. Some early experiences were resounding successes: Shakespeare, Julius Caesar, and Marie Curie gave fascinating interviews.

Other interviews were failures – Jesus, for example, remained elusive. Some trips simply didn't work out because the journalist was in the wrong place or the wrong time, but they usually came back alive.

The science of time travel is kept deliberately vague. I think it's so that the Tempus Program will never face any competition. Not that they'd allow it. As far as I could gather from my own experience, two enormous electromagnets are placed above and below a chair made of pure quartz crystal. A lightning bolt is teased out of the sky, and its electric current is passed through the beam of magnetic pull, and the resulting 'force field' is able to send whatever is in that chair to another place and time.

Time travel can only happen during a storm. I gather it has something to do with the particular resonance of the quartz molecules with lightning, but that's just from overheard conversations. Nobody felt they needed to explain it to a mere Corrector, especially not one taken out of the prison system.

When I'd started the mission, I was sceptical. Selected from thousands of prisoners because of my background as a French history major, I still didn't believe I could make a difference. There were other ways of correcting a major mistake. The TCF could have erased a large enough portion of history to accommodate the changes the journalist had wrought.

However, the energy expended in such an endeavour was enormous and cost an astronomical sum. It's the last resort. Don't ask me how it's done it's used only in dire need. Mostly, they use Correctors like me to set time right.

What's the difference between a Corrector and a journalist, you ask? When a journalist is sent back in time, he or she is left there for exactly twenty hours and then brought back with the magnetic beam to fame and fortune.

When a Corrector is sent back in time to correct a mistake, they are left there to fend for themselves for ever. It's a life sentence. Usually the 'volunteer' is taken out of prison. I'd had one year to learn everything I needed to know to survive in a world two thousand years removed from my own. I had a limited chance of survival, but if I did my job well I'd receive a full pardon and my name in the roster of Humanitarian Awards. What an honour! From a criminal to a hero in the space of a day. This was how long it would take the TCF to verify my work in the history book, located in a vacuum at the North Pole.

Because face it, how could anyone know if time had actually been changed? If you changed the past, you automatically changed the future, right? Wrong. Well, almost wrong. Most of the butterfly theory is correct. Little things can have enormous consequences. However, big things, things you assume would alter history, are usually swallowed up in what scientists call the 'Molasses Theory of Time'.

To make sure time isn't changed in any irrevocable way, scientists placed a detailed history book in a permanent molecular magnetic beam located in the exact centre of the magnetic pole of the Earth. The beam doesn't send the book anywhere, but it does keep it from becoming altered. A replica of the book is kept in another room, in a normal environment. After each time trip the books are compared. The differences show up within a day. Any discrepancies are fed into a computer and the results analyzed.

If there is no danger of time moving from its flow, then the book is closed and everything continues on its way. If, however, the changes make the flow of time deviate, then something is done to put it right. Within a year, a 'volunteer' Corrector is found and trained and sent to live and die in the past. After that, the possibility of correcting time becomes improbable and likely to influence the present in calamitous ways. Or so it's theorized. Possible time change has never been allowed to go that far. The TCF *always* erases it.

Because of the high cost, little alterations to the continuum are ignored, and time, like thick molasses, keeps flowing as it should. Those changes never affect our present because the flow of time tends to glide over flaws without a bubble in its surface. Nor does the history book have the name and date of birth of every human being who ever lived on Earth. The faceless mass remains anonymous. A person could go back in time and fade into the background, and no one would ever be the wiser if he did his job well.

I got to my feet and looked around, but there were no signposts or any indication where I should go. Finally I shrugged, chose a direction at whim, and started down the road. I had no idea if I was going in the right direction, but I knew I'd eventually find out. Besides, I had to go somewhere, right? At the first crossroads a sign would likely tell me which way to get to Chartres, where I had to find a certain Jean de Bourbon-Dampierre.

I walked all day. The city of Chartres, a prosperous town of about a thousand souls, was on a flat plain, and the cathedral was visible for kilometres. Unfortunately I'd started in the wrong direction and it was only three hours later that I discovered my mistake and had to retrace my steps on the rutted dirt road.

Seven hours of walking in perfect freedom after five years of prison life. Seven hours of walking in a straight line, more or less, after years of walking around and around a courtyard. I saw grass and blue sky, although the grass was still dead, it being early March, and the sky was a frosty grey-blue that promised cold weather. I didn't mind. I was free. The feeling was intoxicating. The road stretched empty to my left and to my right for several kilometres. The very tip of the cathedral spire showed in the distance.

My head spun, and I had to sit down. I gazed ruefully at my feet in their thick leather shoes. They were well broken in because I'd walked with them for six months in the prison. It wasn't that my shoes, or my feet, hurt. It was the fact my stomach was empty and hunger was making me dizzy. I would have to wait until I found an inn, though, I had nothing to eat with me. I had nothing but the clothes I wore, my shoes, and a small leather pouch full of coins and a few trifles the historians at the TCF had allowed me to take. I groped for my purse and panicked when I didn't find it right away. When I found it I sighed with relief, but a new worry assailed me. Most of my apprehension came from the thought of not being able to complete my mission in time. What if the boy was not here? What if I'd been sent back to the wrong day, or even year? I bit my knuckles and tried to empty my mind. It was easier to bear if I just didn't think about it.

When I recovered my calm, I dug the purse out of my deep pocket and opened it. The coins inside were supposed to last me two years. There were three heavy gold ones, some silver and many, many copper and bronze coins. I took the gold coins from the purse and weighed them in my hand. They were valuable, and if I lost them or if anyone stole them, I'd be in trouble. I didn't know how likely theft was, but I didn't want to take a chance.

I searched in my leather pouch for the sewing kit. It was an antique, probably from a museum. The TCF historians had approved some of the items on the list of things I'd asked for, and this was one of them. I sewed the gold coins into the inside waist seam of my kirtle. Perhaps I should have done it before. It hadn't occurred to me then, but now the reality of my situation hit me. I spaced them evenly and made sure that they were secure. Then I did the same with the silver coins. One silver coin I put back in my purse.

My clothes had been made by historians. I wore a linen under-shirt, also called a chemise. Over that, I wore a sleeveless gown – the kirtle – and for warmth I had a cloak. Kirtle and cloak were made of finely woven wool. The undershirts were plain linen. I had woollen stockings that tied over the knee, and a coif, which was a head cov-ering made of bleached linen, to cover my hair. Everything had been well but plainly made. However, laces now tightened waists and gores flared skirts. Fashion had just started.

I didn't have many belongings. In a leather pouch, worn tied to my belt, I had the sewing kit, a change of undershirts, a cake of soap, and a few simple pieces of jewellery, which I could sell if need be. I had nothing else. Even my bones had been treated to remove any trace of modern surgery. There was nothing to show I came from the future, down to my fillings that had been replaced by an ivory-coloured composite that wouldn't shout 'Strange Person from the Future!' even if I died and was dug up centuries later. (The Time Senders think of everything, believe me.)

The only thing I hadn't changed was my face. A jagged scar down one side from temple to chin, sectioning my lower lip and ending halfway down my throat. It was a fearsome scar, but I had refused all offers to have it erased.

As I walked towards Chartres, the cathedral spire grew like a pine tree pushing itself out of the ground. Then the rest of the town's buildings sprouted around it. Rooftops and chimneys rose out of the grey fields, and stone houses grew like squat mushrooms. Bare fruit trees, shrubs, and winter gardens appeared. I spotted a few people outside, hurrying through the gathering dusk.

The road I walked went straight across a flat plain, but Chartres crouched in a slight depression upon the banks of a river. The last things that came to my view were the main street, winding around the base of the massive cathedral, and the sullen black river flowing sluggishly under the bridge.

I wanted to find an inn, eat something hot, and lie down in a soft feather bed. At the entrance to the town, the gatekeeper directed me to the only inn, a large stone building near the church. To my relief, his words were easy for me to understand. The historians had done their job well, and I'd had many holograms and tapes from this period to learn the language and familiarize myself with the environment. The tight knot in my chest eased somewhat as I approached the tavern and peered inside.

A huge cauldron simmered inside the great chimney and the scent of roasting meat made my mouth water painfully. I rapped my knuckles on the lead-paned window and waited until a woman opened the door.

'I'd like a room for the night and some food, please,' I said.

'No rooms left here, and the dinner won't be served until after vespers.' The voice was quiet but firm. Before I could open my mouth again the door was shut, the latch dropped and I found myself leaning against the wall in order to stand upright. For a moment I wanted to cry. My face screwed up, and I pressed my cheek on the rough stone and closed my eyes.

'Pardon, Mademoiselle?' The voice came from behind me, and I turned wearily.

Two blue eyes stared at me from beneath thick black brows. The boy had a peaked face scored with deep lines of hunger and suffering that made him look ancient, although I doubted he was more than ten years old.

He stepped closer. 'If you're hungry, the Church has food for the crusaders. They're arriving and they want bread. Come with me, I'll show you. That's where I'm headed.'

I'd heard of bands of thieves that used children as bait. He'd probably lead me to an alley, where I'd be set upon and robbed. 'How do you know?'

His voice dropped confidentially. 'I'm joining the crusade. I want to go to the Holy Land.'

'I see.' I eyed him warily, but he didn't look like a thief. The fact that he was joining the crusades didn't surprise me. From what I'd learned, everyone wanted to go.

The crusades had been the world's first publicized event. Recruiters were everywhere, promising untold riches and salvation without repentance.

His face suddenly tightened. 'You won't be saying anything to Madame Latrainée, will you?'

'I don't know who she is. I just arrived in the city.'

'I know, I saw you coming down the road. I've been watching since yesterday, waiting for the crusaders.'

'And you've seen everyone who's come into the city?' I asked him, suddenly interested.

'Of course I did. At first I thought you were one of them, but you're all alone.'

'The crusaders in this group are nothing but poor peasant youths,' I said. This was from my memorized speech for dissuading Jean. 'They're heading straight for their deaths. Listen to me, er, what's your name?'

'Charles.' The boy looked at me sideways, his eyes a deep, navy blue.

'Sharl,' I pronounced it as he did. 'Listen to me. This crusade is ill-fated. These crusaders will never make it to the Holy Land. King Louis is only planning on landing in Tunis in order to establish forts from which to attack Egypt. It's far, far away from the Holy Land. What will happen if you are captured and sold into slavery?'

His steps faltered, and then he shrugged. 'A slave here or a slave there, what difference? Here I sleep in the stables, I have food when the master remembers to feed me, and I have clothes when I can steal them from the washerwomen at the river. Otherwise I am just a slave, *"do this, do that"*, and no hope to do anything else.' His voice broke and he frowned. 'I was thinking of running away to Paris, taking a chance there, and then I heard of the crusade. Maybe I'll have a better chance with them. At least they get fed when they come to town.'

I looked at my companion and for the first time noticed how dreadfully filthy he was. His hair was matted, snarled, probably crawling with lice. His face was not only peaked, it was pale and unhealthy. He held himself stiffly. I wouldn't be surprised to discover old fractures on his limbs from beatings he'd obviously suffered.

When he walked, he limped. I bit my lip again. Children made me cry. Whether they were healthy and happy, or miserable, they were all reminders of what I'd done.

My knees trembled and I leaned on a wall to stay upright. I took a deep breath.

'Charles, I, I . . .' I hesitated. What could I do to convince him?

10

I looked at the doomed child, his face drawn and illuminated with the fervour of faith and a terrible hope. Hope for a better life, hope that would be completely shattered.

My hand slid down the mossy wall as I sank to the ground, and my eyes brimmed with tears. It came to me just what punishment Tempus U had devised for me. I turned away from Charles. If I couldn't save this child, who *could* I save? It was hopeless.

'Are you all right? Shall I get help?' Charles sounded anxious. He poked my arm, then, when I failed to respond, pounded me on the back.

'I'm fine, I'll be fine.' I got to my feet and stared over his head at the huge church spire. Suddenly, bells began to toll. The air shook with each clang. Each hard ring broke the sky into a puzzle of grey pigeons flapping loudly through the evening. Each thunderous toll shook me from the soles of my feet to my head. My face vibrated with the sound.

Charles' little face blanched and he swallowed convulsively. 'Vespers is starting,' he said. 'We won't get anything now until it's over.'

'Well, we might as well sit down in the church.' I sniffed and wiped my face with the back of my hand. 'Let's go, shall we? Maybe our souls will be saved.'

'God forbid,' said Charles and crossed himself neatly.

I looked at him askance, surprised by his irreverence, but he just shrugged and led the way to the great stone cathedral.

Chapter Two

Time travel is reserved for an elite, highly trained few who are sent back for a few hours or days. However, on certain occasions, a Corrector is needed to rectify a mistake in the past. Correctors are sent on a one-way trip back in time with a specific mission. Correctors are both extremely important and disposable. Do your job well, and your name will appear on the gold board in the main hall of Tempus University. Fail, and you will be erased from Time.

Preface from Tempus University *Corrector's Handbook*

We arrived in the cathedral at the last stroke of the bells and just managed to squeeze onto a bench. Charles was as slight as a wraith and I wasn't much thicker, though I was tall. We were packed in, but we still shivered – the chill from the stone floor seeped up our legs.

At the front of the church, the noblemen and rich families had thick rugs under their private benches and bright coals in braziers burned warmly next to their pews. In the middle part of the church, townspeople had mats made of woven rushes underfoot. Here at the back were the peasants and the poor. Some of them even held animals on their laps or at their feet to keep warm; we sat next to a woman clutching a small goat. Our breath made white clouds in front of our faces as we chanted in Latin. The pressing crowd made me feel light-headed, almost panicky, and I clutched the wooden pew in front of me to steady my nerves.

I tried to take my mind off my panic by staring at the stained-glass

12

windows and stone carvings. I knew that the cathedral in Chartres had just been rebuilt after a fire destroyed it. The relic it housed, the Virgin's cloak, believed to have been lost in the fire and found miraculously intact after four years, had roused the builders to a fever pitch.

They had finished the vaulted ceiling in less than twenty years. Now, in March of 1270, the nearly completed cathedral astounded me with its beauty. The setting sun lit up the west side of the church, making the windows glow. The red glass became molten ruby, the yellow burst into flame, and the blue shimmered like the sunlit sea. Figures etched into the coloured glass seemed to come alive as the last rays of the sun flickered over them. I fixed my eyes to the magnificent windows, each worth a fortune.

The night grew steadily darker as the evening service wore on. The stained-glass windows lost their bright colours and faded to monochrome. I tried to hear what the priest was saying, but it was nearly impossible. We were in the back, and microphones had yet to be invented. Once I thought I heard 'suffer the children', but I pinched myself hard and the darkness faded from before my eyes. I must have fallen asleep and dreamed it.

Then the bells rang again, louder from inside the church. Half-deafened, we made our way through the crowd outside to the barns at the back of the cathedral, where the group of young crusaders prepared to sleep in the hay.

Women in warm cloaks stood over steaming cauldrons of cabbage soup and carved thin slices of smoked ham, doling out supper to the rag-tag bunch. The crusaders crowded around the hams, snatching at the slices as soon as they were cut. They had rarely eaten meat, I think.

There were youths of all ages, though most looked in their late teens. They huddled close to the tallest woman, who was busy filling bowls with soup. The youths wore rough woollen robes over leggings of the same stuff, and some had sleeveless tunics made of leather or sheepskin. Their clothing was poorly made, patched and torn, and crusted with filth; and I realized that these people were the unwanted ones, the ones who could be spared, and who would not be spared.

Their faces were pinched and sallow, but in their eyes dark pools of hope glimmered. People were actually feeding them here.

As I watched, the woman in charge handed a child a bowl and made to pat him fondly on the head. The child flinched. Then he hugged the soup to his chest and ate voraciously, first dipping his fingers in it to fish out bits of cabbage.

Another group stood in a circle, chatting in hushed tones. They were older, and among them was a youth who stood out despite his efforts to blend in. Everyone else suffered from starvation or ringworm, neglect or abject poverty. This boy was straight as a young elm, his hair was nicely trimmed, and his ears didn't have the black coating of dirt the others' had. His clothes were rough, but of good quality. His cloak had been dyed, and his woollen tunic was tightly woven. Moreover, his eyes had none of the painful hopefulness the others had. He looked around with the keen and appraising gaze of a hawk.

I heaved a sigh of relief. I had found my assignment. I recognized him from the hologram the journalist had brought back with him. Now all I had to do was to get him back home. But first, I had to eat or I would faint.

Charles took my hand and practically dragged me over to the soup. The ham was a thing of the past – not a scrap of meat was left.

'We have no bowls,' he informed the woman.

'You'll have to give them back.' She dipped a ladle into the cauldron and served us two wooden bowls full of steaming soup.

'Thank you, Madame,' said Charles. When I didn't say anything, too overcome with the odour of food to speak, he jabbed me with his elbow.

'Thank you, Madame,' I echoed.

We sat on a pile of dry straw to eat. Another woman handed out bread. There were no spoons, knives or forks. Napkins were our sleeves. We drank our watery soup and sopped it up with bread. When the first edge of my hunger was gone, I had a hard time finishing it. It was simply unsalted and unseasoned cabbage boiled with ham bones. The cabbage was tough and the bread was stale.

14

The crusaders obviously appreciated the meal. They probably got fed once a day when they were in a town, but what did they eat along the route? My heart squeezed in my chest. They looked so frail, their arms and legs too long, the soft covering of childhood prematurely stripped away, leaving their bones and sinews exposed and vulnerable.

My hand shook, and the bowl I held dropped and rolled in the straw. Charles sighed and picked it up. 'The soup's gone, but there's some cabbage left,' he said.

'You can have it.' I noticed that no one was offered a second helping of soup, and not many had got slices of the smoked ham. Judging from the way the youths gnawed on the pieces they did manage to get, it was inedible anyway – as hard as shoe leather. I shivered. Perhaps shoe leather tasted good to these poor creatures. Perhaps it would taste good to me after I'd been here for a while. My stomach heaved with anxiety and I clenched my teeth to keep my meal down.

Nothing I'd ever experienced, nothing I had studied on the holograms, could have prepared me for the reality of this time, I thought, my head aching. Not for the cold that penetrated the buildings, the poor food, the clothing, or the hard life the people lived.

Our barn shelter was made of stone, had an earthen floor, and the only heat came from three small, carefully tended fires in the centre of it. The smoke rose to the rafters and swirled around before escaping through the many holes in the roof. Rain would probably come through those very holes, soaking anyone underneath, so I prayed it didn't rain. The straw prickled, and the food was nearly inedible. I folded my arms over my knees and rested my forehead on them. I hated this century. I'd only been here a day and I already hated it.

Moreover, I was stuck, stuck here for all time.

I didn't cry. I had money, more money than these people had ever seen in a lifetime, with the exception of Jean, the young lord. I could rent a room, take a bath, and sleep soundly in relative warmth. I looked at Charles beside me. The food had put colour in his cheeks and his head nodded sleepily. His eyes fluttered closed, his long lashes sweeping his cheeks. His face, in repose, lost its lines of suffering. In the firelight, he looked again his age. His cheeks had smoothed and his mouth softened, and his face seemed surrounded by a nimbus of light. I blinked, sending tears down my cheeks, and his face came sharply back into focus. So much for my not crying.

I wiped my face and got stiffly to my feet. 'Stay here, I'll be right back,' I said to Charles. I took off my cloak and covered him with it, making a bed for him in the straw.

He didn't protest. With a small yawn, he snuggled into its warmth and two seconds later he was sound asleep.

I made my way outside to the public latrines, small wooden sheds sticking out over the river. Through the hole in the bench where I sat, I saw swirling black waters.

After, I went back to the barn and sought out Jean de Bourbon-Dampierre, recently of Paris, runaway.

I waited until he was finished arguing about whether or not they should leave the next day at dawn or let the youngest children rest a bit, and whether or not they should go towards Orleans or Le Mans. When that was settled – they would leave the next day at dawn, and they would head for Orleans – I waited until they were out of earshot, stepped up, and tapped Jean on the arm.

'Excuse me, my lord,' I said deferentially. 'Your father has sent me to bring you back home. Your mother is suffering greatly from your leave and would have you return.' In truth, no one had been sent to find him. His father was away on business, his mother was in the countryside and didn't even realize he'd gone, and his tutor had barely glanced at Jean's scribbled note saying he'd gone to visit friends. The circumstances made it so that Jean's disappearance wouldn't be noted for a full month, which was why I had been sent back just days after he'd left. If I could get him back home soon, Time would continue blithely on its way, and I would be free to make my life wherever I pleased – Paris, Orleans, or even the south of France.

The historian in charge of my education had insisted that Jean was very close to his mother. He'd been sure that a few words to Jean about his weeping mother would send him running back home. Historians can be such fools.

The boy looked at me scornfully. 'He sent a woman to bring me back? Why not the guards? Who are you, anyway? Where is my father? Has he decided to show an interest in me at last?'

I held his gaze. 'I was sent, yes. The guards have better things to do, don't you think? My name is Isobel. Your parents will both be pleased to see you safe and sound back at the court.'

He hesitated, expressions of anger, confusion and distrust chasing themselves across his face. Finally he said in clipped tones, 'I am sorry to inform you that I have decided to join the crusade. We are on our way to the Holy Land to free—'

'To free Jerusalem from the infidels. I know, I know.' I launched into my prepared speech. 'Nevertheless, your crusade is doomed. You are *not* heading to the Holy Land, you're just going to Tunis. If you are captured, you'll be sold into slavery. Look at your companions. They have no money, no way to ensure their safe passage. Did you really think you'd be able to get a ship to take you across the inner sea just because of your faith? Or that you could actually fight?'

Jean lifted his chin. 'Of course I can fight. I intend to join the king's army.'

I pointed. 'Look at that child over there, he's only five, maybe six years old. He walks ten kilometres a day. Then someone must carry him because he's exhausted. Poor food and neglect have weakened him. He knows nothing about fighting. What he needs is food and rest and someone to care for him. He's never had that. You don't have any excuse. You have a family, warm clothes, and have always had good food in your stomach. Don't throw it all away. Be thankful for what you have.'

'How do you know all this?' Jean's eyes hardened. 'Are you a soothsayer?'

'Don't be ridiculous,' I said. 'I have eyes, I can see and I have common sense. You have it too, so use it.'

'I cannot,' he said, looking suddenly sad, surprising me. 'I cannot abandon my companions. We've marched from Paris together. What will they think of me if I just leave them?'

'Whatever they think, they won't think it long. Half of them won't live to see the next harvest, or they'll become slaves. They'll sell you for ransom, or kill you. You're too proud to submit to chains.' My voice was sad too, and very quiet.

I couldn't keep my eyes away from the tiny, dirty child. Jean followed my gaze.

'His name is Antoine,' he said. 'He comes from Lille. He has already walked so far. I only carried him a little way.'

'We can carry him back to Paris if you wish. I'll find someone to care for him.'

Jean searched my face, not speaking for a long moment. 'You look so innocent,' he said finally. 'You seem so sure of what you say, and yet so afraid. You speak of the future as if you really know what will happen. Your eyes and skin are as clear as an angel's, but you have a fearsome scar. Are you a seraph? One of the fallen ones? Have you come to warn me of my fate?'

'I am no angel, believe me. Neither am I evil. I have simply come to take you home.'

'Tomorrow,' said Jean. 'We'll speak about it tomorrow. Tonight, I'm tired, and I would sleep now.' He spun on his heel and left me, walking quickly through the crowded barn.

I didn't follow him. I was too tired to follow anyway. The day had shattered me. Instead I went back to Charles, who slept deeply in my cloak. I took our bowls back to the women, and then I lay down next to him. Shivering with exhaustion, I too fell asleep despite the prickly hay.

The night was cold, and the damp seeped into my clothes. I woke up at least ten times. Each time I peered blearily around, panicked, forgetting where I was and why I was there. My chest ached – stress always gave me pains there. I took slow, deep breaths and tried to calm my fluttering heart. The night seemed to last for ever. It was never still. People shifted in the straw, spoke in whispers, or cried out with nightmares.

At five in the morning, the church bells began ringing again. Some of the crusaders got up and went to Mass. Charles didn't stir. I raised my head and saw another fire being lit beneath the great iron cauldron. Women, dressed warmly in thick cloaks, breathed clouds of white in the frosty air while they prepared breakfast for the crusaders.

I thought the voyagers would be welcome to stay a few days, but I also knew the townspeople really wanted them to go on their way. While they were here, the militia was on the alert. It was a time when a child of ten would be thrown in prison for stealing a loaf of bread, and prison meant certain death. The militia, freemen culled from the townsfolk, stood guard around the barn and made sure the older boys didn't slip into the town to steal.

I was standing in line to be fed, Charles right in front of me, when I heard a depressing titbit of information. Two of the women who ladled the soup spoke to each other in low tones. The youths around me didn't even glance at the women as they gossiped softly. I tilted my head to hear them better.

'They must be off by noon, poor dears. Look at that one – skin and bones he is. He won't get far.'

The other woman, who wore a fine red cloak, snorted. 'Do you really believe they're crusaders, Jeanine? They look more like villains to me.'

I started, then remembered that *villein* was a word employed to describe the poorer peasants or serfs.

'I can't see them freeing Jerusalem, that's the truth,' the woman called Jeanine said with a sigh. 'But I admire their faith. Remember when the last crusade came? King Louis was so young and his men were so handsome, and the horses so bold. I was only seventeen, but I remember seeing the king as if it were yesterday.'

'Now he's so old and so feeble they say he must ride in a litter.'

Jeanine crossed herself. 'Poor King Louis. His three sons have taken the cross and ride by his side. They will give him strength.'

'Jean-Tristan was born in Egypt during the last crusade,' said the woman in the red cloak. 'They say he's a handsome man and nearly as pious as his father!'

'They failed to free the Holy Land from the infidel,' said Jeanine as she doled a ladle full of soup into a bowl and handed it to a thin boy dressed in sheepskins.

'Perhaps this lot has a chance. Some say it isn't a question of might, but of faith.'

The other woman pulled a face and shook her head. 'God bless them. I wish them well on their way.'

Jeanine nodded. 'And on their way they must go. At noon the militia will be here to escort them from our town.'

'Seems hard to cast them away like that. Would some want to stay? I cannot see that child over there freeing Jerusalem from the infidel. Saladin be cursed! Now *there* was the devil, the very devil himself.' The woman in the red cloak shivered.

'Died in Damascus, he did. My mother was still alive when the news came. She stood up and danced on the hearth and her over sixty!'

'I remember that. I was a young girl then and madly in love with a knight I saw riding off to fight.' The woman sighed and shook her head. 'I wonder if he ever came back. In any case, he never passed through this town again.'

'That small child won't even make it to the next village.' Jeanine shook her head.

'Perhaps someone had better keep him here.'

'Who?'

'Why not you? Your brood is grown and you've a place at your hearth,' Jeanine said persuasively.

'I couldn't. Who knows where the mite is from, or who his people are? Perhaps he's a changeling. I wouldn't dare take him home.'

It was my turn now to get my bowl of watery soup and chunk of hard bread. I'd been listening carefully to the whole conversation. Now I spoke up. I hoped the lie I was about to tell would be believed.

'Excuse me, mesdames, the child you speak of is named Antoine. He comes from Lille. He's no changeling. He was simply one child too many in a poor family. They couldn't feed him, so they sent him on a crusade. The village priest blessed the child before he left and gave the family a sack of grain for their efforts. If you take him in you'll be sparing him a certain death.' I spoke quietly with my eyes cast down. I was afraid the women would take offence, but they didn't.

The woman in the red cloak handed me my soup. 'I'd take the child to spare him the long walk to Montpellier, but I'd need a coin to feed him and clothe him. We're not rich folk.'

'If you take him, I'll give you money,' I said. 'If you promise to treat him well.'

'Do I look like a cruel person?' She sounded indignant.

'No, I apologize.' I took my soup to my place in the straw and sipped it slowly.

Believing Antoine would be cared for here in Chartres reassured me. I felt a small measure of peace. Charles sat beside me and ate noisily, pausing now and then to wipe his mouth on his sleeve.

'I heard what you said to her,' he said, pointing with his chin.

'Do you think that I did the right thing?'

'Perhaps. Who can say? I know that woman, she has a good reputation. She helps feed the poor when the Church asks her to. She's here now, and that says much for her. I think Antoine will be treated fairly if you can give her a coin. Can you?'

'I can.' I opened my purse and dug out the silver one. It was a nice, heavy coin and I knew it could feed a small child for half a year. 'This should do, don't you think?'

Charles looked and his eyes grew wide. 'A coin indeed. I think that will do nicely. You have just bought Antoine a home. Pray he appreciates it.'

'I will,' I said.

When the woman saw the coin, she raised her eyebrows. 'That's quite a sum. I'll take the child home with me. I have a pallet for him there. I promise he'll never want for food, and I won't make him sleep in the stables.'

'I believe you,' I said. We looked at the subject of our conversation, Antoine. He sat by himself, his bowl in his lap and his face pinched with fatigue and ill health. I wondered if he would last the winter.

The woman must have sensed my unease. 'He'll be fine. He has nothing a full belly and warm clothes won't put right. I won't make him work hard until he's full-grown, and if he proves himself able, he'll have a place in our workshop. There's always work there. My husband cuts stone. He's working on the cathedral.'

I nodded, reassured. I knew the cathedral would be under construction on and off for at least two centuries. Fire would destroy it twice more. Workers would always be needed for it. If Antoine became a stonemason, he would be lucky indeed.

We ate breakfast and then crowded once more into the cathedral to hear mass before being escorted out of the town. The priest spoke for so long a plague of yawning descended upon us. I could barely understand what he was saying, but a few words caught my attention.

'The road to Montpellier is long and arduous. When you get to the Holy Land, seek the tomb of Agnes de Courtenay and pray for aid. She will help you on your quest.' Agnes de Courtenay had been the mother of the defunct king of Jerusalem, Baudouin IV. Would her spirit, even if it were able, really help a ragged mob of youths? Doubtful. She'd never done anything except help her own cause. Besides, this crusade was only headed to Tunis over three thousand kilometres away from Jerusalem. Not exactly close to Agnes's tomb. I sighed. The priest droned on and on, and finally the bells rang, liberating us.

I managed to find Antoine in the crowd, and I told him I'd found him a place to stay. As I paused on the steps, the woman with the red cloak approached.

'My name is Dame Sara,' she said, taking the boy's hand. 'Will you come with me, then, and see your new home?' she asked, her voice kind.

Antoine nodded, his face pinched with worry.

I went with them, too, as it wasn't far from the cathedral. The house was large and well built. Its floors were planked with wood, and the stone walls were covered with heavy cloth to keep the chill away. There were three fireplaces, one in the kitchen, one in the great room, which served as a living, dining and bedroom for the family, and one in the annex, a large room where the workers slept. Behind the kitchen was the larder, where several smoked hams hung amidst other salted and smoked meats.

The family was evidently prosperous. They certainly didn't need my silver coin, I thought bitterly. But then I realized that anything could happen in those days. A dry spell, a sickness in the livestock or crops, and all was lost. A silver coin would guarantee Antoine food and lodging for a year.

I followed Sara around her home without a word and tried to keep as much out of the way as possible. Antoine was kindly received by the other occupants of the house.

Sara's husband nodded and smiled. He was a tall, well-knit man with huge hands that looked as hard as the rocks he cut. Sara said she had two daughters, married and living in neighbouring villages.

A cat sat in a curl next to the fireplace, and as we opened the door and let in a flood of weak sunlight, an old woman looked up and blinked at us.

'Grandmother, this is Antoine. He'll sleep next to you and keep you warm this winter.' That was Antoine's introduction to his bed-mate. He stood uncertainly, his finger in his mouth, but the old woman put her knitting down and motioned him near.

She peered at him and touched his cheek gently.

'A fine lad.' Her voice was still strong. 'Antoine is your name, and a good name it is. Do you see the cat? Have you ever touched one? No? Well, you must pet her gently or else she'll scratch. Her name is Grisette. If you're quiet, you can hear her purring.'

Antoine forgot to be shy and was soon seated near the fire stroking the cat. His face, which had been pinched and grey, relaxed, and colour came back into his cheeks.

'He looks better already.' Sara nodded and I handed her the coin I'd promised. She took it and tucked it into a small purse tied to her waist. 'I won't lie to you. This will buy him a year with me. At the end of that time, if I find he's a good boy and willing, I'll keep him. However, if he causes trouble I'll turn him out.'

'He's but five years old!'

The woman shrugged. 'I'll do my best. I'll treat him well. It's up to him now.'

I knelt next to the small boy and took him by the chin. 'This woman is giving you a chance to stay with her and with the cat.' His hand tightened on the animal's fur. 'For your own good you must obey her. If you're a good boy you can stay here and learn a trade. You must promise to be well-behaved.'

Something in my voice must have reached him, because he put his thin hand on my arm and squeezed it. 'Don't worry,' he lisped, 'I'll be good.' His eyes were huge in his starving face. They were lined with red and had deep bruises of fatigue around them, but they were bright eyes, deeply knowing for such a young mite.

I nodded. 'Farewell, then. I wish you well.'

He didn't reply, and Sara escorted me to the door. 'Don't worry, young miss. I'll tend to him. You can go to the Holy Land now and free Jerusalem. May God protect you. I'll care for your child.'

That gave me such a shock I was speechless. She hadn't believed the story I'd made up about Antoine. However, I reflected later, it was just as well that she thought he was mine. At least she thought she knew his mother and that the child wasn't a feared changeling.

Once I left the house, I found Charles waiting patiently for me on the street. 'The others have already left,' he said.

I was surprised to see him. 'Thank you for waiting,' I said, strangely touched.

Charles nudged my arm. 'We'd best be off,' he said in his deep, raspy voice. 'The villagers won't want us staying around.'

Yes, we were off, and my assignment still unfinished. Now I had to find the stubborn Jean de Bourbon again and escort him home. I hastened down the road. Townsfolk lined up along it. To wave, to wish us well, and to make sure we were really leaving. I felt a pang of terror and prayed that Jean would listen to me when I caught up with him. I had no wish to go on a crusade.

This much I knew. Despite the people believing this Crusade was heading to the Holy Land, it was only going as far as the ruins of Carthage in Tunis. Since the base of Muslim power had shifted to

Egypt, Louis did not even plan to march on to the Holy Land. Now, any war against Islam fittted the definition of a Crusade – but try to explain that to the people. They only wanted to free the city of Jerusalem from the infidel. Louis needed their taxes so he loudly proclaimed this invasion, destined to recapture Tunis and construct forts from which to attack Egypt, a crusade. It was an ill-fated mission and I had no intention of participating.

Chapter Three

Thirteenth-century clothing featured long belted tunics with various styles of surcoats or mantles. Dyes were becoming popular, but do not wear striped material as this was reserved for prostitutes. New laws regarding clothing reflected the Church's burgeoning control of civil populations.

Tempus University *Corrector's Handbook*

Charles and I crossed the bridge and took the road leading south. As if to reward me for taking care of Antoine, the sun came out. Its bright rays lit up the town of Chartres and the outlying countryside. In the fields serfs laboured, picking up the omnipresent rocks and stones. It was late March, and it was time to plough, to rake and to prepare the fields for planting. In the vineyards, men cut the grapevines back and burned the twigs. Smoke rose from small fires in thin spirals and disappeared in the clear air.

We caught up to the crusaders after about an hour's walk and I searched for Jean. In the daylight I could study the crusaders better. It was a relief to see that Antoine had been by far the youngest of the group, and aside from three or four spindly adolescents, most were robust youths or young men and women. Crusaders were not all valiant soldiers. The Church urged all common folk to take part in a crusade. They were expected to fight with sticks or their bare hands, I supposed, for none were armed. They were poor, their clothes in tatters for the most part, and I felt almost too well dressed with my thick woollen cloak. Many of them had acne scars, blotchy complexions, and chapped cheeks and lips. They looked unhealthy. And though few had the slightest bit of grace or brightness in their faces, all had the fervent expressions of fanatics, with eyes that burned and voices that rose to a high pitch when they spoke of the Holy Land and killing the infidel.

I started to wonder if the crusades weren't a ruse to get rid of undesirables in some towns. I could picture the mayor, or whoever was in charge, going to the local group of hoodlums and describing the delights of disembowelling the enemy. He'd urge them to do their sacred duty and off they'd go, caught up in a fervour of bloodlust and faith a powerful combination in any time. And most of them really thought they were off to the Holy Land. They didn't know where Tunis was, and they didn't care.

I stumbled on a rock and stepped on my hem. Before I could fall, a strong hand caught my arm, and I found myself staring into Jean's keen eyes.

'You've been searching for me,' he said, tossing his head like a strong-willed colt.

'That I have. Will you follow me to your home now?'

'No. I've decided to go on this crusade to fight the infidel, after which I plan to join the order of the Templars as a soldier. You can go back and tell my mother I'll buy her souvenirs from Jerusalem. My father should be content to have me out of the way for a year or so. Tell *him* I'll be back to claim my inheritance.'

My throat constricted and I thought I'd probably faint. I had been expecting to find a youth. Sixteen was, to my thinking, still a child. However, Jean was a head taller than I was, and his expression was a grown man's. I had rarely seen such determination in anyone's eyes before. We stopped walking and the rest of the group flowed around us like water in a stream. Charles glanced back, saw we weren't moving and trotted to join us. I motioned for him to stay away, and he sat on a clump of grass to wait.

'I heard what you did for Antoine.' Jean's eyes softened just a bit. 'It was a good deed, and I'm sure your soul will be judged more kindly because of it when you die.'

I licked my dry lips. 'I didn't do it for my soul. Jean, I can't let you go on this crusade. I'm sorry. I *must* bring you back to your home. My life depends upon it.'

That gave him a pause. 'What crime did you commit to merit that punishment?'

I shook my head mutely. 'I made a promise to bring you back. Your mother misses you so much she's made herself sick with grief.'

'I won't go back home until I've fought against the infidel and won a place for my soul in paradise. Then I will buy a relic in the Holy City and bring it back for my mother.'

'Your mother is desperately worried about you, Jean,' I said. 'She's ill. You *must* come home *now*.'

'I won't go back until I've fought, and then I'll take my place at the head of my family. I won't return until I can prove to the whole world what a coward he was to refuse to go on this crusade.'

'Perhaps your father has good reasons,' I said. 'Did you ask him?'

'He thinks far too much of material things and not enough of his soul. The pope has blessed us all, and while we are on the crusade we will be exempt from communion or confession.'

I frowned. This was not going as planned at all. According to the Tempus U historians, my mission was simple. Jean, they'd told me, was a dutiful, submissive child. They had no idea, I thought bitterly. 'You're too young to fight,' I snapped, my nerves fraying.

He ignored me. 'After we secure Tunis, I will go to Acre. The Templars will certainly accept me in their order.' The last words he spoke were whispered in my ear although we were quite alone now, the group having passed us by. Charles was dozing on the side of the road.

'The Templars? Don't be ridiculous. Besides, they're monks, and you're not.'

'True.' He shrugged. 'Then I will go on a pilgrimage to the Holy Land.'

'It's three months' march to Jerusalem from Tunis,' I sputtered. 'How will you get there? Please, Jean, forget this folly.'

'I told you, I have money. I will pay my own way and go either

28

by ship or by caravan.' His green eyes glinted with excitement. 'I can't wait. It's going to be a wonderful adventure. Come, we're falling behind.' He turned and, with a decided stride, left me.

'Charles?' I called. The boy sat up and rubbed his eyes, yawning. He got to his feet and trotted over to me.

'I'm with you.' He shoved his hand into the crook of my arm. His eyes, however, followed Jean's broad back as he marched down the road.

I gritted my teeth. This wasn't how my mission was supposed to go. I intended to bring Jean back home, and I would, even if it took longer than I'd expected. There was no time limit to my mission. All I had to do was make sure Jean went home, married, and had children. I was stuck here for the rest of my life, so unless something went radically wrong with my plan, I wouldn't be erased.

We walked all that day, not stopping for meals, and we slept when we came to a small hamlet that offered us the shelter of its hay barn for the night. The next morning we ate boiled oats prepared by the villagers, and we walked some more.

The days passed in a blur. I was starving half the time. My stomach, unused to the coarse food, revolted. I'd been used to getting more calories, to rice and pasta, to meat that hadn't spoiled, and to bread without mould or bits of stone. I chewed everything carefully, fearful of cracking a tooth. Half the time, my stomach hurt because of hunger pangs, the other half of the time because the food had made me ill. In prison, my diet had been carefully monitored. While training for the program, they'd given me bread made from rye wheat and gruel made from boiled oats to get me used to the food. But so far, I'd not had any rye bread nor tasted any oats.

What I did get was stale bread, old apples, a few bits of salted meat, and hard cheese. To drink, now and then, we got ale – wine was for the wealthy – and anyway, it was March the crops hadn't been sown. We were eating last season's leftovers.

I didn't have the energy to do anything but shuffle along the road. The crusaders prayed and I prayed but for different things, believe me. I wanted decent food and a chance to talk Jean into going back home, but Jean had taken to hanging out with a rough bunch and often got into arguments with them. I didn't like their looks and stayed away from them.

Charles kept close, like my little shadow. He was a godsend to me. Thanks to the idiot Tempus U historians, I had been woefully unprepared for this mission. Charles made sure I was all right and gave me titbits of advice.

'I don't like the looks of that lot either,' Charles said to me. We were sitting in a washing shed. It was raining and this was the best shelter the village had to offer. But my spirits were raised by the scent of cooking meat. Someone had offered a whole suckling pig to the group and it was roasting on a spit beneath a tree, not far from us. This was the first time I'd seen fresh meat, and I was desperate to start eating. I stared at the roasting pig and swallowed hard, my mouth watering. Everyone stared at it, actually, and I think they would have eaten it raw if the cooks had let them.

Tending the fire, along with the farmer who'd donated the pig and three burly townsmen whose job was mostly to keep the hungry crusaders at bay, were Jean and another young man. The group of rowdies sat at the other end of the shed, playing dice and squabbling among themselves.

'I'm hungry,' I said. That was about all I thought of anymore. Eating and sleeping. I looked around. 'Where will we sleep tonight? There's no straw here.'

'The villagers will bring some, don't worry.' Charles patted my arm.

I worried anyway. The washing shed had a good roof and three walls, but the middle of the floor was taken up by a stream-fed pool, surrounded by stone slabs that slanted towards the water. We had scarcely the space to sit, much less lie down.

Just then a cry rang out. *'Supper is ready!'* There was a rush towards the meat. A couple of people fell in the washing pond with resounding splashes. One girl hit her head on the stone and slipped underwater. No one stopped to help her.

The water was only knee-deep, but the girl was unconscious. I grabbed her and tried to pull her out, but her clothes were soaked and heavy, and I was weak.

'Charles, can you help me?' I cried.

He did, and we managed to haul her onto the floor. She sputtered and got to her hands and knees, water streaming from her mouth and nose. Blood flowed from a nasty gash on her temple.

'Shall we take her to the village?' Charles asked me, worry in his voice.

'Can you walk?' I asked the girl.

She nodded, and we took her arms, helping her to her feet. No one paid the slightest attention to us as we left the shed.

'It's still raining,' muttered Charles, wrinkling his face. 'We'll be walking through mud tomorrow.'

It was already muddy. The cow path leading to the village was sodden. By the time we made it to the cluster of houses we were soaked and filthy.

'Call for help,' Charles suggested, and I did. Heads poked out of houses, and one kind soul trotted over to us. He was a sturdy young man with a thatch of black hair and black eyes. Rainwater streamed from his felt hat.

'Where are you from?' he asked the girl, but she was too muddled to reply. 'She isn't a Cathari, is she?' The man frowned at us.

I had no idea what he was talking about, but Charles shook his head vehemently.

'Of course not! We're crusaders!'

The man looked closer at the girl. 'Is she married?'

The girl, dazed, shook her head and collapsed in his arms. He carried her into a small cottage that, despite being tiny, was well built and warm, thanks to a roaring fire in a large chimney. There was no glass in the windows and the roof was thatched, but it was clean, the floor was planked, and there was even a curtained bed and an oaken chest in one corner – signs of prosperity.

An old woman, who had been sitting by the fire, hurried over and took the girl's arm, leading her to a bench. Charles and I waited to make sure she'd be safe, and then we left. I was reluctant to leave

31

the cosy farmhouse, but there was hardly room for all of us in the main room. The old woman had started to examine the girl's wound, while the young man held her hand and patted it in a kindly fashion. They hardly noticed when we left.

'I don't think we'll see her again,' Charles predicted.

'Did you see how the farmer was looking at her?' I asked.

'As if she were a fine, fat heifer,' said Charles with a grin, and then he sighed. 'It must be nice to have a house for one's own. I never lived in a house.' He glanced back over his shoulder at the humble dwelling.

'Never?' I was shocked.

'No. I was born in a barn and lived in the stables. I've never slept in a bed,' he added with a shrug.

'Charles, why did the farmer ask if she was a Cathari?' I asked.

'Shhh!' He looked shocked and glanced about to make sure no one could overhear. 'Cathari are part of a heretic sect that broke off from the Church. There was an uprising in the south, and all the Cathari were massacred. No one talks of them, and if you're suspected of being a Cathari, you're turned over to the authorities and they . . . take care of you,' he said. 'Don't let anyone hear that word from you, and pray you are never accused of being a Cathari. It's worse than being a witch.' With that he crossed himself, looking grim.

We slogged through the pasture and arrived at the washing shed. All that was left of the pig was a pile of white bones without a scrap of meat. I swayed and had to grab the tree to stay upright. Next to me, Charles swallowed hard, his face wan.

'How could they?' I cried. I peeled myself off the tree and staggered to the fire.

Nothing. There was nothing. I picked up a rib and gnawed at it, then tossed it into the sputtering fire. I felt like screaming.

'Don't worry,' said Charles, an angry glint in his eyes. 'I'll think of something.'

I paid him no attention, too absorbed in my bitter disappointment. I stared at the bare bones and was fighting back tears when I heard an angry cry. Charles had been caught dipping his hand in Jean's purse.

'You thief!' Jean cried. He grasped Charles by the arm and would have sliced his hand off at the wrist if I hadn't intervened.

'Stop!' I grabbed Jean's hand, where a wicked-looking knife glittered.

'Stop!' echoed Charles. A bony little knee went straight to Jean's crotch.

Jean dropped the knife and doubled over, gasping. 'I'll kill you,' he hissed, when he got his breath back.

Charles danced out of his reach. 'You're wicked to be so well-fed and strong while we have to beg for each morsel of food. Look, Isobel is starving right before your eyes. How do you think you can earn a place in Paradise if you can't even help your companions? Will you let her starve while you stuff your face? You finished the whole pig while Isobel was helping someone. You should be ashamed.'

Jean sheathed his rapier. He opened his mouth to retort, but I glared at him. When he noticed my regard, he flushed an angry red. With a curse, he turned on his heel and walked away.

The next day, Jean approached us and apologized. He even gave me his breakfast, a bowl of watery gruel. I took it and shared it with Charles. I was still angry. My stomach hurt constantly.

'Are you feeling better?' Jean took my elbow as we left the washing shed.

'I'll be fine once I get something to eat,' I said. I was seriously considering taking one of my hidden coins and buying food for myself, but I was terrified the loutish group would learn I had money and steal it. 'You should watch out for those men,' I said, nodding in their direction. 'They're nothing but trouble.'

Jean shrugged. 'They're fighters. They're going to war.'

'They're louts,' I said. 'Jean, you have to go back home. These others aren't your friends. Look at them!'

I called our companions 'the others', which didn't endear me to them. I had trouble remembering their names and I couldn't talk to them about anything. I found their fervour offensive and their zeal embarrassing. When we came to a new village, I cringed on the periphery of the group while they spoke to the persons in charge and insisted on food and shelter.

Although I had money sewn into my kirtle, I never used it and kept it well hidden. I told anyone who asked that I'd given my last coin for Antoine's care. The villages gave us shelter in the form of barns or haystacks, and the people gave us food as well, even if it wasn't good food.

If I succeeded in my mission I'd be here for a lifetime, and I'd need all the coins I could get. I'd taught myself how to sew, and if I could find a little farmhouse like the one in the last village, I could settle there, and maybe Charles would stay with me. We could raise chickens or something.

Though it was a time of peace and safe borders, the common people had only just begun to prosper. A middle class made of talented and trained artisans would slowly flourish and create new towns and villages. The farmers, too, would eventually find a steady market for their goods and prosper as well. France would have nearly a hundred years of peace before wars and plague ravaged the land. The state would grow stronger, and education, art, and literature would flourish. A small golden age was approaching if I could live long enough to enjoy it.

I eyed Jean sourly. Because of him, I was likely to embark on a disastrous crusade and probably lose my life, or he would die and we'd all be erased. Not a very cheerful thought.

Jean caught me looking at him and he frowned. My expression was not the most amiable at that moment. 'What is it, Isobel? Did something bite you? Is your stomach aching? I'm sorry about not saving you a bit of meat last night. Is that why you're upset?'

I snapped at him. 'Why can't you simply go back to your home, where you belong?'

He didn't reply. It was a question I asked him at least twice a day, and he'd taken to ignoring it. 'You'll never believe what I heard in the village,' he said.

'I don't suppose you heard that they've called the crusade off.'

34

'No, the king *is* going to Jerusalem after he secures Tunis. Then he means to free Antioch.'

'That doesn't sound reasonable.' If I remembered my history correctly, Louis would die during the crusade. Was it in Tunis, or was it in the Holy Land? Had he been planning to go all the way to Antioch? Where did Jean *get* his information? I scratched my head. Confusion and lice made me do that often. 'Where will he embark?'

'In Aigues-Mortes, the port he built the last time he left France to fight the infidel.' Jean looked pleased with himself. 'I heard he is pledging free passage to all those who will come and fight with him.'

'Wonderful,' I said. I looked at Charles, who hadn't missed a word of our conversation. 'What do you think?'

'A free trip with the king is better than begging a ship from a slave trader.' A spark of mischief lit his eyes. 'Now that we have free passage, we're sure to reach the Holy Land. I can't wait to see it!'

'We are *not* going to the Holy Land, we're only going as far as Tunis,' I said to Charles, who ignored me. I sighed. 'You,' I said to Jean, 'had better not get killed. If I don't bring you back safely to your family, I'll be arrested.'

Jean's eyes widened. 'What?'

'I made a promise to bring you back to your mother alive. If I fail, I'll probably be thrown in prison.'

'Why?'

'Because I already got paid. But I lost the money on my way to Chartres. If I bring you back, I'll get more money. If I fail, I'll be tossed into a jail cell and left to rot.'

I made that part up, but it was convincing. Since Jean hated his father and thought him capable of anything, he believed my story. I'd embellished it as we marched, acting as though I allowed him to drag the frightful details out of me. He believed me though. My life truly did depend on his well-being; he heard that ring of truth in my stories.

Both Jean and Charles, like anyone in those days, adored stories and songs. They were important in that time when entertainment was rare and only came from troubadours or storytellers. I had made up a good story, and Jean fell for it. Not to the extent that he was willing to give up the crusade, but I'd persuaded him not to enrol in the archers, to leave the fighting to the trained soldiers, and only to make the pilgrimage to Jerusalem to pray for the deliverance of the Holy Land from the infidel, and not to join the Templars. I counted the months in my head. A month to get to Tunis. Three months at least to get to Jerusalem. Then back again to Paris. It could be a year before I knew if my mission had succeeded. I sighed. A year? Who could tell? My calculations were rough. I based everything on my studies, but they could never take into account delays due to weather, to illness, or attacks by bandits. And speaking of bandits, I eyed our travelling companions warily. I had every reason to make sure they never found out I had money.

Charles stayed near me. He didn't like the other travellers any more than I did. His wry humour was worlds away from their fervour, and I tended his minor cuts and bruises without comment. One time they weren't so little, and I knew that one of them had thrashed Charles, although he never told me who.

When we walked, I was careful to lag behind the rest of the group and keep Charles with me. Jean walked behind with us, silent and deep in thoughts he rarely shared. He was the most reserved person I'd ever met. He was also the most determined and, once he realized I needed food, he always made sure I got some.

The idiot Tempus U historians had got everything wrong about him. He loved his mother, but wasn't going to run back to her. He wasn't a child, he was an adult.

After a month, we reached the south of France. The weather became warmer, and I took my cloak off and folded it, tucking it into my belt. I had hated the rain and cold, but the heat was unbearable too, with sweat making a prickly rash on my body. I itched and stank and most days I found myself wanting to strangle Jean and just get it over with.

On one particular day, the sun hammered us mercilessly and my mood was black. Jean walked alongside me without speaking, and his presence grated on my nerves.

'Are you thinking such lofty thoughts that our words would interrupt you and bring you crashing to Earth?' I said.

He looked at me warily. If Charles had dared the same statement he would have riposted with a quick insult, but he was more circumspect with me.

I wasn't finished. 'Does your silence mean you have taken a vow? Will you decide on obedience or celibacy? You can't have both, you know. You're far too unyielding.'

'Why don't you leave me alone with my thoughts?' he asked.

'The road is long and I'm bored. I'd like you to tell me a story for once. Charles has none to speak of. While your king traipses off to the crusades, sick with dysentery, his lady wife pines for him. Shall I tell you a secret, Jean? Your king won't come back alive.'

Charles, who had overheard, gave a sharp gasp.

'Don't speak evil of our king,' Jean snapped.

I think I was a bit mad that day. The sun beat upon our bare heads and the road was white, dusty and devoid of shade. I gave a bitter laugh. 'Truth is not evil,' I said.

'If you weren't a woman I would thrash you,' he said, after thinking about it for a while.

'I'd like to see you try.' I clenched a fist and waved it at him. I'd never been in a fight in my life, not even in prison, but I wanted to hit him. Why wouldn't he listen to me and go back home?

His face darkened and he took a step forward, but Charles caught his cloak. 'No, no, Jean!'

'It's "my lord" to you, villein!' He turned on the unfortunate child and raised his hand.

I darted in before he could strike. 'If you want to hit someone, hit someone bigger and stronger than you are.' With that, I swung my arm back and hit him across the face with a rousing punch.

He sat down in the dust, more stunned than hurt, and stared as I hopped about, hugging my bruised knuckles to my chest. 'What demon has possessed you?' He let Charles haul him to his feet.

'Is there a demon called frustration?' I asked.

He took my hand and examined it, rubbing the red spot on the knuckles and shaking his head. 'Didn't anyone teach you how to hit?'

'Heavens, no!' It was so unbearably hot. I plucked at my sweaty shift, wrinkled my nose at my own sour body odour, and burst into tears.

Jean and Charles looked at each other. We had fallen so far behind the others that the dust from their footsteps wasn't even visible. There was a small dip in the fields, and a copse of dark trees seemed to beckon.

'Let's go over there and see if there's a stream or a spring.' Charles jutted his chin at the woods, and we agreed. Jean took my arm at the elbow and helped me across a dry ditch and onto the ploughed field. We walked the distance in silence. The only things we heard were the liquid notes of a bird.

'A thrush means water,' Charles said, with evident satisfaction.

We stepped into the shade and I sighed. The relief of being out of the sun was sublime. A glittering stream gurgled and splashed between banks of fern and nettle.

We found a small, sandy beach and sat down. I took off my shoes and put my feet into the water. Jean and Charles stripped and washed themselves. I waited until they were finished and left me alone. Women in this time were expected to be modest, though the people were far from prudish.

The boys soon finished and told me they would be right out of sight, but within hearing. 'If anything bites you, call out,' said Charles. I'm sure he meant to be reassuring.

I took off my clothes and plunged into the stream. With handfuls of sand, I scrubbed myself. I had a cake of soap in my purse, which I used with delight. I washed my clothes as well, scrubbing them with sand and rubbing them on a flat rock to remove the grime. Afterwards I carefully hung them on branches so they would dry quickly.

A hot breeze eddied through the woods. I was surprised; it was May in France, albeit the south of France. I hadn't realized that the Sirocco, a wind straight from the Sahara, could be felt as far north.

The air blew hot and dry as if from an oven. In a few days, we would be in Montpellier. Our long march was almost over. The arid lands we trampled through were nothing like the desert we would soon see, though. I wondered what I would do for clean clothes and baths where we were headed. The thought of not bathing made me cringe.

Well, it could be worse. I hadn't yet had my period, which was a blessing, but I assumed it was because the Tempus U doctors routinely sterilized their Correctors. One day they'd taken me to the prison medical building and the doctors had put me to sleep.

When I woke, they informed me that I was now sterile, that my appendix was gone, that my tonsils were out, and that I'd been vaccinated against every sickness I could think of. Their words replayed in my head as I sat with my feet in the water. I would never have children, and I was stuck here. The hopelessness of my situation sank in. I was alone in a dreadful century with a recalcitrant runaway, a waif, and barely enough money to buy me a year of decent living. And my soap was half gone.

I lay on the beach and sobbed, heedless of what anyone would think. After a while, I sat up and dried my tears. Several nervous coughs from a deep thicket made me nearly smile.

'Oh, you can come out. I don't mind if you see me naked.'

'We mind!' It was Charles, his voice indignant.

'Why? I saw you!'

'It's not the same.'

'Wait a second.' I picked some leafy branches and covered my sex, sitting with my feet in the water and my head in a spot of blue shade.

The boys came out of the bushes in single file. Charles grinned at me, but Jean refused to glance in my direction. His ears were very red.

'If I were you, I'd wash my clothes and dry them.'

Jean snorted. 'Wash my own clothes? Who do you take me for?'

'An intelligent person. Obviously I was mistaken.' I said. 'If you won't wash, you'll pest.'

'I pest already.' He shrugged. 'I'm crawling with lice and I stink. So what?'

'Horrors! I'll wash them for you,' I said. 'I prefer walking next to someone who doesn't smell like sewage.'

'So do I, but I don't mind if you pest,' he said. He glanced at me then looked away with a frown. 'Is it so important to be clean?'

Charles made a face. 'When the dirt's gone from behind my neck I catch cold easier.'

'Good Lord, Charles, let me see your neck!' I exclaimed.

After I saw his grime-coated neck, I made him shuck off his clothes and bathe again, scrubbing this time with sand and my soap. Jean did likewise, but only after chiding me never to take the Lord's name in vain again.

They didn't ask why I'd been crying. People were always crying then, from exhaustion, from hunger, from despair. There were so many reasons, but they'd never have guessed the real one. Charles glanced at me once or twice, a question hovering on his lips, but that was all. Jean seemed bothered by my nudity and wouldn't look at me until I'd put on my shift. Afterwards, he looked at me, tilting his head to the side.

'You should always wear your hair down,' he said, as I struggled to comb out the tangles.

'I want to chop it all off.' The mess of tangles and snarls exasperated me, though I'd spent the previous year allowing it to grow long so I'd fit in in the past. In prison we kept our hair short.

'No!' He pushed my hands away and smoothed my hair over my shoulders. 'I used to braid my sister's hair, but hers is dark. Yours is fair and thick, like a sheaf of ripe wheat.'

I was flustered, but Jean's hands were deft and he soon had my hair in tight braids.

'Thank you,' I said.

His hands lingered a minute on my hair, and then he shrugged and stepped back.

'I miss my sister,' he said.

I gritted my teeth. The Tempus U historians hadn't said a word about Jean's sister. What else hadn't they known?

After our clothes dried, we dressed and made our way through

40

the dusk to the next town, where the crusaders had already requisitioned a hay barn and a large, simmering pot of soup.

Like me, Charles was always famished. The smell of the soup brought a flush to his thin cheeks. Jean waded into the crowd and fetched two bowls, one for him and one for me. His chivalry didn't extend to Charles, but the boy was used to that and had elbowed himself to the front of the line.

'Thank you,' I said, as I took the soup from Jean.

He frowned and looked down at his bowl, then sat down next to me. 'Isobel,' he said.

'Yes?'

'How did you get your fearsome scar?' He asked the question in rushed tones, his face slightly reddened.

I sipped my soup and peered over the rim of my bowl at him. He stared back at me, not eating. His cheeks were flushed, whether by the sun or temerity I couldn't tell. His eyes sparkled, flashes of green emerald. His hair, newly washed, was as shiny as a raven's wing. 'I fell through a window,' I said, finally. I didn't know how to tell him I'd shattered a windshield with my face.

'You could have died,' he said.

'I nearly did. It's horrible, isn't it?' My hand strayed to the scar and traced the line of it from my temple to my throat. When my fingers reached my lip he caught them.

'No,' he said.

I was surprised. 'No?'

'Who saved you, a fine physician? Was he a monk?' Jean's fingers tightened around mine and I looked at our hands, entwined. I shook my head and wondered why I was suddenly so lethargic. I should pull my hand from his grasp, my mind said. My hand tingled strangely. His touch made my chest tight.

My mind scolded, but my spirit had stopped listening. Warmth crept over me. The hay beneath us was soft and fragrant. My breathing quickened. I felt my cheeks grow hot. I didn't dare meet his eyes.

'What are you doing?' Charles bounded over and seated himself cross-legged in front of us.

Jean whipped his hand away as if it was burning, and I cupped shaking hands around my bowl of soup and tried to compose my thoughts.

'I asked Isobel to tell me about her scar,' said Jean, after a moment. He gave a shrug. 'She cut herself on a glass window.'

Charles gave me an appraising stare. 'Glass can be very dangerous if you're not careful.'

Jean yawned. 'After tomorrow we should arrive in Montpellier. Then it's just a short ways to Aigues-Mortes.' He folded his cloak around him and snuggled into the straw. A few minutes later he was asleep, or feigning sleep. With Jean, I never knew for sure.

Charles collected our bowls and returned them to the village women gathered around the fires. I made my way to an outdoor latrine pit and searched for something to clean my teeth. Hygiene was the biggest problem I'd faced so far, hygiene and hunger.

When I found a small hazelnut tree, I broke off a few twigs to use. In prison I'd read of an ancient toothpaste recipe that came from Egypt and was used by a certain princess, but for that I'd need ground chalk, a pinch of ashes, oil of clove, and the urine of a young virgin.

I contented myself with the twig and an occasional vinegar rinse.

Chapter Four

Why were levels of interpersonal violence so high in the Middle Ages? Historians have pointed to the prevalence of alcohol and the fact that most people carried knives on a daily basis. Try to stay indoors at night and avoid taverns and rowdy gatherings. (If you do get stabbed, see Chapter 15, Section 5: disinfecting and cauterizing wounds.)

Tempus University *Corrector's Handbook*

The night was agitated. Noises constantly woke me as mice scurried about in the hay in search of food, barn owls hooted, dogs barked nearly constantly, and just before dawn, a fight broke out between some of our fellow crusaders. I sat up, blinking and trying to see through the darkness. Next to me, Charles emerged from a pile of hay. He yawned loudly.

'What is it?' he asked, scratching his head.

'I can't see,' I answered. The fight was getting louder and others woke, peevishly calling for some quiet.

I heard a sharp scream and then came the sound of a body hitting the earthen floor. A steady cursing sounded now, and agonized wails. Someone was hurt, apparently. Somebody else blew on the coals in the brazier, adding straw to coax a flame. The brazier was set in the doorway of the barn to keep out the chill, and now it cast a reddish light over the scene. The noise had woken the village, and a constable and guards with torches came within minutes.

The squabble was over a girl. She sat in a pile of hay, her black hair a tangled mess, and she pulled at her lower lip with dirty fingers as the constable tried to get her version of the story. The two young men who'd fought were both dead. They'd been fighting with knives, and mortal wounds had been dealt by both of them. I recognized the fighters as two crusaders I'd liked to stay away from because of their irascible tempers.

The girl stared dumbly at the carnage on the floor and wouldn't say a word. After a while the constable led her away. Some villagers loaded the bodies upon a cart, the torches were doused, and we were left alone in the barn with the coppery smell of blood and the echoes of screams in our ears. When the light cracked the sky open, I huddled in a corner, trying to will myself back into my time.

It didn't work. A touch on my shoulder, and Charles was whispering that we should leave. 'The townspeople will want us gone after last night's fracas. Jean is waiting for us at the gate. Come.'

I unfolded my stiff limbs and walked slowly out of the barn, avoiding the black stains on the floor. The other crusaders slept or preened like chickens in the straw. I hardly glanced at them. My blood was iced with horror.

It was time to go. I wanted only two things, to get Jean back to Paris and then to slit my wrists. Well, maybe not slit my wrists – that wouldn't help my mission but I couldn't deal with the constant violence. All the lessons the Tempus U psychologist had drilled into me about eliminating stress by deep breathing and relaxation seemed like flimsy twigs trying to stem a river. I bleakly wished the self-satisfied psychologist was here now, to see how *he* would deal with the horrible splatter of blood, urine, and faeces.

I could barely keep myself together that day. Perhaps it was the fight; more likely it was depression settling over me. The dusty road wound between huge cliffs that cast a deep violet shade. Above our heads, the sky was raw blue. The cliffs themselves were red, and the grass was yellow. In the distance was the sea. I could smell it now. Salt in the air left a faint glitter on our skin.

44

Fatigue made my head spin and made me clumsy. I stumbled repeatedly. Charles grabbed my arm and urged me on. When the sun was straight overhead, Jean spotted a recess in the rocks, and we climbed a narrow goat path to a small cave. Other travellers had left a pile of tinder, but we had nothing to cook so we lit no fire. I simply sat and shuddered as the full horror of my situation registered on my mind. Charles watched me closely for a while then said he'd go find water. I think he'd decided I was dying of thirst.

I was parched, but it made no difference. All I could think about was how to kill myself. My mission started to fade into the background, I could hardly remember it anyhow. What was I supposed to do? Why? Why bother? I was going to die anyway. I might as well be erased so none of this would ever have happened.

Jean slid over to me and took me in his embrace. Immersed in my own thoughts, his actions took me completely off guard. The feel of his arms around me was like an electric shock. No one had touched me in so long, aside from the doctors in prison. I turned to him and clung, pressing my shivering body to his.

His hands slid down my sides and his breathing deepened. My head spun. I didn't realize what was happening until he'd already lifted my dress over my head. By then it was too late to stop. Desire rose within me, sharp and compelling. All thoughts fled at his touch. Surprise and longing took hold of me. I arched my whole body towards him and offered myself wantonly.

It was over very quickly. Just the touch of my bare skin made him cry out. I hardly had time to draw him into me before he shuddered and spent himself. His breath was ragged, sweat stood out on his brow.

I couldn't move, completely under the spell of raw passion. My body had been wakened by Jean's touch, but my mind was strangely lethargic. Locked in a tight embrace, the stuffy heat in the cave making our bodies slick with sweat, I couldn't think of anything but assuaging my desire. After a minute, he hardened again and we made love once more. This time I took control of the situation and showed him how to give me pleasure. It was soon done – nothing could have been drawn tighter than my lust. We cried out in unison, he in surprise, I in release.

He rolled off me and lay panting on the floor. I sat up and drew my shift over my breasts. With hands that shook, I smoothed my dress down over my legs.

Jean watched me with a puzzled expression, as if he couldn't quite place me. 'I'm sorry,' he said. 'Did I hurt you?'

I closed my eyes. I wanted the silence to become visible, to cloak me and cover me in darkness so I could melt away.

'No, Isobel, look at me!' Even his pleas were stern. Perhaps he couldn't help it. He was used to giving orders.

I put my hand out blindly and touched his face. Slowly I drew my fingers down his cheeks, over his chin, then back up to his forehead. I searched his face with my hand, looking for something, some sort of salvation, but all I felt was the smooth cheeks of youth and fuzz on his chin where a beard should have been. If only he'd been older.

Sixteen! Oh God, I'd just lain with a sixteen-year-old. I was nine years older than he was. No . . . I shook my head. Who was older? He'd been born more than thirteen centuries before I had – I was younger than Jean by nearly a thousand years.

A giggle burst from my lips. I buried my face in my hands and, for the first time in two weeks, started to laugh.

'Isobel!' Relief, and a hint of anger, coloured his voice.

I raised my head and looked at him. 'I'll be all right,' I said.

'I don't know what happened, I felt, I wanted . . .' He moved closer to me and gripped my arm. 'Will you marry me?'

'Oh, Jean.' I sighed. My sorrow was lessening. I could feel its weight easing off my body, and I could move without the feeling of lead in my limbs. 'You don't have to marry me, for heaven's sake. All we did was make love. You can't go and ask the first girl you lay with to marry you. You have to get to know the person, fall in love with her, want to spend the rest of your life with her, have children . . .' My voice tapered off.

'Will you have a child?' he asked, his eyes very bright.

'No, I will not,' I said. The depression departed, but I was exhausted. My head ached. 'Let me sleep now. I won't marry you and I won't have a child. We can make love again, whenever you want to. It's better to ask first, instead of just falling upon me, though.' I yawned. 'It's all right, don't worry.'

'Why are you crying then?' He pulled my head down to his lap and stroked my cheeks.

'I don't know, I think I'm just tired.'

'Then sleep, Isobel, sleep.' His voice, I realized, could be very gentle.

I slept.

All my life I'd been prone to depression, but prison had made it worse. Sometimes it was all I could do to get dressed in the morning. When I was depressed, everything seemed wrong. The sky was too bright, the trees too close together, even my feeling of touch was altered so that things were too rough or too spiky. My mind and my body would get out of synch, and I would struggle to keep an appearance of calm while fighting rising tides of panic or crushing waves of sorrow. The efforts drained me, and I would finally fall asleep from sheer exhaustion.

From experience, I knew these bouts of depression never lasted long, although they were crippling. I didn't try to fight them anymore. I only tried to ride through them. From prison doctors I'd learned how to deal with my condition, and so I slept. Whenever I drifted awake Jean still held me lightly and stroked my temples and hair. It was comforting to be touched by another human being.

When I woke fully it was night, and there was a small, bright fire. Charles had snared or stolen a rabbit from somewhere, and the smell of grilled meat tickled my nose. I sat up, blinking sleepily. I felt nearly normal again. The healing powers of sleep had worked their magic yet again.

Jean and I looked at each other, and our smiles were twin flashes of white. His eyes sparkled, and I'm afraid to admit mine were probably glowing as well. We didn't speak. I stood up and made my way out of the cave towards a clump of bushes. A clean, comfortable bathroom with running water would have been my first choice, but I'd have to be content with a shallow hole dug in the ground and, hopefully, a small spring or stream to wash up in.

In the darkness, I stumbled into the bushes. On my knees, I dug a hole using a stick and when I finished using it as a toilet, I covered it with dirt again. The gurgle of water alerted me to the presence of a stream.

As I searched for water after doing my business, my mind wandered. It usually did that after a bout of melancholy. I remembered Jean's arms around me and I stopped, tipped my face to the stars and took a deep breath.

It had been so long since I'd felt loved. The last time had been just before the accident. I'd been in my second year at the university, taking classes in French history, and I'd spent the weekend with my boyfriend during a break in my studies. My boyfriend and I had made love in his dorm. Afterwards I'd looked at my watch, sighed deeply and told him I had to hurry or else I'd miss my flight. I'd slung my bag into the trunk of my car and turned once more to wave at him as he leaned out the door. The hiss of steam from the engine in the deep, tranquil night air had hypnotized me, already relaxed from our lovemaking.

Why had that child been outside in the dark? Why hadn't his parents kept him in his bed? Children never went unsupervised in my time. They were too rare. Too precious. A butterfly net had been clutched in small hands and a collection jar hung over his shoulders. He had been intent on his prey, the nighthawk moths that floated like white ghosts in the heat of the summer's night.

So intent was he that he never noticed my car's headlights. I had been thinking of my boyfriend and how much I would miss him. I'd closed my eyes for an instant, better to imagine his face. When I opened them a second later, I swear it was only a second, another face stared at me. A white, moon face, trapped in the blinding glare of my headlights, paralyzed by the vision of the car rushing toward him.

The shock had been terrible. I'd swerved in a last, desperate attempt to avoid the child, but the corner of my fender caught him on the chest and flung him into the night.

My car hit a tree, and I crashed through the windshield. Steam had escaped from the cracked boiler in a white, billowing cloud. As I faded into unconsciousness, the child's parents had rushed out of the house. His mother's screams accompanied me into hell.

I woke in the prison hospital, three weeks later. My trial had been held 'in absentia' while I lay in a coma, though they'd waited until I awoke to pronounce the formal verdict. Considerate of them. I was found guilty and sentenced to life in prison.

After the war and the Great Divide, everything had changed. Laws were stricter. In other circumstances, I would have been executed. But as a young woman with working ovaries, the State kept me alive. And then one day, a man came to see me about a voyage back in time. If I accepted, I could live out the rest of my life in the Dark Ages. I only had a small mission to accomplish.

I shook my head sharply, chasing away the bitter memories.

In the dark, I saw the glint of moonlight on water. I approached and found a small, bubbling spring. The water was icy. Shivering, I washed with my dwindling sliver of soap, then heard Jean calling me. His voice floated over the night.

'Isobel! Isobel!'

I rinsed, dressed and went back to the cave, braiding my hair as I walked. My shoes were in the cave, but my bare feet were getting tough. I didn't notice the sharp rocks anymore. Once inside I was nearly overcome by the warmth of the fire and the rich scent of roasting meat. I swayed.

'Are you feeling better?' asked Charles, a wrinkle of worry between his brows.

I nodded. I didn't trust my voice yet. The memories were still too sharp, but time was slowly eroding the edges. Soon I'd be able to remember my trip into hell, and then, perhaps, I'd be healed.

We arrived in Montpellier late the next day. The sun was setting, casting a red glow over the ancient city. Montpellier had been

49

founded by the Romans as a trading post. Now it was the second or third most important city of France, with some 40,000 inhabitants, more people than I, or Charles, had ever seen. We gawked as we entered the gates of the city, and Charles clutched my arm as if afraid to lose me in the bustling crowd. Only Jean, familiar with Paris, was blasé. Temples and churches abounded, and as we arrived, the air was split by the sound of ringing bells.

Charles made a face.

'Vespers,' he said. 'I suppose it will be a two-hour wait until dinner.'

We straggled into the nearest cathedral and sat while the priests chanted mass. The wooden bench was hard, and I couldn't help shifting about on it. Jean sat very still, his eyes fixed upon the priest, his lips moving silently along with the Latin prayers. On my other side, Charles struggled against hunger and sleep in resigned silence, his head nodding now and then. I heard his stomach growl and he shot me an amused glance from beneath his long lashes. I giggled.

'Shhh,' hissed Jean.

When the service was over, we filed out of the church to search for lodgings. I'd persuaded Jean to try to find an inn and distance ourselves from our fellow travellers, whom we'd managed to avoid for two days now. I admit to selfishly wanting to spend a night in a real bed, with a hot bath and some decent food. The other crusaders could fend for themselves, my mission involved only Jean. I wondered if I could seduce him into forgetting the crusade. I'd try, at any rate. As we walked, our hands entwined and I felt almost happy.

As fate would have it, we stumbled upon the other crusaders as we passed the great gilded doors of the church. A shout, a rough hand shoved me aside, and a loud voice said, 'Is this the man?'

'Yes, it is!' The shout came from one of the louts Jean had often argued with along the way.

The crowd drifted out of the cathedral and pressed around, obviously looking for entertainment. Women pulled their children out of the way as the crusaders jostled one another, and Charles and I found ourselves in the midst of a shoving match between townsfolk and crusaders as they tried to get a better view of what was happening.

Jean struggled gamely, but two armed guards held him tightly. They wore cloth badges sewn onto their tunics. I assumed they were town constables.

They held his arms, not his mouth. 'What do you want of me?' he cried angrily.

One of the crusaders, a tall man I knew by sight, stepped forward from the crowd and pointed at Jean. 'You killed two men near Orange, and then you fled. Have you forgotten already?'

'I did nothing of the sort!' cried Jean. 'They killed each other. I proclaim my innocence!'

Charles yanked on a constable's arm. 'It was a brawl between two knaves for a bitch in heat!'

I too stepped forward to intervene, but there were too many people shoving, shouting and milling about. All I could do was watch, impotent, as Jean was led away, kicking and struggling.

When the crowd let me pass, I had lost sight of Jean, and Charles had disappeared. Several bystanders told me Jean had been taken to the city prison, which, as I discovered, was a dismal building near the port. Just past its black turrets, I could see the tips of tall masts, and the scent of salt water came in gusts from the sea.

I saw Charles slumped glumly on the steps. The guards on each side of the door didn't even glance at him. They ignored me as well, and I motioned to Charles to follow me.

We stood in a nearby alley and spoke in whispers.

'What shall we do?' he asked.

'I was about to ask the same of you. How can we see Jean?'

'We could ask the prefect,' he said. 'But I think he'll want money.'

I darted a glance at the prison. 'Let's go find lodgings. Perhaps we can get help there.' Before we left, though, I did go to the prefect and ask for the name of someone who could represent Jean. I also warned him that Jean was related by marriage to King Louis and that I planned to go to the king's camp and report Jean's arrest. Anyone of royal blood, I knew, could not be held in a prison that was not especially for nobles, and could not be tried unless it was by a jury of peers. If I could prove Jean was noble, he would be remanded to the king's representative of the region.

Jean had doubtless told the same tale. The man listened gravely, gave me the name of a 'fine *prévôt,* a sort of lawyer, well schooled in defending murderers', and told me the faster I saw the king, the better, for Jean's trial would be next week if no word about his nobility was forthcoming. I was taken aback at the pace of justice, but my studies hadn't included the intricacies of murder trials.

My heart pounded painfully as I nearly dragged Charles through the city looking for a likely inn. Once settled, I sent a message to the lawyer and invited him to meet me for dinner.

The inn was large and expensive. I had wanted something decent, and now with Jean in prison, I needed to impress a lawyer. I wanted him to think we were nobility and therefore try his best. The doubtful looks the innkeeper cast upon Charles and I disappeared when I pulled out my purse. I paid for a week with one of my heavy silver coins. Included in the price of the room were a maid, all the hot water I required for bathing, and meals for myself and Charles – my valet, I told the innkeeper – and the services of a messenger. The innkeeper agreed and respectfully asked what else I'd need.

At that time, it was not unusual for a woman to travel alone. The innkeeper showed no surprise and led us to a spacious room with a four-poster bed, a fireplace, a chest for clothing, a desk for writing, and a straw-stuffed pallet on the floor for my valet. I bid the maid to bring a table and chairs for supper in my room, as well as a hot bath. Soon, to my delight, there was a tub in front of the fireplace. Servants carried buckets of steaming water to the room, and I made Charles wash as well, much to his disgust.

I ran a sponge over my body, brushed my hair until it shone, and pinned the braids in two rolls over my ears. Luckily for me, the styles of the times were elementary. Women wore dresses that reached their ankles and their hair in braids, tucked into a hairnet or pinned to the head. Some wealthy women wore tall, pointed hats with scarves attached, but the Tempus U historians hadn't provided me with the trappings of wealth. They had given me clothes that put me in the upper middle class.

I pulled on my baggy stockings and tied them around my knees with the ribbons attached to the tops. Then I put on a fine linen shift with long sleeves. Over that went a sleeveless kirtle. There was no underwear and no bras. The clothes were made of wool, and, if I hadn't worn my linen shift, would have itched horribly. Nothing was too fancy, but everything was of good quality, and my kirtle had laces to tighten the waist and gores to flare the skirt. I put my belt on, then tied a gold ring to a green ribbon and looped it around my neck, and hoped the grass stain on my hem wouldn't show in the dim firelight. I scrubbed Charles' face again and told him to act the part of my servant.

'Your servant?' He frowned. Before he could argue further, there came a knock at the door.

'Answer!' I whispered, 'And ask who's calling. Then announce him like royalty.' I pushed him towards the door with an imperious nod.

'Who's there?' called Charles, shuffling his feet and rolling his eyes at me.

'Monsignor Houdebert, *prévôt royal*,' was the response.

I raised my eyebrows at Charles. '*Prévôt royal*?' I mouthed. He shrugged. I had no idea what that was, but I was to find out the *prévôt* , or provost, administered justice in the name of the king. It was sort of like a lawyer.

I waited until Charles opened the door to my room before standing and offering my hand to be kissed. The lawyer, Monsignor Houdebert, bowed over my hand, kissed the air several inches above it, and smiled without showing his teeth. He wore a short robe made of good-quality cloth, dyed deep blue. His belt was leather, set with eagles cut out of shiny brass. His short beard curled around his chin. His eyes were blue-grey and very deep-set under fair brows. His hair was dark blond, streaked with grey, and he wore it cut square and just touching his shoulders. It was straight, but he'd crimped it sharply with curling irons at the ends.

'Thank you so much for coming so promptly,' I said. 'Please be seated. I have taken the liberty of ordering our meal. I hope you appreciate grilled sardines. I was told they arrived fresh this evening on the fishing boats.'

'That will be perfect.' He seated himself on a chair and leaned forward upon his cane. I suspected that he carried it more for show than for use, for he was still a man in his prime and without any limps I could see. Perhaps it held a hidden weapon to use if he was set upon by thieves.

I looked at him closely. He met my gaze seriously, in silence. Finally his wide mouth curled in a smile – the corners had been smiling for quite some time. 'Do I meet your expectations, Mistress de Bourbon-Dampierre?'

I blinked, then remembered I'd given Jean's name to the lawyer.

'You are younger than I thought you'd be,' I said, feeling flustered.

'I hope that doesn't disappoint you.' The dimples at the sides of his mouth deepened.

A knock sounded on the door. 'I believe our dinner has arrived,' I said. Charles uttered a loud sigh of relief and opened the door to let in our maid, laden with a tray and a pitcher of wine.

The dinner was simple but good. As the cook had assured me, the grilled fish was fresh. There were no vegetables – we ate our fish plain, with bread. Creamy goat's cheese and dried figs were our dessert. The wine was not bad at all, a light rosé the lawyer told me was made in the hills behind Montpellier. I let Charles have a glass, and after dinner he curled up in a corner on my cloak and fell asleep.

Houdebert and I looked at each other. I poured him more wine, and he sipped it, settling back in his chair and plucking at an imaginary speck of dust on his stockings.

'So, I hear your cousin has been arrested for the murder of two men?' His voice rose in question and I nodded.

'That is correct,' I said. 'Jean is innocent. We were sleeping soundly when the fight broke out. By the time a lantern was lit, one man lay on the ground, dead with a knife in his craw, and the other man was trying to staunch a wound that, alas, proved fatal for him.'

Houdebert folded his hands underneath his chin and stared at me. 'Why do you say "alas"?'

'Because then he would have been arrested, and not Jean.'

'And why do you suppose that your cousin,' he seemed to hesitate slightly, 'was accused?'

'I believe it was because the other travellers in our group disliked him. You must realize that he isn't of the same class, and he can be quite arrogant at times. The other voyagers accused him of hoarding money for the trip to Antioch. Jean denied this and cited King Louis' promise to take the crusaders free of charge, but that didn't change their attitude. They argued often about that, and I think they wanted to punish him.'

'What more can you tell me about the night of the killings?'

I was glad he'd stopped saying murders. 'A woman was involved. I saw her today in the crowd, so she's still with the crusaders. She wouldn't say anything in the barn, but perhaps she was in shock.'

'I will find her and speak to her tomorrow,' promised Houdebert. 'Right after I've seen Jean de Bourbon-Dampierre. If he is of royal blood, he can only be heard by a peer. No one else can take his statement or pass judgment upon him.'

'That would be a good place to start.' I stood, intending to dismiss him.

'I don't know about that,' said Houdebert. He gave me another one of his appraising glances. 'I think the best place to start would be right over there.' He indicated the high bed with a small jerk of his chin. 'If it pleases you, my lady.'

I was stunned, although I tried not to show it. Another particularity of this century, I remembered, was that people didn't think of sex as a sinful. On the contrary, they believed that it led to good health. Fornication was not only tolerated, it was encouraged. The

55

more the merrier, so to speak. The Church didn't yet claim sex was sin. It was just flexing the young muscles it would use in another two or three hundred years, culminating with the war between Protestants and Catholics. Right now, the Church and its Inquisition were still fledglings.

The crusades were the first holy wars it had fought, and Church and state, though closely linked, were not yet inextricably united. The Inquisition, an ecclesiastical institution used to suppress heresy, was gaining the power it would wield for the next five hundred years, but its main concern right now, as I had learned from Charles, was with the Cathari and with sorcery – not sex. The kings of France had largely ignored the church and its power because they saw themselves as all-powerful and divine. Religion was for other people. The current King Louis, later known as 'Saint Louis', was the first truly pious French king. The results of his leadership would be spectacular in several ways, provided I could turn Jean on the correct path.

Right now, though, the king was ill with dysentery, cranky with lice, and eager to be sailing towards Tunis, where he would die. He didn't know that, of course. But I did.

'Your skin is as smooth as the finest silk,' murmured Houdebert. He was a skilful lover, lithe and thoughtful, unhurried and absorbed in his delight.

I arched my back and shivered. It had been so long, so long, and suddenly, in the space of two days, I'd had two lovers. My body ached with pleasure. I caught my breath as he bent over my nipple. A hard throbbing started deep within me and I abandoned myself, my hands holding tightly to Houdebert's narrow hips.

He chuckled appreciatively and nipped my shoulder, then quickened his movements as his own passion swept over him. The heavy curtains surrounding the bed muffled his groans. I hoped he wouldn't wake Charles because I wasn't up to explaining my method of hiring a lawyer.

Afterwards, Houdebert dressed, bowed over my hand, kissed it firmly this time, then turned it over and kissed the inside of my wrist. He left quietly, drawing the door shut behind him. *Monsieur Houdebert!* I bit my lip, torn between laughter and tears. What was his first name anyway? Dare I ask? Or would I go through life thinking of that skilful lover as Houdebert, *prévôt royal*?

Satisfied I'd done everything I could to obtain Jean's freedom, I tugged my covers under my chin and slept deeply.

Chapter Five

Keeping out of trouble is easy if you avoid contact with people.

Tempus University *Corrector's Handbook*

The bells for matins rang through the city and woke everyone with ears.

Charles unrolled himself from my cloak in the corner and yawned. 'How did you sleep?' he asked.

'Very well, thank you.'

'Mr Houdebert seemed very proficient,' he said. I peered at him closely but decided it was an innocent remark. Thinking about the lawyer brought a furious blush to my cheeks. Instead of responding to his comment about the man, I asked Charles to fetch a servant to draw my bath.

I bathed while Charles devoured breakfast. Then I dressed with care and took one of my gold coins from its hiding place. I showed it to Charles, and luckily he'd finished eating because he nearly choked.

'It's for Jean,' I said sternly. 'Mr Houdebert said I'd have to pay for his food in prison and his linen, and I must buy a proper dress in which to go see the king. There will be enough left over to pay the lawyer and bribe a magistrate if things go badly in court.'

'I should think so,' said Charles, awe in his voice and eyes. 'May I touch it?'

Charles and I bought fine robes, one for each of us and one for Jean, still in prison.

The magistrate in charge let us bribe him in order that Jean have a good meal, a wash, and a chance to put on his new clothes before the audience. Then I hired a man with a white donkey to lead me to the king. It wouldn't impress him if I arrived on foot in the army campground.

His camp was on the road to Aigues-Mortes, about a four-hour trotting ride from the town. There were far too many people with him to lodge in the city, so Aigues-Mortes, a port on the far end of a dead-water bay, was expanded to launch the crusade.

The donkey and my guide trotted all the way, and the weather was fair so I made good time. I arrived at noon, just as the king was finishing his second round of prayers for the day.

My fears of not being able to approach him were unfounded. He received all visitors according to rank. I was dressed in a good robe, my hair was clean, and I must have looked like nobility, for I only had to wait a little while before my name was announced.

King Louis was elderly and frail, and his hands shook as he motioned to me to advance into the cool shade of his blue tent. His eyes, though, were full of kindness. I don't think I ever saw such a compassionate regard. His blue eyes were pale and cloudy with age, but lit from within by a munificence that seemed to confer a glow to his whole face.

Once in front of poor doomed King Louis, I felt very timid. I bowed as was the custom and addressed his feet when I spoke.

'Sire,' I said, choosing my words carefully. 'Your cousin, the Sire de Bourbon-Dampierre, has asked me to look after his son, Jean. As his guardian, I have followed him on this crusade. He is determined to fight the infidel at your side. Jean is headstrong and brave, but he has got into trouble with some scoundrels in Montpellier. He has been unjustly accused of murder and needs your help.'

'Ah?' The king raised his eyebrows. 'That is a grave accusation. I will write to the magistrate at once. How did Jean come to be in Montpellier?'

'He heard of your new crusade and wanted to join it. His father, your cousin, forbade it, but Jean disobeyed him and ran away. When the Sire de Bourbon-Dampierre found out, I was sent after him. If you wish, I can bring him back to his father.' This was my last, wild hope. If King Louis ordered it, Jean could be sent home, perhaps even escorted home. I held my breath.

My hopes were dashed at once. The story brought a smile to the king's wan face. 'It does my heart good to hear of such enthusiasm in a boy,' he said. 'I'm proud to hear he wants to join my crusade. I will make room for him in my cortege as soon as this unfortunate incident is cleared up and make sure my son, Jean-Tristan, welcomes him. I'll dictate a note for the magistrate, and you can give it to him.'

A tall man seated next to the king wrote the letter. The royal scribe, I surmised, as I noticed his inkwell, parchment and quills. After, he sealed the letter and handed it to a page who then handed it to me with a little bow.

The king sank back into his cushions and waved his thin hand. 'Go now, my child, and have no fear for Jean. I shall look forward to seeing you before we leave. We will have a grand adventure in Tunis, and after, we shall free the Holy Land.'

'Amen,' I said, my heart sinking. Saving Jean from prison only to have him shipped off on a doomed crusade was not the best of plans, but I could do nothing else.

I mounted my little donkey and the driver took her bridle and led her off again at a smart jog. We were back in Montpellier well before sunset.

I went straight to the prison, and asked to see the magistrate. He received me, took my letter, and waved me out the door. 'The page will see you out,' he said.

I'll never know if he knew what happened to me. I'll never know if he did it on purpose. When I left his office, a man was by the door. I assumed it was the page and told him to see me out. I should have known better. The man was far too old to be a page.

We went down the hallway, then he opened a door and motioned me through. I didn't hesitate, even when I saw the door led to a small room. I turned, meaning to ask where the exit was. He never let me speak. He hit me, knocking me to the ground.

In my first year of prison, I'd been beaten and raped by a sadistic guard. When I'd tried to tell the warden, the beatings grew worse, so I'd learned to close my eyes and wait for it to finish. When this man knocked me down, my first reflex was to submit. He soon grunted, finished his loathsome business, and stood up.

He leered down at me. 'If you say a word to anyone, I will personally go into Jean's cell and stab him to death. And no one will be the wiser,' he ended with a coarse laugh.

I don't think I fully realized what had happened to me. I lay on the floor, my face numb where the man struck me, my robe bunched around my waist.

He adjusted his breeches. 'Don't bother coming back again, unless you'd like another go.'

With that, he opened the door and left.

I pulled myself to my feet and stood, shaking violently.

I was in shock, so I'm not quite sure what I did next. I remember going to the inn and asking for another bath, which made the innkeeper mutter balefully. Then I sat in a large tub of boiling water, but perhaps that part is just wistful imagination.

My face was bruised, my whole body was sore, and I couldn't stop trembling.

I crawled into my bed and huddled under the covers. Jean found me there after they set him free.

The trial wasn't a trial at all. The king's letter went straight from the magistrate to Prévôt Houdebert, who gave an order, and Jean was freed within the hour. A very efficient system indeed.

Jean sat on the bed and pulled the covers back. He saw my face and frowned.

'What knave hurt you?'

I just stared at him. Shock made speech impossible.

He cursed, took me in his arms and stroked my hair. 'I will kill whoever did that to you.'

That jarred me out of my shock. 'No, no, please,' I cried. I had visions of Jean in prison once more, and the thought of approaching that horrible place again made me shudder. 'I fell down the stairs, my robe caught on a . . . a something. It's nothing, I promise.'

'My poor Isobel.' His voice was tender again. His hands, caressing my back and my head, strayed towards my bodice and I felt his breathing deepen.

A sort of blind panic took over me then. I can't explain it, but it must have been an after-effect of the rape in the prison. I screamed and thrashed, pushing him off the bed. Then I dove under the covers and sobbed so hard I started to choke.

Jean was stunned, though not into immobility. He reached under the covers to drag me out. I wouldn't be comforted, drawing in huge gulps of air and sobbing between each breath. He sent Charles to get some brandy. I also heard the word leeches, but that didn't sink in until I saw the innkeeper's wife standing over me holding a shallow bowl full of black, slimy worms.

'Poor lady, she's in a bad way.' She shook her head and clucked. 'I wondered about her when she came in near sunset, all bruised and pale. Looked to me she was about to puke. If she had a bad fall, it's the shock. If it's her liver, the leeches will set her right. Hold her up now and give her a glass of that brandy.'

A cup of burning liquid was poured down my throat, then I watched numbly as the innkeeper's wife rolled up my sleeves and applied the leeches.

Voracious creatures, they latched onto my arm and seemed to swell immediately.

I hadn't the slightest bit of strength left to protest or struggle. If I'd been in my right mind, I would have screamed, but I'd been beaten into docility long before my voyage through time. Now I simply sat, my arms on pillows in front of me, while the leeches did their work.

They drank their fill and dropped off. The innkeeper's wife plucked them off the covers and plopped them back into a wooden bowl full of water. She waited until they'd all finished, then she dried my arms, wiping off the ribbons of blood. 'She'll be fine tomorrow,' she said. Then she cocked her head. 'The bells will start soon. It's nearly vespers.'

Charles heaved a huge sigh, whether of relief or annoyance, I don't know. Then he perched at my side and stroked my cheek. 'Are you well now?' he asked.

I nodded. I did feel better. My head felt as if it were full of helium and would float right off my shoulders any second. There was no more blood in my veins. I felt as light and pure as an angel. I smiled. The brandy didn't hurt either. I'd ask for another cup, as soon as I got the power of speech back.

Jean stepped forward, though he didn't get too close. 'Was it my fault?' he asked, hesitant. Though the bells pealed outside he made no move to attend vespers.

I shook my head slowly and mouthed the word 'no'. Then darkness swooped upon me. Drunk, bled to faintness, and numb with shock, I slept for two days.

When I woke, Charles told me, as he helped me to my feet and laced my dress up, that Jean had been to see King Louis and that we all were to accompany the king on his voyage. We would be in the secondary court, not on the same level as the royal family, of course, but we would be considered nobles, since Jean's father was such, and we'd pay our own way, which meant buying a tent, bedding and pack animals to carry everything. However, we'd have the protection of the royal guards, and Jean would benefit from that as well. He wouldn't be in the infantry, marching to battle. As part of the court, he'd be expected to stay near King Louis.

I was relieved and terribly worried at the same time. The chances of dragging Jean back to Paris before we embarked for Tunis were growing very slim indeed.

The future hung from a thread, and I was supposed to make sure nothing changed. That thread grew thinner every day, and worry sometimes gave me blinding headaches.

We spent another two weeks in Montpellier at the inn, and during that time, I didn't see Maître Houdebert again. He wrote me a charming letter and reproached me for not visiting him, *'pour le remercier'*, but I was still in shock and it took days for my bones to stop aching. Of those two weeks, I remember only bits and pieces.

Jean chafed at waiting. He had grown up in the court and knew the king's youngest son, Jean-Tristan. They hadn't seen each other since they were ten, and Jean was worried that his friend had forgotten him.

'I was ten the last time I saw him,' he reminded me for the twelfth time in one day.

I looked up from the stocking I'd been darning and tried to look interested. 'I'm sure he hasn't changed much. Now, can we talk about maybe going back to Paris?'

He ignored me about Paris. He usually did. 'No, he's changed. He's a knight now, he has his own troop of archers, and he's got a warhorse.' His voice cracked and he frowned. 'He hasn't got a wife with him, though. She stayed home.' He brightened, and the look he gave me was downright lascivious.

'Go see him and stop bothering me. I'm sure he remembers you. Didn't you say you both went to Navarre one summer?'

Jean scratched his head, and then looked at his nails. I'd realized not long after I came here that most people automatically did this to check for lice. He heaved a sigh and nodded. 'I'll go today to speak to him. Of course he'll remember me. We were friends, once.' Despite the confidence of his tone, his face puckered with worry.

When he left to find Jean-Tristan, I tried not to fret. I wanted Jean to find his friend, but I was sure that if he did, he'd never return to Paris. He'd want to fight with the prince's regiment. That would be better than if he fought in the rank and file, but I still hoped I could convince him to go home.

He came back that evening glowing. When I saw his face, I knew. 'You saw Jean-Tristan,' I said.

'He gave me this!' With a flourish Jean whipped aside his cloak and held out a helmet. A jaunty red plume waved at me as my heart plummeted to my feet. 'I'll even have my own shield. Jean-Tristan has asked his own smith to paint my arms upon it.'

I touched the helmet and smiled at Jean. 'You want to be a knight like Jean-Tristan, don't you?'

He nodded, too excited for words. Then he set the helmet carefully on the wooden chest and turned to me. His fingers fumbled my laces and he leaned into me, burying his face in my neck. 'He's a knight, but I have this,' he whispered hoarsely, and his hands reached into my dress and cupped my breasts. Jean hesitated. 'Are you feeling up to making love to me?' he asked, his expression worried. He hadn't tried since I'd pushed him away.

In reply, I pulled him to me and kissed him. My body tingled with delight as his eager hands undressed me. His enthusiasm was contagious. I hugged him to me and gasped as his movements quickened.

'When you become pregnant, then you'll have to marry me,' Jean said as we lay side by side on our bed.

'No, Jean, and stop asking me.' I frowned. 'I hope we don't run into that group of crusaders again.'

'Who, the ones that accused me of murder?' Jean nuzzled my neck. 'Don't worry about them. Maître Houdebert had them banned from Montpellier. I hear they've left the city.'

'That's a relief.' My heart had given a little flutter at the mention of my charming lawyer, but Jean's next words chased him out of my head.

'The ships are coming to Aigues-Mortes. The king has sent messages to the crusaders to join him there. We'll be leaving tomorrow.'

'Are you sure you won't reconsider?' I brushed a lock of hair from his face and looked into his eyes. 'Please? Can we forget this and go back to your home in Paris? Your mother misses you.'

'Will you marry me then?' he asked, his face suddenly stern.

'Will you go back to Paris if I say yes?'

He thought about it for a minute, then his mouth quirked into a grin. 'No, I suppose not. I'd rather fight with King Louis than get married. Once we return, we'll marry.'

'I cannot marry you,' I said gently. 'You don't understand now, but you will someday.' He had to marry someone else, someone who could have children and found a dynasty, but I couldn't tell him that. I knew he wasn't in love with me. It was just youthful infatuation.

He shrugged and kissed my shoulder. 'We'll talk about it later. Right now I have to go and get our supplies ready.'

Finally we joined the huge encampment and marched to Aigues-Mortes. The crowd had grown to such proportions that the road was clogged with traffic. Upon arriving in the bay, every parcel of dry ground was taken up by tents, horses, people or carts. People were even obliged to camp in the marshes, resulting in a surfeit of illnesses.

Jean, with his usual arrogance and forcefulness, found us a decent spot to set up our tent. It was the first time we'd set up our camp. Charles and I proved to be totally inept. I put the stakes in backwards, so that they shot out of the ground at the slightest tug. Charles tangled the lines and managed to poke a hole in the roof with a tent pole. Jean sighed, pushed us out of the way, and soon had our little tent standing jauntily. I unloaded our belongings and Charles took care of the donkey. The tasks were thus distributed: Jean set up the tent, I took care of the baggage, and Charles led the donkey to graze and to water.

Our tent was very nice, except for the hole, I guess. It was made of green velvet and the material was thick and well-sewn. The tent poles were ash, and very straight, and we had an awning that gave us shade. Jean bought a rug for the floor and a small brazier for cooking and for warmth.

We stayed only a short time in Aigues-Mortes. There were too many people there. The grazing land was soon stripped, and the water became rank with waste. As soon as possible the ships were organized and everyone loaded.

My hopes for escorting Jean back to Paris vanished altogether when we stepped aboard the ship that would carry us across the Mediterranean Sea. From the upper deck, I watched Aigues-Mortes dwindle in the distance. I trembled in fear. The thread holding onto the future was stretched to the breaking point. We were heading towards certain death, defeat and disaster. How could I save Jean? If I couldn't, erasure would cost me my life and the lives of everyone in this portion of time, and history would be rewritten from the point it picked up again. My thoughts were in turmoil.

The ship plunged into a trough, rose with its bow towards the sky, plunged again, veered, rocked, and half the voyagers rushed for the sides.

I stood a moment longer and felt the wind whip my robe, tease my hair out of its braids and shred the last of my hopes for a successful mission. I turned my face to the sun and decided to face my own future with courage. Then the ship plunged again, and I too rushed to the side and lost my breakfast.

By dinnertime, I was ready to die. I considered throwing myself right off the ship. The deep blue swells looked more inviting than the rough wooden planks of our cramped quarters. But Jean kept me inside the cabin and wouldn't let me commit suicide.

'You'll feel better in a few days,' he said sympathetically, while I retched miserably into a wooden bowl. He handed the bowl to Charles and waved him away.

Charles gave him a look that would have singed Jean's hair, had he noticed, but he took the bowl and emptied it anyway. He'd been busy doing that all day.

'Have another salt cracker,' Jean said.

'You're a loathsome sadist,' I said, when I could unclench my teeth.

'What's a sadist?' asked Jean.

I remembered belatedly that the Marquis de Sade hadn't been born yet, but I also recalled Jean hated Latin studies. 'It's a Latin word,' I said. 'Didn't you learn it?'

'I despised Latin,' he said. 'The sailors told me you'd be better after a good night's sleep, and they said to eat a cracker after every bout of sickness. Have some water now and then try to sleep. It's dark now.'

'How can you tell if it's dark? There's no window in this miserable cabin. It's always dark, from what I can see,' I answered peevishly.

Jean just shrugged, too excited to be on a ship bound for the crusade to notice my ill temper. He'd much rather have been on deck getting in the way of the sailors than attending to me, but the exasperated crew had ordered everyone below. So I ate the cracker, drank the water, and was ill once more.

To take my mind off my seasickness, I thought about King Louis. In the eyes of the king and the rest of the court travelling with him, I was Jean's legal wife. There was nothing odd about that because most people married very young, and I supposed I looked young to them, with my clear skin and fair hair.

Too, there was the fact that Jean had introduced me as his wife, which left me gaping longer than I would have liked. The king thought I was a 'charming and devoted wife' to have come to see him while Jean was locked in prison. He paid me several very flattering compliments, waved his royal hand, and Jean led me away.

Later, when I asked Jean what in heaven's name he was thinking, he merely grinned.

'I have decided to make you my wife,' he said. 'For one thing, it will make my father absolutely furious. You did say he wanted to imprison you, didn't you?'

I gritted my teeth. 'I prefer a more romantic reason to marry someone.'

'Well, I'm sure we'll find one,' he replied, with a cheerful leer.

We shared a tiny, cramped room in the pitching ship. Charles slept on the floor, and Jean and I huddled on a narrow cot that folded down on leather hinges.

I was sick for a day, but as Jean had predicted, I felt much better when I woke up.

This lasted until I found out there was no fresh water for bathing, brushing my teeth or washing my clothes until we arrived in Sardinia, our first stop. We had to wash in salt water, our clothes were rinsed in salt water, and salt permeated everything on the ship, even our skin, with a fine, silver dust.

Jean and I sailed with the nobles. It was fitting, Jean explained, that we shouldn't be with the villeins. First came the king's ship, and nobles took up the next fifteen ships. Jean would have preferred to be with his friend Jean-Tristan, but he was in a separate ship with his troops. Soldiers and archers piled into twelve other ships – ten ships carried supplies, although I knew from my research they would prove woefully inadequate, and there were even boats full of curious fishermen, bobbing alongside for a while.

The rest of the crusaders – the commoners, and probably the group we'd travelled with – were packed in thirteen other ships. We spread out upon the ocean, not so close as to bump into one another, and made our way the best we could.

Caravels with deep keels and swinging booms hadn't been invented yet. The ships in the thirteenth century were wide, had very short keels, and rolled like corks on the sea. Their sails were square, like the ancient Viking ships, and I wondered at times if our prayers were the only things that kept us afloat. We were at the mercy of the wind and when it blew contrarily, the sails were lowered and the anchors thrown out to stop us from being blown right back to France.

Only two days after we'd set sail, two storms rushed across the water, sweeping over our flotilla and sinking three of the ships carrying our fresh water. Another ship, loaded with horses, sank right after another storm. The sailors were picked up and loaded onto a different ship but not the horses. I watched, horrified, as the poor creatures thrashed out of the debris and then swam after the ships, whinnying pitifully. They could swim nearly as fast as the ships sailed, and being strong swimmers, they followed us for hours. One by one, though, they grew exhausted and drowned. Their plaintive neighs echoed in my ears for days.

The storms were brief but violent. After each one, the sun came out and scorched us. We would make our way to the deck and search for the king's ship then the others.

Our mouths moved as we counted silently to see how many had been lost.

After eight days of this sort of two steps forward, one step back movement across the water, we arrived in Cagliari in Sardinia.

*

Once the ship docked, we all got down on our knees and gave thanks. The prayer went on and on, but for once I fervently agreed with everything the priest said.

We were the eighth ship to arrive. Next came the knights and their horses, loaded on ships that smelled like manure. The villeins arrived the next day, and the king anxiously scrutinized the horizon for his best archers, all on another ship.

I thought the old adage 'never put all your eggs in one basket' could be changed to accommodate archers in a ship, but they all arrived safely after two days. Twelve other ships sailed into the harbour, ten with infantry and the others loaded with more rag-tag villains and crusaders. Everyone fell to their knees as soon as they reached dry land, then fetched their belongings and merged into the squalor that was the encampment.

The natives didn't appreciate our coming. They retreated into a large fortress a few kilometres away and refused to sell us any fresh produce. Or if they did consent to sell, it was at prices so outrageous everyone complained bitterly.

There were several distinct camps set up on shore. One consisted of the nobles and the king, one held the noble soldiers, one held the rest of the soldiers, and one was made up of the crusaders. The latter camp had the noisiest bunch and the least well-prepared. Whole families had joined the crusade and children played around the docks, scrambled underfoot, fell into the water, and generally got in the way.

One afternoon I sat on the docks and pulled three children out of the shallow water myself. Though it wasn't calm by any means, it was more orderly on the docks than in the camp or the village. Out on the docks, it was easier to stay out of the way of archers practising their archery, knights exercising their chargers, and messengers running between the various parts of the encampment. Add to this the general hustle and bustle of merchants hawking their *exorbitant* wares and natives coming to gawk at the crusaders, and you get a general idea of what the encampment was like.

We were only halfway to Tunis, and already I was exhausted by the voyage and dreaded another week at sea. Jean, however, practised fighting nearly every day with Jean-Tristan, and Charles slipped like a shadow everywhere, listening to every conversation he possibly could.

We set up our tent on the outskirts of the king's camp. Charles was now our official page and he gloried in his new-found prestige. He had a role to play and he puffed his chest out and followed Jean whenever he went to the court. I thought he would be no trouble, as he was a bright lad. Then I caught him playing dice for money with another page. Though playing cards and dice was tolerated, gambling wasn't, and the priests stalking about the camp were very strict. To most, the crusades were a holy endeavour and sin would certainly doom them. The priests punished anyone caught sinning in public in a terribly painful fashion. The Inquisition was starting to rear its ugly head.

'Charles, I will never, *never* forgive you if you're caught gambling and the priests cut off one of your hands,' I told him. He glared sullenly at the ground and rubbed his ear where I'd boxed it.

'You didn't have to swoop down on me like a madwoman. You scared me out of my wits,' he said.

'I hope so. Imagine if you'd been caught by one of the fanatics? You'd be in the infirmary right now, minus one hand. Don't be foolish, Charles. I won't have it. Either you promise never to play dice or cards again for money, or I'll sell you to the first slave dealer I find in the Tunis.'

'You wouldn't!' he gasped.

'Try and see,' I hissed. 'Now go outside and fetch me a bucket of hot water.'

'You just took a bath yesterday!'

I eyed him. 'And when did you last take one?'

He looked horrified. 'Before we left Aigues-Mortes. Don't you remember?'

'Make that two buckets.' I wrinkled my nose. 'We'll have to wash your hose as well. It looks as if you sat in a pile of manure.'

'It was the only place we thought we'd be left alone to gamble,' he grumbled.

71

I shot him another angry glance and he left, dragging two buckets after him, his shoulders slumped and his head bowed. As soon as he thought he was out of sight he tossed the buckets into the air, caught them and trotted off towards the kitchens where huge cauldrons of water were always heating.

'You were far too lenient,' said Jean. His voice came from the shadows of our tent where he reclined out of the hot glare of the sun.

'You would have cut his hand off right away, I suppose,' I said drily.

'Come here.' He patted the bed beside him. We'd been lying there all morning, except when I'd gone off in search of Charles.

'I want to bathe first,' I said, stretching my arms above my head.

'I'll help you undress.' His eyes gleamed in the darkness. The tent cloth was so thick only tiny pinpricks of light filtered through the roof.

I laughed softly. He was insatiable. With the normal, healthy appetite of a sixteen-year-old, he made love to me two or three times a day. Whenever he could and even sometimes when he ought not, he slid his hands beneath my shift to fondle me, his green eyes darkening.

He caught me by the hand and pulled me down on top of him. 'I wonder why I never thought of getting married before. This is the best sport in the world.'

I nibbled his earlobe. 'If you get hit by an arrow or stabbed, you'll lose your health and your ability to make love. Wouldn't it be better simply to go back home?'

'Will you marry me then?' he asked. His voice grew husky as he pushed my dress up over my head.

I shook my head. 'I'll never marry you, Jean, but I'll always be your lover.' I sighed as he ran his hands over my rib cage, his fingers splayed, and caught my breasts in his palms.

'But why?' He bent his head to take a nipple in his mouth. He tugged it, sending delicious shocks of pleasure through my body.

I arched against him, unable to resist his ardent passion. He was so urgent, so eager. He hadn't learned to be subtle. With a fierce cry, he threw himself onto me, thrusting, holding me tightly to his chest. I wrapped my legs around his slim hips and drew him into me, as eager as he was. His body was finely drawn and made to give pleasure. We bucked against each other, shivering as the delight seized us. Our hearts hammered madly and our hands entwined. There was a moment when there was no sound, when there was a sort of shock in the air. It crystallized around us, locking us together, and then it shook us apart.

When I regained my breath and opened my eyes, Jean was staring at the tent ceiling, his eyes cloudy. 'Why won't you marry me?' he asked.

'I can't,' I said softly. 'It doesn't matter, anyway. We can stay together as long as you like, and when you fall in love with another girl you can get married.'

'I'm in love with you,' he said.

'No, you're not. You're in love with making love. It's normal.' I tried to keep my voice light as I rolled over and groped for my robe. 'Charles will be back any minute.'

'I do love you, Isobel,' Jean insisted. His voice wavered a little. 'Please tell me why you won't marry me.'

'Please don't ask me anymore,' I said. 'It tires me to repeat the same thing over and over. What difference does it make? We're together, and that's all that matters for now.'

'Is it because of my father? I know you owe him a favour, but you kept your promise. You found me.'

'I swore to bring you home,' I said.

'I'll go back. I swear by all that's holy, and on King Louis' head, I swear to return.'

'Shhh!' I sat up, furious. 'Don't say that!'

'Don't say what?' He raised his eyebrows. 'I made a pledge. That should make you happy.'

I slumped back onto the bed, my head aching. 'It's nothing. A premonition, I told you before. King Louis isn't going home. This whole crusade is doomed.'

73

'You could be burned as a witch if anyone heard you saying that.' Jean put his hand on my lips, then leaned over and kissed them. 'Your lips are like rose petals, and your skin as soft as milkweed.' His voice caught in his throat. 'You're an angel cast out of heaven for some misdeed, and I found you. You're my seraph. I will marry you, Isobel.'

'I'm no angel, and there's no future for us,' I said sadly.

Chapter Six

The basic idea was that in order to defeat the Muslims and retrieve control of the Holy Land it was best to attack from Africa, and the first step was Tunis. The Crusaders needed a rallying point after sailing across the Mediterranean. If the region could be controlled, it would provide a solid base from which to attack Egypt. The Crusaders would land near Tunis, set up camp in Carthage, and wait for reinforcements. Carthage, a once mighty city, was now in ruins. Tunis, the neighbouring city, was the seat of the government and trade of the region. (Note to Corrector: you will not need to study this closely as your mission will not include actually going on a Crusade.)

Tempus University *Corrector's Handbook*

In the evenings, after eating whatever we scrounged up, we'd sit just outside our tent under the awning, and I would tell a story. Charles would lie on his back, his head on his arms, and listen without a word. Jean interrupted the most. He had to know every detail about every character in the tale. When I told the story of Cinderella he wanted to know what the father did for a living, what wicked things the stepmother had done, and how ugly, exactly, the stepsisters were. Then he listened sceptically to the part where the fairy godmother changed Cinderella into the belle of the ball.

'I don't see how she could do that,' he said with a shake of his head.

'Do what?' I'd got to the part where Cinderella was admiring her glass slippers.

'Change a vegetable into a coach. It wouldn't work at all. You could hollow it out, but you couldn't affix wheels to it, and a woman could hardly sit in it.' He snorted.

'It's a fairy tale,' I said, exasperated. 'Haven't you ever heard one before?'

'No, and I prefer the story of King Arthur.'

'Let her finish.' Charles plucked at my sleeve. 'What happens next to Cinderella?'

'The prince sees her, falls in love and asks her why her robe is covered with vegetable seeds,' said Jean.

I bit my lip to keep from laughing. 'Well, more or less. Perhaps those stories are too childish for you, Jean. Did you study the Greek myths?'

'Only the Roman versions, and even those our teachers told us were abridged. Mostly we recited Latin verbs and practised rhetoric.'

'That must have been interesting,' I said.

'You're joking, of course.' Jean pulled a sour face. 'We also had to do sums, and I hated mathematics. We studied French poetry, Latin, and some Greek. My favourite lessons were the natural sciences, studies of beetles and birds, and astronomy. Our tutor was only interesting when he spoke about the stars,' he said, pointing upwards.

'I never learned to read or write,' said Charles suddenly.

We both left off admiring the sky and stared at Charles instead.

'I want to learn,' he said.

Jean laughed. 'A villein learning to read? Now I've heard everything. I suppose you'd like to study Latin and science as well?'

'And maths and Greek.' Charles nodded. 'That would be wonderful. You have no idea how lucky you are, my lord.'

I opened my mouth, and then shut it. Jean looked at Charles as if he'd suddenly sprouted horns. Charles' chin was propped on his knees and he gazed out over the camp, his eyes very big in his face, and very sad.

What would it hurt? Charles surely wouldn't change the timeline. 'If you want, I can teach you to read,' I said.

'You can read and write?' Now Jean stared at me instead.

'Of course.' I frowned, and a thought crossed my mind. 'Don't you know any women who can read or write?'

'Yes, of course I do. Noblewomen are educated. You must be noble.' He cocked his head, considering. 'I wondered about that. Was your family in disgrace? Was that why you were forced out into the streets and impoverished? Was that why my father could force you to fetch me home?'

'Noble? Me? Don't be absurd.' I squinted out at the camp and changed the subject. 'Have you heard what the council is discussing?' I asked Charles.

He listened to every bit of gossip, and he loved to tell us about it. 'They're trying to decide when to leave,' he said. 'The king waits for his brother, but most people think we'd better press on now. The natives are unhappy with our presence and would have us depart. The Tunisian emir al-Mustansir, so they say, is eager to become a Christian. He would welcome King Louis, in return for a baptism. The king's counsellors also say that if the emir proves to be obstinately heathen, there are treasures untold to plunder in his city. They say he's in the habit of furnishing the sultan of Egypt with funds and soldiers for his wars against the Christians. Since this is a crusade, attacking Tunis would be the same as attacking the sultan of Egypt, so it would count for fighting to free Jerusalem from the infidel.'

'Oh,' I said, looking askance at Jean. 'That's not very fair, is it?'

'What?'

'Attacking someone if they don't prove to be as tractable as you thought.'

Jean shrugged. 'It's war.'

'I don't approve of war,' I said.

Charles gave a little laugh. 'You don't approve of many things, Dame Isobel.' He'd taken to calling me Dame, playing along with Jean's charade of our marriage.

'What do you mean?' I asked.

He cocked his head. 'You don't realize it, but you're always criticizing everything. You complained about the ships, the crowds, the

77

soldiers and their weapons, the knights, the diplomats, and even King Louis. What, if anything, pleases you? Will you tell us?'

I drew my knees up, imitating Charles, and put my chin on them. I suspect my eyes were sad as well, because suddenly I felt the crushing weight of the future upon me. 'I like the king. I think he's a wonderful person. He's kind, and truly good. He has no business making war. His heart isn't in it, even I can tell.'

'The Marmaluks have gained too much ground in the Holy Land. We must reclaim what's ours by holy right. We need a base from which to attack Egypt and overthrow them. Tunis is perfect.' Jean spoke with all the misguided fervour of a crusader.

I held my tongue. Who was I, after all, to condemn? What was happening had already happened, and nothing could change the outcome. Fate had already decided who would win and who would perish. I only hoped that Jean would be spared, because of all the people on the crusade, only he and I were out of place. Everything we did, no matter how unimportant, could have huge repercussions in the future. I was walking a razor's edge, and it exhausted me.

I closed my eyes and leaned against Jean's arm. After a minute, he hugged me close.

His body was warm, and I moulded myself to him. In the distance, an argument rose over the murmur of the crowd. The bickering was soon hushed and laughter took its place. I could also hear the steady slap of waves against the ships, thuds from the horses' hooves, muffled cursing, and the whisper of a breeze in the rigging. Fatigue claimed me and I fell asleep, the sounds of the night all around me.

We left soon afterwards. The council had decided we'd sail directly to Tunis, and for once the winds were clement and blew us across the sea in two days.

Arriving at the coast, the king sent the admiral of his fleet with two ships to reconnoitre a landing. We waited, hanging over the railing, watching the shoals of silver fish darting in and out of our ship's shadow.

'Look at that one,' said Charles, pointing. 'It's the biggest one yet.'

'No, that one is,' said Jean, pointing at another. The shifting water was making me giddy, so I lifted my head and peered towards land.

I noticed sails and shaded my eyes to see past the dazzle on the water. 'The admiral is heading back,' I said, 'and he seems to have another ship in tow.'

'Diplomats, do you think?' Jean squinted at the growing sail on the horizon.

We were anchored not far from the king's own ship, and I could clearly hear the voices carry across the water. When the admiral's ship approached, he hailed the king and presented his trophy.

I choked, and then giggled nervously when Jean asked me what I'd heard. 'Is it a diplomat from Tunis, come to welcome us to land?'

'No,' I said, trying to steady my voice. 'The idiot's gone and captured a merchant ship. He's begging the king for reinforcements, as there are three other ships being held captive by his second ship in a cove nearby.'

'He's rather exceeded his instructions, hasn't he?' Charles gave me a wink.

I frowned. 'Silly fool,' I said. 'No, not you. That's what Louis just said to his own admiral.' I cupped my hands around my ears and leaned forward to pick up the king's comments to his son, Prince Philip, standing by his side. 'He's telling Philip that he's going to anchor here while we wait to see what the Tunisians will do.'

'What would you do if you were the Emir of Tunis?' asked Charles, his eyes wide.

'What I would do would be totally impossible at this time and age.' I turned to look at Jean. 'But I think you'll get your wish to fight. The king has arrived in Tunis and has declared war as surely as if he'd fired a crossbow.'

Jean looked both pleased and worried and excused himself to go see to his armour.

Charles pursed his lips. '*Silly fool*. He said that?'

'That's just what he said,' I replied. I sat in a patch of shade and scratched my head. 'Damn lice.'

We were anchored in the mouth of a wide harbour, out of reach

79

of crossbow shots. The weather was infernally hot, it was the twentieth of July in the year 1270, and half the sixty thousand people in the king's fleet would be dead in less than a month.

The next morning I woke to the sound of wailing trumpets.

The noise had insinuated itself into my sleep and taken over my dream, twisting it into a nightmare where a child screamed and screamed without drawing a single breath.

I sat bolt upright, my chest heaving in fright. The noise didn't abate with my awakening. Rather, it grew more insistent. I flung off my light covers, snatched my grubby kirtle from the peg on the wall, and stepped over Charles' small form on the way out the door. The ceiling was so low I bent over double, and as I climbed the narrow ladder leading to the deck, I felt like I was climbing out of a dark well. Below deck there were no lamps, no windows, and no air. I was gasping when I made it to the top.

Jean was already perched on the railing, his feet drumming excitedly on the wood, his eyes glowing. 'Look!' he cried, pointing toward shore. 'The Saracens have arrived!'

In the indistinct light of dawn, I could make out a huge crowd of men and horses milling on the beach. I looked to the right. Another small army was camped on the bluff overlooking the harbour. On the left, tents were scattered across the land, and I could clearly see the glitter of light on the metal spearheads.

My head swam and I gripped the wooden railing until splinters dug into my palms. Unexpectedly, my stomach heaved, and I retched over the side of the ship.

'Are you all right?' Jean hopped off his perch and put his arm over my shoulders.

'It's just nerves.' I wiped my mouth with a shaking hand. A shiver of fatigue washed through me, so I sat down on the deck.

'There's a whole shipload of sick people,' said Jean conversationally. 'They've all got swamp fever.'

'Oh great,' I said. 'Malaria. That's just what we need. I suppose King Louis is going to attack the Saracens?'

'He's planning to do that, yes.' Jean's face fell. 'Our ship won't be fighting, though. We're going to retreat a way back and keep the king's ship covered.'

'That sounds like a sensible idea, don't you think?'

'The knights have been getting ready. I can hear the clanging of armour coming over the water. The sound carries well in the early morning. The horses have been kicking the sides of the ships.'

The noise of iron-shod hooves striking the wooden planks was distinct. The knights must be the first ones off. The ship crews, protected from arrows by large wooden panels, manoeuvred the ships backwards towards the beach. The ships carrying the mounted soldiers were simply hollow vessels that the horses surged out of in a tight group down two enormous gangplanks. There were thirteen of these ships, one having sunk on the way to Sardinia.

Our fleet boasted ten of another type of ship, designed for the archers, with towers and shields. These, including the king's own archers on their own special ship, would cover the cavalry's flanks. The ships holding foot soldiers bobbed around the edges of the battle, searching for an opening to land.

The full force of the king's army landed that afternoon and drove the Saracens out of the harbour without much trouble. The knights galloped their heavy chargers out of the bowels of the ships onto dry land, the archers rained arrows on the hillside and the foot soldiers charged gamely up the beach.

The Saracens retreated towards Carthage, their fiery horses galloping with their tails held high in the air like flowing flags.

Jean, Charles and I cheered.

'What happens next?' asked Charles, his face pink with excitement.

'We set up camp.' Jean sounded morose, disappointed to have missed the action.

'There will be other battles,' I said, just as gloomily.

'We'd best get our things in order if we're leaving the ship,' said Charles, ever practical.

I looked out over the water, towards the king's ship floating so

81

close to ours. All the flags waved jauntily in the hot breeze, and the king sat under his awning and waved his thin white hand at the soldiers on shore. His face was serene, joyful with the painless victory. However, it wasn't a victory, really. The Saracens had simply wanted to see exactly what kind of an army the French king had brought. Now they knew.

Two days after we'd arrived in Tunis, we left the ships at last. The army set up camp on a swampy island just off the shore. There was no fresh water and no grazing land. We were miserable, the weather was hot, there were swarms of blood-sucking insects, and an alarming number of people were falling ill with malaria and dysentery.

After three days of planning, the king's forces attacked the fortress of Carthage. They were aided by five hundred longbowmen and four battalions of foreign knights who sailed into the harbour from the kingdom of Naples. Even the sailors armed themselves and went to do battle.

I watched black smoke rise from behind the fortress and shook my head. 'They shouldn't have burned the wheat fields. Now we'll have nothing to eat if we stay for a while.'

'The emir of Tunis will capitulate, and then we'll trade and have plenty,' said Jean. 'Does this seem too tight?'

I tugged at a string holding his breastplate in place and shook my head. 'No, and don't forget your helmet.'

'I won't.' His green eyes glittered. 'It's such an honour that Jean-Tristan asked me to accompany him.'

My first misgivings overcome, I had to admit I preferred knowing he was with the king's own son, thus heavily guarded and on horseback, rather than on foot and surrounded by itchy-fingered archers. Jean-Tristan had sent him a shield, and to Jean's immense delight, some armour that fitted him nearly perfectly.

I sighed. 'Be careful, all the same.'

'I will.' He leaned forward and gave me a kiss.

I held him tightly, wincing at the contact of hard metal. Besides the breastplate, he wore a belt with flat metal tongues hanging down from it, metal thigh guards, and a length of chain mail around his throat. I thought he looked very dashing, and told him so. He turned crimson with pleasure and adjusted his helmet on his head.

'What is *that*?' I pointed towards the top of the helmet where a scrap of familiar-looking cloth was tied.

His voice, coming from the depths of the helmet, was muffled. 'It's your undergarment, my lady. I took it as my token.'

I was speechless, but Charles uttered a stifled shriek of laughter before darting out of the tent and out of Jean's way. Well, now I knew where my makeshift underpants had ended up. I'd searched for them all morning.

A groom led Jean's mount up. A stocky bay animal with soft brown eyes and a black mane and tail, he wasn't as big as the war-horses, but then Jean didn't have a full suit of armour on. The horse was a cob, actually, but Jean was too thrilled that he was actually going to battle to care.

He pointed towards the smoke. 'Look over there. The crossbow-men have taken position!'

'Where will you be?' I asked, one hand on the cob's reins, the other on Jean's knee.

'Look for the flag belonging to the Count of Nevers,' Jean said. 'Now let me go, woman, I'm off to war.'

'You must have been waiting for weeks to say that, my lord,' I teased, though my heart wasn't in it.

Jean grinned. 'More than weeks. All my life, my lady.' He nodded once, making my underwear flap, and then cantered off to join his battalion.

Charles and I made our way to the group of noblewomen, children, ladies-in-waiting and pages. It was the first time I'd had contact with these women, our ship being one of the few with no family groups.

In the very centre of the crowd sat the young princess, Isabella of Aragon, who was Prince Philip's wife. She wore fine robes, with a long gold chain wrapped around her slender neck. She couldn't have been more than twenty-five or so, with skin the colour the French called *bisque* and very dark brown hair. Her eyebrows nearly met in the middle, which was considered a sign of beauty.

I had yet to see Prince Philip closely. From a distance, he was of above average height with dark blond hair and his father's rangy build. He was hardly ever with his wife since he was in charge of his own cavalry and group of knights. I'm sure Jean would have given away everything he held dear to be a part of *that* group.

The crowd around the princess consisted of no less than twelve handmaidens, although most could be called matrons. She had a jester, three jugglers, a Spanish midget, and five pages. Most of the pages and ladies-in-waiting lay on pallets. When I got closer, I saw they were drenched with sweat and flushed with fever, and several doctors hovered around, peering into eyes and whispering together.

A large awning sheltered the princess and her retinue as well as the rest of the noblewomen and children. Though we too found space at the very edge, its shade was scant comfort from the sweltering heat. Charles and I watched some people playing cards or throwing dice, although most just sat and bit fingernails or scratched lice.

We were on the outskirts of the crowd, as befitted my dubious rank. Jean might claim to be married to me, but to most people, I was on the same level as a courtesan. In a sense, I suppose that's what I was.

Proof of that came when a page from the princess asked if I knew any songs or stories to while away the time. Many courtesans at that time were schooled in the art of entertainment and could play a lute or recite poetry in a pleasing voice. Noblewomen could as well, but they weren't expected to perform. As I didn't have a title and my family was unknown, it was normal I was thought a courtesan. It wasn't an insult, so I wasn't offended.

I stood and curtsied. I *had* studied court etiquette, after all. I cleared my throat. 'I shall recite a poem, if that pleases your majesty.'

'It does.' She inclined her head. 'We adore verses.'

I nodded and a bit nervously, I admit, began one of the many poems I'd learned in prison. It was by a poet called Rutebeuf who had lived about fifty years before, and I expected that the company would have heard of him.

'La Complainte par Rutebeuf.

"The Plaint by Rutebeuf (c.1225–c.1285)
Misfortune never comes alone:
And troubles of my own
Beset me in the end.
What became of all my friends?
With whom I was so close, and loved so dearly?
Those who truly mattered,
Have simply scattered.
They were too unsteady
And unready.
If they have dismayed me,
They have betrayed me.
For as God has beset me with
Ills from every side,
None came to my aid:
The wind, I think, mislaid
Them. Love is gone:
My friends took it along,
The wind whistled at my door:
And called them away evermore." '

When I was finished, there was an uneasy silence, made even heavier by the suffocating heat. The princess shifted on her chair, then smiled and said, 'Had we known you were so melancholy by nature, we would have insisted upon a song! Nevertheless, it was a pretty piece, and well recited. In truth, I feel it quite apt for these circumstances, for aren't we all alone when misfortune befalls us? Let us hope that our friends have more courage than the poor poet's friends did. Thank you, Dame de Bourbon-Dampierre, for that is your name, is it not?'

Her voice was musical, and she spoke with the accent of her native land. She had a lovely smile, with one tooth charmingly crossed over the other in front.

'That is my name, yes, but my first name is Isobel.'

'The same as my own!' she cried, and clapped her hands. 'Come closer to me, so that I may see you better. My eyes are not strong and I fear you are rather a blur.'

I was escorted to her chair, and I curtsied again. My lessons on how to curtsey must have been more successful than I thought, because the myopic princess complimented me upon my grace. Then she enquired after my young husband. Perhaps she didn't put much as emphasis on the word 'young' as I thought, but I blushed. It was a source of embarrassment for me. I still couldn't believe Jean was my lover. He was nine years my junior and he exasperated me, especially at times like this, when I had to pretend he was my husband.

'He is fighting alongside the Count of Nevers,' I said.

'My dear brother-in-law, Jean-Tristan, speaks often of your husband,' said the princess, squinting at me. 'What a frightful scar you have. What happened to you?'

'I fell through a window when I was a child.' I repeated the story I'd made up.

The princess turned to the lady-in-waiting on her left. 'Doesn't she look like one of the angels carved from marble in our palace chapel? The one with the crack right through its face. The resemblance is uncanny. I think you will bring us luck, Isobel, our melancholy angel. Will you stay by my side today and take my mind off the battle? The heat is so terrible, I can't imagine what our dear husbands must be suffering inside their armour.'

'Of course, your majesty.' I couldn't bear to think about it either. The sun reverberated off the water, scorching the ships docked behind us. I could smell the overheated wood, the linen sails, and the bittersweet scent of tar and pitch. Underneath it all there was a heavy, cloying odour of sweat and faeces that we'd never escape as long as we stayed grouped in such a small space.

I'd gone from the cold of spring to the heat of the African summer in the five short months I'd been in this time. Nowhere had I found the least bit of comfort except in the soft bed in the inn at Montpellier, in the arms of Prévôt Houdebert. I felt my cheeks turn scarlet and I looked down at my feet.

'Don't worry, my melancholy angel, I'm sure your young husband will come back tonight, victorious.' The princess smiled at my distress, thankfully not divining its source.

I blinked back tears of self-pity and returned her kind smile. 'I pray that the fortress will have more shade than this swampy island.'

'If we win we will find out,' she replied. 'What games do you know?'

'Do you have any cards?' I asked. If we were going to be here all day, at least I knew how to play tarot, a card game popular at that time.

We played tarot all afternoon, though wilting with heat, our hands slipping with sweat on the cards. Stinging drops of perspiration ran down our temples and necks, and everyone's face was crimson.

Two ladies-in-waiting and one page played with us to make a game of five. Three other ladies-in-waiting tried to cool us with large fans made from hundreds of tiny blue feathers. The air felt good, though it stirred up the odours, and twice I had to excuse myself and go be sick.

I leaned against the wooden planks set up to hide the septic ditch from sight of the court. Shivers ran up and down my back. The smells were making me ill. Nothing could have prepared my nose for the rank scent of a thousand people who rarely bathed all using the same toilet facilities an open pit dug in the marshy ground. I leaned over it and retched again. Then I walked to the seashore and splashed water on my face. Overhead, gulls screamed, attracted by the offal and garbage. In the sea dark fins often surged out of the glassy water, proving that sharks also appreciated the waste that the sailors tossed overboard.

I didn't wade for long. Though the odour here was less intense and the water felt good on my feet, the sun beat mercilessly upon my head. As soon as I'd rinsed my mouth with salt water and combed my hair with wet fingers, I made my way back to the awning.

Charles tugged at my sleeve. 'Are you all right?'

'Yes,' I sighed. 'It's just so hot, don't you think?'

'I'm thirsty,' he said, 'but there's no more fresh water. I looked in the barrels, and their bottoms are all dry.'

'Tonight we'll have some,' I said, with more reassurance than I felt.

'The princess is waiting for you to finish the game.' He looked up at me a bit shyly. 'She seems to appreciate your company.'

'Shall I introduce you?'

'No, I'll stay here.' Charles had joined a group consisting of the pages of lesser noblewomen. In the middle of a grass mat, I caught sight of white bones, the knucklebones that they used to play dice.

'Don't get caught,' I said.

Charles shrugged. 'It's too hot for the priests to go walking around with their black cloaks, and the guards are all off fighting.'

When I returned to my seat the princess leaned forward, touched my arm and asked me, 'Is this your first pregnancy?'

I didn't think I'd heard her correctly, so I said, 'Excuse me?'

'You're pregnant. I know the signs because I've had four children already.'

I gaped at her, at a loss for words. Finally, I managed to choke out, 'Pregnant?'

'Well, yes, of course. Don't you recognize the symptoms?'

'Symptoms?' I was too shocked to do anything but repeat what she was saying.

'You're nauseated, and I see you wince when your arm brushes against your breasts, as if they hurt. Your skin is very pale, yet you have that look pregnant women get, a sort of glow. How far gone are you? Not three months, I suppose, for you're still very slender.'

My hands were shaking so badly I dropped my cards. The princess picked them up, clucking in pity. 'Look at all these trumps, and the twenty-one as well! You could have bid a *guard* easily.'

'I didn't have any kings.' I stared at my hands. Sore breasts, I thought. They had been horribly tender lately, but that didn't mean anything. I wasn't pregnant. The Tempus U doctors had taken care of everything, or so they'd said. It was ludicrous.

'But you had four dames, three knights and one valet,' said the princess, counting on her fingers. 'That makes twenty-six points, plus the twenty-one that makes five more. Thirty-one points all together. What a splendid hand! Good thing you dropped it; I would have bid against you. I had the one, the excuse, and all the kings.' Her voice was light.

'That would have been poor judgement,' I said, mindless of the shocked looks I got from the ladies-in-waiting. 'You had to pass. If you had all the kings, I would have called you and we would have played together. It only makes sense.' I hardly knew what I was saying.

'Of course, how silly of me! Do you want my physician to look after your pregnancy? He's an Arab, and quite proficient. I'll tell you a secret as well.' She leaned over and whispered loudly. 'I'm pregnant too! Isn't that wonderful? Two months gone and terribly sick in the morning. My nausea gets better in the afternoon, though, unlike you. You're sick all day long, aren't you?'

I nodded. 'I'm not pregnant,' I said, my voice cracking a bit. 'It's impossible, I assure you, it's quite impossible.'

Chapter Seven

'Eight to ten weeks pregnant,' said the physician. He sat back on his heels and smiled at me in satisfaction. 'I'm never wrong.'

I stared at him in shock. 'It's not possible.'

Jean poked his head into the tent and asked, 'Well?'

'Two months pregnant,' said the doctor. His narrow dark face split in a large smile. He had perfect, white teeth. He patted my belly. The Church had yet to make it sinful for a woman to be touched by a man, so doctors were allowed to assist in childbirth. As many of the doctors in that time were Arab, and very well educated, medicine was practised the way the ancients had practised it.

Religious beliefs throughout the medieval world had yet to make science obsolete, and medicine was still an art. The man in front of me had studied in Alexandria, had lived and worked in Paris, and had travelled to the Byzantine Empire to learn the different techniques of the Orient. If he said I was pregnant, chances were, he was right.

Jean's face glowed so brightly it seemed to light up the entire tent. 'How wonderful! I shall send a letter to my mother right away. She'll be so happy!' He took the doctor by the arms and hugged him. 'How wonderful!' he repeated. 'We won the battle, we're moving into the fortress tonight, and my wife is pregnant!'

I shifted on the bed, more than a little uncomfortable. I still couldn't believe I was pregnant. Didn't the doctors at Tempus U make me sterile? *How* had I got pregnant? And whose child was it? The baby could have been conceived the night Prévôt Houdebert had shared my bed, or worse, when the man raped me in the prison.

I turned over on the bed and buried my head in the pillows with a frustrated sob. Agonizing over the paternity of the baby was the least of my worries. Now Jean would insist on making me his legal wife, and I had no business wedding him. According to the imbecile historians, Jean had to marry and found a dynasty. I was only in the way!

My sobbing redoubled. The only way out of the mess was to commit suicide, since I was likely to get erased anyway.

Jean sat down by my side and took me in his arms. He smelled good, he'd taken the time to wash. When he'd cantered up on his lathered cob after the battle he'd looked more dead than alive. His face had been covered with blood and his hair matted with sweat. The unaccustomed weight of his armour combined with exhaustion caused him to fall with a resounding crash when he'd dismounted.

I'd thought he was seriously wounded, uttered a frightened scream and fainted. That was why the doctor had been called.

The whole day had been too much. I shattered into a million broken pieces, and the doctor gave me a drink to calm my nerves.

Jean had to hold me until I fell asleep. He couldn't pry my fingers from his tunic.

That night the entire camp moved into the fortress the crusaders had wrenched from the infidels. The fortress was old and not in good shape. It had been built on the ruins of Carthage, and all around us were Roman columns and the vestiges of Roman villas. There were even partial mosaics on some walls, and there were paved courtyards and a cobblestone road. However, there was none of the grain the crusaders had hoped we'd find nor any sort of fresh food at all. Luckily, the valley was rich with grazing land and a stream ran through it, giving us fresh water. Women, children, the sick and the wounded were installed inside the fortress. Sentries were posted on the roof. Most of the nobles got rooms, and Jean managed to find a small room in a turret overlooking the sea. I was pathetically glad to get away from the smelly, soggy island. The fortress had a large septic ditch dug quite a way away, and the cooks soon had huge fires going in the kitchens. The smell of roasting meat raised everyone's spirits.

Jean, Charles and I put our belongings in one corner, spread our pallets on the floor, and looked at each other.

'What shall we do now?' asked Charles.

I wrinkled my nose. 'I want to bathe.'

'Why don't you lie down,' said Jean.

'No, I want to have a walk. I've been cramped on a ship or in a tent for far too long.' I scratched my scalp and grimaced at the feel of my greasy hair. 'Isn't there anything that kills lice?'

Charles looked sympathetic. 'You can boil rosemary and thyme in oil, strain it, cool it and mix it with clay. You leave it on your head until it dries, and then you comb out all the nits.'

'Does that work?' I asked, a spark of interest in my eyes.

'Not usually,' said Charles. 'Usually we wait until winter, and they die of the cold.'

We went to fetch water, each of us carrying an empty goatskin slung over our shoulder. There was a long line of women in front of us, and the road was dusty. We were parched from walking. Charles looked at the line and sighed. 'Why don't we cut across the fields?'

It was a good idea, except there was a marshy place and the mosquitoes were ferocious.

Well, perhaps we would have got malaria anyway.

'If I die, will you send this to my mother?' Jean asked me. His eyes were bright with fever, and his face was flushed.

I dipped the cloth into the water and wiped his forehead. 'You're not going to die, it's just a touch of malaria.'

'Take it anyway. I want you to have it.' He pressed his ring into my hand.

'It's yours, and you're not dying.' I pushed the ring back on his finger, smoothed a lock of hair off his face, and smiled. I'd trimmed his hair to combat the intense heat and his fever. With it cut so short, he looked younger than ever. My smile wavered. His forehead was burning hot, but he was young and strong. I didn't doubt he'd recover.

There were no complications, his breathing was clear, his urine normal, and the white of his eyes stayed white. I kept the doctors, with their leeches and their endless bleeding, away. They'd already killed one woman who hadn't even been that ill.

'I want to marry you, Isobel,' Jean whispered.

'Don't think about that now.' I stroked his brow, but he pushed my hand away.

'I promised my sister I'd marry someone wealthy, but I can't imagine life without you. Do you think she'll forgive me?' His voice wavered, and his eyes were so bright I doubted he knew what he was saying.

I dipped the cloth into the water and wrung it out. The water was tepid. In the heat nothing was ever cool, not even the breeze. 'I don't think she'll hold it against you if you marry someone you love.' I draped the damp cloth on his forehead and watched his eyes flutter closed as he fell asleep.

Charles was sick too, but less so. His youth and energy soon overcame the fever, and he was up and walking about now.

I didn't get sick. The Tempus U doctors had vaccinated me. I was immune to the pest, cholera, malaria, dysentery, and even the flu. Apparently the only thing they hadn't done right was sterilize me. I was now three months pregnant, and my breasts hurt so much that even the lightest brush of cloth made me wince.

I sighed again and rubbed my face on my sleeve. Jean's short haircut looked very tempting to me in this heat. I thought of doing the same, although women were expected to have long hair. Coming into fashion now were tall pointed caps with coloured silk veils attached to the tops. The princess had one, and so did several of the richer noblewomen. Perhaps I could make one, then cut my hair short and hide it with the hat.

It wouldn't have pleased Jean, who loved my hair. I liked my hair well enough when it was clean and louse-free, which was a difficult thing to maintain. The week before, in desperation, I'd tried Charles' remedy for lice, followed by the princess' remedy. Then I'd asked the doctors and received several different recipes. The one with lye in it nearly burned my scalp. It did, however, kill the lice.

Now I dosed the chalk and vinegar more carefully and avoided putting too much lye into the mixture. Once I'd got the potion recipe down, I cut off Charles' hair and treated him for lice. Then I did the same for Jean even though he was ill. We were perhaps the three cleanest people in the camp. Even when Jean and Charles were sick, I insisted on washing them every day.

Most people, including the doctors, were sceptical of my hygiene practices. The princess told me that I'd wash the skin right off my body if I continued to bathe so regularly.

'Furthermore, I never bathe while I am pregnant,' she said, shaking her head emphatically. 'It's very bad for the baby. He could drown.'

I assured her I'd only take sponge baths.

Since we moved to the castle, Jean and Jean-Tristan had been nearly inseparable, and even while Jean was sick, Jean-Tristan visited nearly every day. I liked the prince. He was the youngest of King Louis' children and had been spoiled since he was a baby by everyone, but that hadn't made him capricious or demanding. Rather, it made him open and friendly, full of cheer, and affectionate towards his family. His blond hair was always carefully combed in the morning, but by midday, it was a riot of tangled curls. He was never at rest and always tried to make himself useful. The most menial jobs were done with a merry whistle when Jean-Tristan did them.

The fighting had all but stopped, and the crusaders were bored. To pass the time, we played cards and told stories, and I was invited to see Isabella at least once a day. I enjoyed her company, although I never stayed long. Her court was stuffy and crowded. I preferred to stay in our tower room in the shade. At least we had a slight breeze. Then Jean and Charles had fallen ill.

They had been sick for two weeks when the first of August dawned hot and clear – the same weather we'd been having for a week. Trumpets called the soldiers to their posts. The Saracens had been skirmishing with us for days. So far, we hadn't lost any men. Well, except the man who'd had the misfortune to fall off the wall when he was drunk, but you can't count that as a casualty of war.

The soldiers were entrenching the camp, and the Saracens seemed more interested in teasing us than actually attacking us. Diplomats rode in and out of camp constantly, to and from the emir of Tunis. I wasn't privy to the messages, but I knew the king waited for his brother, the King of Sicily, to join the crusade. I also knew his brother would arrive too late but didn't say that, of course. Until reinforcements came, we'd stay put.

The outbreaks of malaria were fewer now, but dysentery had spread through the camp, and the king decided to confine his sons to their ships. Prince Philip insisted on staying with the king, which meant Isabella stayed as well. The other two princes, Pierre and Jean-Tristan, went to their ships.

Jean-Tristan had come that morning to ask if we would like to accompany him aboard his ship. I had no intention of getting on another ship. My seasickness would be worse now – even thinking about a ship's movement made me queasy. Down on the water there was no wind at all, no shade and no respite from the heat. The ships' holds would be like ovens. I was therefore glad when Jean refused.

'I'm still not feeling well, *mon ami*,' Jean answered. His face was wan, but his fever had broken. 'When I recover I'll join you, if you wish.'

'I would like that very much,' Jean-Tristan said. He leaned down and kissed his cousin, and then he bowed to me. I curtsied back and walked him to the doorway.

'Will he be all right?' he asked me in a low voice. 'Shall I ask my father to lay his hands on him to cure him?'

I shook my head. 'That won't be necessary.' King Louis was reputed to have a healing touch, and soldiers were always asking him to touch their wounds. He regularly made the rounds with his physicians to lay his hands on patients. So far in the encampment there were at least fourteen people who claimed he'd cured them with his touch.

Jean-Tristan nodded, and his face was sombre for once. 'I was born in Damietta, Egypt, you know, during the last crusade. My father was captured by the Marmaluks, and that's why my mother called me Tristan – to mark the sad occasion. But my father returned unharmed, and the time I spent here as a child makes me feel at home here. I can't wait until we capture Tunis and make our way to the Holy Land. It will be interesting to see how much of it I remember.'

'So why do you look so serious?' I asked.

He frowned. 'It worries me to see Jean so ill.'

'Don't worry,' I said. 'Jean is strong and his fever has broken. In two days he'll be as good as new. We'll come visit you on your ship.'

Jean propped himself up on one elbow. 'Don't lose all your money before then, cousin. I intend to beat you at cards and win your allowance from you.'

Jean-Tristan stuck his tongue out and laughed. 'You're right. He's getting better.'

I curtsied once more, Jean waved weakly and then I went to the window and watched the young prince ride off towards the bay.

Two days later, he was dead. He fell ill, along with the king's emissary, and both of them died of dysentery within twenty-four hours.

When the news of Jean-Tristan's death reached the encampment, there came a shocked silence. Then low moans sounded, as women started to wail and men pounded their chests in grief. Jean, still in bed, sat up and cupped his face in his hands. Tears seeped through his fingers, and his shoulders shook. He made no noise as he wept.

I thought of the poor king and went to the window again. From our room we could see beneath the awning and into the royal tent. The king sat in his habitual place in the shade, but his face was hidden in his hands and he wouldn't speak to anyone, not even his priests.

I had known, of course, what was to happen. But knowing

something and living through it are very different things. I'd let myself get close to Jean-Tristan. In the back of my mind his death had always been a fact in a history book, and when I'd met the living man, the spectre of his demise vanished. Was it because these people had been dead for centuries when I studied them? I didn't know, but I couldn't associate these vibrant, living people with the shadowy figures in my history books, all long dead. I refused to think of who was next to perish.

I gazed over the encampment. Black flags unfurled and sagged in the torpid air. Sobs rose from the king's tent as his guards wept uncontrollably.

I went to Jean and put my arms around him. 'I'm so sorry,' I whispered.

'I should have gone with him,' he choked.

'Thank goodness you didn't. You would have died, too,' I said with a shudder. My arms tightened around him. I closed my eyes, too frightened of the future to think. Jean was safe, it was all that counted for the time being.

Jean-Tristan's body was dismembered, his heart salted and put into an urn, and his bones boiled and scraped clean then placed in a wooden casket in the hold of the king's ship. The August sun blazed overhead, the crusaders mourned their dead, and the Saracens watched and plotted.

Chapter Eight

'Cette précieuse Couronne du sauveur vaut mieux que tout l'or de
l'univers'
(This precious crown is worth all the gold in the universe)
Engraving on the medallion made for the crown of thorns attributed to
King Louis IX.

Tempus University *Corrector's Handbook*

The days passed. The horror of Jean-Tristan's death hung over the
encampment like a dark shroud. Blistering heat tormented us, and
there seemed to be no end to the misery we endured.

The twenty-fifth of August dawned, a sweltering morning, and
news was shouted from the battlements that the ship of Louis'
brother, Charles I, the King of Sicily, had been spotted a half a day's
sail away.

The camp's spirits rose, and the smell of smoke tickled our nostrils
as the cooks lit the fires to roast meat for the celebration feast. The
camp needed to be cheered – the king had been ailing for some
time now. Some said it was sorrow over losing his son, and a few
thought that it was fear for Prince Philip, though he was no longer ill
and was out of danger. Some even said he was pining for his wife. In
this day and age, it was considered important to have sex nearly every
day, and the king had been celibate for nearly six months.

Jean's illness was not fatal, but I wanted him to regain his strength.
Used to having sex two or three times a day, Jean had chafed at

being ill and celibate. He'd insisted that a bout of lovemaking would set things right and wanted to get a physician's opinion to sway me, but when Jean-Tristan died the shock brought his fever back. He grieved to the point where he was nearly prostrate.

I tried to raise Jean's spirits with card games and stories, even offers to make love, but he simply turned his head to the wall.

'Leave me alone, Isobel.'

'Jean, look at me, please.' My voice was gentle. I took his chin in my hands and turned his face to mine. His eyes were red-rimmed and swollen from crying.

'I am wretched. My prince is dead, and I'll never see him again. I was to have gone to Nevers with him to stay at his court. We would have hunted with his falcons, and . . . and . . .' He choked and new tears spilled down his cheeks.

I brushed them away and shook my head. 'Jean, you're a man now. You have to understand that fate has other plans for you.'

'I'm not a man,' he said.

'You are.' I stroked his cheek again and laughed softly. 'Haven't you felt your beard coming in? It's so dark it looks as if your face is sooty. You'll have to shave now. Look, I got you a razor. Do you want me to do it for you?'

He dashed the tears out of his eyes with his fists and rubbed his cheek. 'It *is* a beard!'

I nodded. 'Shall I ask Charles to fetch some hot water?'

'Knowing you, you've already done so, and he'll be here in a minute with a bucket.'

'I guess you know me too well,' I said, relieved.

'Have you been crying too?' He looked closer at my face and frowned. 'You have, haven't you? What is it?'

I sighed. I had to warn him, but it depressed me more than I'd thought it would. I truly admired the frail king. 'Prince Philip and his wife are both ill with the fever, but they'll recover. The doctors aren't afraid for their lives.'

'But?' Jean sat up straighter now and took my hands in his. 'You look so melancholy. I heard what the princess called you, and I think it suits you well. The melancholy angel. She thought you'd bring good luck. She hasn't asked for you again, has she?'

'When misfortune strikes, friends tend to evaporate like smoke in the wind. She's right not to call for me, though. I will not bring any luck to this crusade. I told you before, Jean. It's doomed.'

His face softened. 'You're prey to your pessimism. The doctors told me pregnant women often get that way. Did you know that I wrote a letter to my mother?' He sat back, a satisfied look upon his face. 'I managed to send it with the king's own courier. She will receive it, God willing, in three months.'

'Fast mail,' I said, almost teasingly. Then my disquiet grew. 'What did you say to her, Jean?'

'I told her I'd married an angel,' he said, kissing me softly. 'And I said you were having my babe. I told her that Jean-Tristan was dead of the flux. Then I wrote that the Emir of Tunis lost Carthage to King Louis. I explained that we were camped here waiting for Charles of Sicily, which was why we hadn't pushed on to the Holy City of Jerusalem. As soon as I get there I'll buy her several souvenirs and try to find a piece of the true cross, although I think it will be hard. Did you know that the last time King Louis was in the Holy Land, he bought the crown of thorns for a veritable fortune? I don't know which boutique sold it, but it must have been amazing. I'll have to try to find that shop when we get to Jerusalem.'

I wanted to correct him the crown had been pawned off to a Venetian consortium by Baldwin II, and King Louis had simply bought it from them. But I managed to hold my tongue and look suitably impressed. Then I frowned. 'We are not married,' I said. 'And I don't think there's the slightest splinter left of the true cross. It's been a thousand years, my lord.'

'We will get married as soon as I shave.' Jean winked at me as Charles came into the room carrying a basin of hot water. 'See? You didn't even have to call him.'

Charles set the bowl down. 'There's bad news in the camp,' he said without preamble.

'What is it?' Jean splashed water on his face and leaned back. 'Will you shave me now, Isobel?'

Charles frowned. 'The king's illness has taken a turn for the worse.'

Jean uttered a cry and stood up so suddenly he nearly overturned the basin. I righted it just in time. He went to peer out of our window. 'I see him. He's lying on a pallet under his awning.'

I stood next to Jean, a strange, tingling feeling growing between my shoulder blades. I was watching history unfold.

A crowd gathered around the royal tent, but there was hardly any noise. Soldiers stood in straight lines, guarding the fortress and the king's tent, but most of the crusaders milled about aimlessly, and silently.

'What's going on?' Jean asked. 'Why is that girl being led over?'

Charles pushed between us and squinted. 'It's the virgin,' he said.

'I beg your pardon?' Jean stood on tiptoes to get a better look.

Charles made a face. 'The doctors say the king needs to make love in order to get rid of the sickness inside of his body. They've fetched a virgin. She will lay with the king, and he'll get better.'

'Why don't they just bleed him?' Jean asked.

'They have, but nothing has helped. He's been in agony since last night, and every hour he grows worse.' Charles pursed his lips. 'She's very young.'

'I'd say she was about twelve. What on earth . . . why, they're taking her clothes off!' I was shocked. 'Jean, that's not—'

'She doesn't mind,' said Jean haughtily. 'It's an honour for her.'

'I don't think so!' I said. The girl dropped her shift and stood naked in the bright sun. Her small face puckered worriedly, and her hands were cupped in front of her sex. Her breasts were tiny rosebuds. After she was escorted to the pallet, the king propped himself up on one elbow and motioned to his head physician.

The sound of their voices travelled upwards. I cocked my head and listened unabashedly.

'What's he saying?' Jean hissed.

'Shhh, his voice is so weak.' I cupped my hands behind my ears and strained to hear. 'He says he won't sully the vows of marriage he

101

took with his wife. He will lie with no one but her. The virgin will have to go.'

'No!' cried Jean, incredulous.

'He says thank you.' I nodded, impressed. 'He's very ill, I can hear it in his voice. Poor Louis.' I was suddenly very sad. He'd been one of the kindest persons I'd ever met. Below us, in the tent, the doctors pushed the girl forward, all begging the king to reconsider. They went so far as to put her right into the bed with him. One held her down, and the others begged the king to have sex with her.

'No,' said King Louis, and he turned his back to the naked virgin and refused to speak again.

'Wow.' I was impressed. 'I don't know many men who would have resisted.' I looked sideways at Jean.

He snorted. 'She's just a child. Besides, when you're ill with the flux the last thing you want to do is make love.'

'I prefer to believe King Louis is a saint,' I said, then clapped my hand over my mouth.

'What is it?' Charles asked.

'Nothing.' I straightened up. 'Come, Jean, let me shave you. You must go and pay your respects to the king before he dies.'

Jean whirled around, his face very white. 'He's not dying!'

Now was the time to tell him. 'I'm afraid he is.' I took his hand and led him to a stool. 'I want you to be prepared for the worst. Your king will die before his brother can come.'

'But . . . but the scouts said his sail was spotted not six hours away!'

'We'd better get you ready quickly then.'

Charles of Sicily stepped ashore almost exactly one hour after his brother drew his last breath. The king's body was still warm when his brother kissed his forehead and then turned and knelt at Philip's feet.

'My nephew, you are now King of France,' he said in a choked voice.

Philip blanched. I don't think he'd quite realized what his father's death meant for him.

Charles' troops pitched their tents a few kilometres away from the king's camp. I thought it a prudent move to avoid the illnesses running rampant through the ranks of the crusaders. There were other reasons the Sicilians and the French didn't get along very well, as we were soon to discover.

That night, Jean and I were both leaning out of our window, as usual, so we spotted the quarrel right after the sentries did. 'Fight! Fight!' the sentries screamed and motioned with their spears towards the seashore.

A man in crusader's garb pushed a soldier and shouted. They scuffled and bumped into a local merchant, causing him to drop his basket of dates. Losing his temper, the merchant smashed the basket on the soldier's head. At his cries, more soldiers came running. The shouting grew louder.

'You'd think that they could let the king's body repose in peace,' Jean said bitterly.

He pulled away from the window and paced in the room. 'I hate it here. Why did I come? This place is cursed. You were right, Isobel. How could I have been so blind? War! Ha! It's nothing but pest, dysentery, and flux.'

I glanced over my shoulder at him and raised my eyebrows, but he was too busy kicking at our bed covers to notice. The fight on the beach had reached epic proportions. At least fifty soldiers, half as many crusaders, and a handful of what looked like native merchants were all involved in the brawl.

'Come look at this,' I said. 'War is also a melee.' I looked upwards to swat at a mosquito and frowned as something caught my eye. There was a shadow on the horizon. 'Uh-oh. I think trouble's coming.'

Jean stopped kicking the covers and rushed back to the window. His youthful enthusiasm for fights sparked his interest. He gazed at the crowd and winced. 'I don't think that man will walk again,' he said.

'Yes, but look, over there on the hill!' I said, pointing.

Jean followed my finger and his face suddenly paled. 'It was a diversion,' he whispered.

He leaned as far out the window as he could. 'Sentries, sentries!' he yelled. 'We're being attacked! Look up on the hillside! You *fools*, can't you see we're being attacked?' He pounded the stone window casing with both fists. Then he turned and kissed me hard on the mouth. 'Idiots,' he said. 'I have to go.'

'Be careful!' I felt his forehead out of habit, but he was fine. A little wan, but done with his malaria.

He shot me a half amused, half annoyed glance. 'I'll do my best to stay out of trouble.' Then he clattered down the spiral staircase, shouting as he went. 'To arms, to arms! We're being attacked!'

He was right, actually. The Saracens had sensed the tensions between the two camps and sent spies while they readied for a surprise attack. Luckily, the sentries hadn't left their posts, and the soldiers were quick to get ready. The horses were saddled and the soldiers armed in less than a quarter hour. The foot soldiers took their places in the trenches and, as the Saracens rode up, engaged them while the cavalry got into position.

The crossbowmen clambered up onto the roof of the fortress and started raining arrows down upon the attackers. In no time, the real battle was engaged.

The emir of Tunis, hearing that King Louis was dead, thought to profit from the tragedy and strike while the French army was leader-less. He hadn't counted on Charles of Sicily and Philip uniting their forces so quickly, or on Philip's leadership qualities. The new king was a natural commander and an excellent tactician. He quickly rallied his troops and riposted with fury. Perhaps part of it was grief – he was mad with it, some said. He rode at the head of his army, waving his great Damascus steel broadsword and bellowing '*Chargez! A mort les infidèles!*'

The army swept in behind him like a wide, prickly curtain. After three hours of hard fighting, the crusaders won. A huge cheer shook the soldiers when the Saracens turned and fled. The emir of Tunis, seeing the battle lost, pulled all his soldiers out of range of the cross-bows and sent his emissaries immediately to sue for peace.

I could see most of the first part of the battle from my window, but it was too far away, really, to see individuals. When Philip's forces pushed their opponents over the crest of a hill, the fighting was lost from sight.

Afterwards, the soldiers trickled back into the fortress, many clutching scraps of the flags that they'd wrenched from the infidels. I looked for Jean among the crowd, but he was nowhere to be seen. I wasn't worried. There was already raucous singing coming from the soldiers' quarters. Flags were hoisted, flapping in the dusty wind. The sun started to set, and the whole world looked as if it had been dipped in gold.

Men continued to pour into the gates, many limping now or being held up by friends. A horse cantered in, saddle empty, scattering people in his way. A soldier made a grab at his bridle and missed, and the horse veered off towards the stables. He knew where his oats were. I started to smile but froze when I recognized the horse as Jean's brown cob.

'Charles!'

'What is it?' He leapt to his feet and strewed chess pieces all over the floor.

'We have to go find Jean. His horse has come back without him.'

'That says a lot for his horse,' said Charles. However, his face furrowed with worry. 'We'll go the back way, there will be less of a crowd.'

I grabbed a shawl and flung it over my head. Charles asked me what I needed it for. 'It's hot as an oven outside.'

'In case Jean has wounds that need binding,' I said grimly.

Charles led me out of the fortress through a back door, but even that was blocked by milling soldiers. We finally wormed our way through and set off down the road at a quick trot. The road wound past the coast before dipping into a low valley. As we jogged, we dodged horses, soldiers and civilians like us, going back to the fort.

Several times we had to leap off the road to avoid being run over by galloping steeds.

'Can't you go any faster?' I begged Charles, tugging at his arm.

'I'm hurrying!' Charles puffed. 'But I'm still feeling weak, if you really want to know.'

'I'm sorry!' I stopped so suddenly he nearly crashed into me. 'You're barely over your fever. You shouldn't be rushing around like this. Go back if you wish.'

He shook his head. 'No, my lady. Jean needs us both. Come, the battlefield isn't very far.'

'How can you tell?' I craned my neck, but we were in the bottom of the valley, and I couldn't see over the hill.

'Can't you smell it?'

I stood still and sniffed. My nose was assailed by a sharp, coppery scent. 'What is it?'

'Blood,' said Charles, his face still. 'The battle must have been harder than I thought.'

Besides the straggling soldiers, the doctors hurried along, carrying their medicines, while men trotted to and from the fort with stretchers. I peered at each one going by me, to see if I recognized Jean, but I saw no one I knew. Other women hastened towards the battlefield as well, their faces drawn with anxiety.

I pulled my shawl tighter around my shoulders. Despite the evening's heat, I was shivering. As we topped the last rise, below us was a plain, and upon it were hundreds, no, thousands of bodies.

Charles yanked me off the road in time to avoid being hit by a wagon pulled by a team of four mules. In it, I saw with a sinking heart, were men with spades over their shoulders. They weren't wasting time before digging graves. In this heat the bodies would decompose and spread all sorts of diseases.

Charles crossed himself, speechless at the sight of the battlefield.

'Come on,' I whispered. 'Jean must be down there somewhere.'

'I hope we get to him before the gravediggers do,' said Charles.

'Oh God, don't say that. He's not dead,' I cried.

'They bury living men, too,' said Charles wryly. 'That's what I meant. Shall we separate? I'll go to the left, you to the right. We'll stay within shouting distance.'

'It sounds as if you've done this before,' I said. 'All right. Let's go.' Dread prickled over my body.

★

Some of the dead men looked so much like Jean that once or twice I cried out, and Charles came running. Each time he found me on my knees, trembling, but from relief.

Each time he pulled me to my feet and shook me hard.

'Isobel! Get a hold of yourself. He's out here somewhere, and we'll find him.'

Night fell but offered no respite from the heat. Torches flickered in the navy blue air as women searched for husbands or lovers, and doctors searched for survivors. There were sporadic shouts when doctors yelled for the stretchers or women screamed as they found what they had feared. Overlying everything was the constant *thunk* of spades hitting the earth, the steady swish of dirt flung over shoulders, and the occasional sharp clang of iron hitting rocks.

I staggered on. The battlefield stank. It was soaked in blood, and once I tangled my feet in someone's intestines and nearly tripped. I uttered a strangled scream, managed not to vomit and stepped out of the slippery mess. It took me a good three minutes to get myself together and moving once more.

In the dark, dead horses became huge, threatening shapes. Wounded horses neighed plaintively, their whinnies blending in with the cries and moans of the wounded. There was less crying than you would think. Most men lay in shock and watched their last stars, their minds already somewhere else.

One or two men called to me, begging for water. I had no waterskin with me. Each time I shook my head and they nodded, slumping back onto the grass, staring off once more into the sky.

I walked, calling Jean's name softly, like a litany, over and over. 'Jean, where are you? You can't be dead the sky would already be cracking open to swallow me.' In my mind, the erasure would start like a huge rip in the heavens, a gaping hole that would suck me into nothingness. Lightning would flash, and clouds would roil and churn as they met the vacuum the Time Correctors would use to erase all the damaged parts of history.

I stumbled on someone's outstretched hand and stopped, head bowed, chest heaving, willing everything to be a dream.

Charles called me. His voice rose over the sound of the graves being dug and the cries of a wounded man being pulled out from under his horse.

'Over here. Isobel, hurry!'

I dashed across the field, leaping over a fallen soldier, a sword, a spear. There was a horse in my path I swerved around it and nearly fell upon Charles, kneeling just on the other side. He cradled Jean's head on his lap.

'He's dead,' he said softly.

I dropped to my knees at his side. In the feeble light, I could see that he was right.

Jean was dead. His face was peaceful but devoid of all colour. I stuffed my fists into my mouth. Horror iced my spine. Jean was dead, my green-eyed boy, my dark-haired lover, dead on the battlefield with an arrow in his side.

'No,' I managed to whisper.

Charles looked at me. His face was dreadfully pale. 'I'm so sorry.'

'No.' I repeated stubbornly.

'Shall we take his armour off?' he asked me gently. 'His mother will want to have it.'

'No!' I couldn't stop. My head shook, and my entire body trembled. My teeth started to chatter.

'I'll do it. You should go back now.' Charles stood, and Jean's head slid off his lap.

'No!' I lunged forward and caught it, let it down gently. Then I crouched over him, my tears falling on his face. 'How could you die?' I whispered to the still body. 'How could you leave me here alone? What will become of me? You can't die, you have to go back to Paris. What about your descendants? Who will rule France now?' My voice shook. 'My God, Jean, what have you done?' My voice rose in a thin wail. I was rocking back and forth now.

'Isobel, please!' Charles took my arm and tugged, but I ignored him.

'Jean, wake up now, please,' I begged. I couldn't see anymore. Tears obscured my vision. Sobs were torn from my throat I couldn't

108

stop them any longer. I lay over Jean's body and sobbed, wailed, and keened all of my fear and despair. The night was split with the sounds of crying, but my wails soared over the rest, drowning them, drowning me.

Charles sat by my side, his hand on my arm, and murmured quietly. I have no recollection of what he said. I have no memory of returning to the fortress, of lying on the pallet or falling asleep. I was caught in black glue that held my mind prisoner. My eyes were open, but all I could see was Jean's white face.

Chapter Nine

The Crusades were a bloody war, but the word Crusade *was used for all religions wars, including the war against the Cathari in the Kingdom of France. The sayings, 'If it can be shown that some heretics are in a city then all of the inhabitants can be burnt' and 'Kill them all, God will know his own' come from the Crusades. Stay as far away from religious conflict as you can.*

Tempus University *Corrector's Handbook*

Charles was curled up at my side. When I stirred, he sat and looked down at my face intently. 'Isobel?' he whispered.

'Tell me it was all a dream,' I begged.

'I'm sorry.' He bowed his head, and tears dripped off his nose. He looked so thin and pale, almost as sickly as he'd looked that evening in France when I'd first set eyes on him.

'How long have I been sleeping?' I asked. I felt so drained it was an effort just to speak. Why hadn't I been erased? Had Tempus U forgotten about me? No, that was impossible. I tried to clear my head, shaking it weakly.

'It's been five days,' whispered Charles.

'What?' I froze, my voice cracking.

'Don't cry, my lady, please don't cry.' Charles patted my arm, an expression of desolation on his peaked face.

I hitched myself up on one elbow then sat up painfully. 'Where is everyone? Why is it so quiet?' For a strange second, I thought we were all dead. The morning sunlight streamed through the window, making the colours in my cloak and on Jean's armour, propped in the corner, glow. The rays glittered off his helmet and set the scarlet plume afire.

'They have left for the hills. The pest is upon us and already three hundred people have died. Can you hear the chanting? The priests think to keep it away with religious fervour.' Charles closed his eyes. 'I never thought I'd see so many people die.' He scrubbed at his eyelids with his fists. 'We'll die too, won't we?'

I slumped against the wall, my head bowed to my chest. A great lassitude took hold of me. In a haggard voice I said, 'Listen to me, Charles. The sickness is caused by fleas. The rats carry them. When the fleas bite you, their saliva deposits the pest in your blood and you fall ill. It isn't always fatal – some people resist better than others do. If you can avoid fleas or rats, it's better.'

Charles looked at me through narrowed eyes. 'When you were sick, after Jean died, you lay in your bed and raved. You spoke of things I'd never heard of, of kings and princes, and travels through time. You said that Jean couldn't die. That it was impossible because he had to start a dynasty of kings and now your mission was a failure. You kept begging the time senders to let you try again. *"Take me back and let me try once more"*, you cried.'

I gaped at him. He was speaking of things that he never should have heard. Now I was sure to be erased, Charles along with me. 'Shhh! You mustn't say those things! If anyone hears you, we'll both be . . . killed,' I said. 'They'll think we're sorcerers.'

'Yes, but what about the magicians who sent you back in time?'

'I can't tell you about them,' I said, horrified that he'd overheard. 'It will be the ruin of both of us. Forget you ever heard anything, I beg you!'

'I'd never breathe a word to anyone,' he said, looking offended. 'You can tell me the truth, Isobel. Besides, I have no wish to be branded a sorcerer and turned over to the Inquisition.'

I rubbed my face. What had I done? Rule Number One was drilled into our heads from day one: never, ever let on to anyone that you're from another time. Better to die than admit you're from the future because it could create a ripple in the time continuum and would practically ensure the erasure procedure had to be used. The historians had insisted.

I sighed. They'd also insisted Jean would be easy to manage, that my mission was a simple one, and that I'd been sterilized. What else had they got wrong? What harm could it do now? I trusted Charles, and he deserved to know the truth.

'I'll tell you, but not today. Right now I have to think of what to do. I failed, don't you see?' My voice cracked. 'I've failed, and when those time senders . . . I mean magicians find out, they will destroy me and everyone around me.'

He pursed his lips and gave me a doubtful look. 'If you say so. At any rate, the mission you dreamed of hasn't failed. You carry Jean's babe. Have you forgotten that?'

I raised my head to stare at him. He looked at me with his wise eyes, his weary face pale and tear-stained but set with a determination I'd rarely encountered. 'Oh my Lord,' I whispered.

'You had forgotten, hadn't you?'

'It may not be his.' My chest shook with each heartbeat and my whole body vibrated like a guitar string.

Charles thought about that, his head to one side. 'Who else knows that?'

'No one,' I said. It was true. Even the historians with their vacuum-sealed book would not know. People's movements and actions aren't recorded, only their impact on the future. Now that Jean was dead, I had to give this child his name. Perhaps it wasn't such a fiasco after all. I licked my dry lips, thinking hard. Jean had never done anything of note – his birth and death had been unrecorded. Only his bloodline was important.

Dizzying relief swept over me.

'Then you'll have to go back to Paris and bear the babe in his family home. You will have to raise him as Jean's son. Will that be too difficult?'

'That's what I'll do.' I rose halfway, and then sat down when my head spun. 'Charles, will you help me?' I begged. 'Will you stay with me, please?'

'On one condition.'

'Name it.'

'That you tell me all your secrets. I want to know by what sorcery you voyaged through time and what you were speaking about when you were delirious.'

I stared at him, undecided. If Charles was right, maybe I wouldn't be erased after all. However, if he knew, or suspected, I'd come from the future, it would unbalance everything according to the TCF historian. The same infallible historian who assured me that I was sterile . . .

A hysterical giggle bubbled out of my lips and I clamped them shut. He waited patiently, his chin on his knees. Then I said, 'We'll speak of this later, and *only* in private. First, can you show me where Jean was buried? I need to see his grave.'

We stood in front of a small mound of dirt. There was a cairn of stones at its head, and for the first time I noticed Charles' hands were scraped and reddened. He caught my glance. 'I made them bury him by himself, not in the ditch with the others.'

'Thank you.'

'He was my friend too,' Charles said.

We stood shoulder to shoulder while the sun rose high into the heavens. The heat made us retreat, finally, to the shade of a cypress. Charles opened his pouch and took out two pieces of stale cheese, some flatbread and a flask of wine. We ate while the flies buzzed noisily around us. In the distance, the waves crashed upon the beach. Faintly from the north came the sounds of the crusaders' encampment. They had grouped in the caverns. Charles told me that the King of Sicily was discussing a truce with the emir of Tunis while Philip made plans to leave. He would bear the bones of his father and brother to France.

'Poor Jean-Tristan,' I said softly. 'Poor King Louis, and poor Jean.' Tears spilled down my face. I didn't try to stop them. My pain was still too raw. Perhaps I'd never loved Jean as he'd loved me, but he had been my lover, and already my body missed his soft caresses. He'd been so handsome, so insouciant, and so enthusiastic. I would never know if I'd truly loved him, unless you could measure love by the empty space it leaves when it is lost. If you could, then my love had been immense, for I now felt as if my entire body was nothing but an empty shell.

Charles patted my shoulder and swatted at a fly. 'Isobel, we had better make plans for leaving.'

'I thought I would send a message to the princess. I mean, to the queen. She is the queen now, isn't she?' I asked.

'Queen Isabella of France,' said Charles.

'I hope she won't hold all this against me,' I muttered. Charles shot me a startled look, and I shrugged. 'She thought I'd bring her good luck.'

'Then I hope she is the forgiving sort,' he said.

She was. 'My melancholy angel!' she cried, as we boarded the ship. She swooped towards me. Her arms were held wide, her pointed cap was askew, and her yellow veil floated behind her like a cloud of pollen.

She hugged me tightly, and I felt her body tremble.

'My poor angel,' she repeated. 'Your husband was so young and handsome. Jean-Tristan adored him and told us before his death that he wanted your husband and you to accompany him to Nevers. You will have to honour his wishes. You must visit his court. I'll make sure that you're welcome.' She pulled back suddenly, her eyes glazed. 'Oh look, they're raising the sails. Are we sailing, then? Where are you going?'

'I am going to Paris to take Jean's armour to his parents,' I replied. 'Your majesty, perhaps you'd like to sit down for a while. The ship is pulling anchor, and we'll soon be leaving. Shall we sit here? It looks rough out there. I fear the swells will make you fall.'

'Of course, of course you must go to Paris. What was I thinking?' She laughed and put her hands on her stomach, where a tiny bulge belied her pregnancy. 'I mustn't fall down, either, it would be bad for the baby. Oh, where is my nurse, Carolina? I hope she isn't sick. I lost all my handmaidens but these two, and my midget died.' She waved towards two sickly looking women huddled behind her. 'My juggler is dead, as is my confessor. I shall have to find another one right away – I can't use Philip's confessor. No, I shall have to find another one. How lucky you were that this plague didn't affect you.' Her voice was high and shaky. She talked as fast as she could, I suspected to keep whatever demons lurked inside her head at bay. Her hands tightened convulsively on her belly.

I led her to a cushion and waited until she sat down, then I looked around for Charles. He stood near the tiller, his face turned towards land. I followed his gaze, towards the hills, where Jean lay forever sleeping. My eyes filled with tears and I blinked them away. It would do no good to cry, especially now.

I put on a brittle smile and turned towards the queen. 'It will be good to go back to France,' I said.

'Yes.' She smiled tremulously.

The long black pennants at the top of the masts flapped in the wind and I couldn't repress a shudder. I sat next to the queen and hugged my skirt tighter around my legs as the ship moved towards the open sea and the breeze grew stronger. It filled the sails and they swelled out above our heads, heavy grey curves of linen. Sails on other ships billowed like storm clouds all around us as they caught the wind. The masts creaked and the sailors cheered. The ships moved out of the harbour.

Charles didn't budge from his post. While everyone else looked forward over the vast water towards France, he stayed perfectly still, staring at the place where so many had died.

The queen tried to remain gay. She chatted brightly about the weather, the birds, the sailors and the ships. However, her voice often cracked and her hands were white on her skirt, the fabric bunching as she clutched at it. Her two remaining handmaidens sat like drooping lilies nearby, not speaking.

Her husband, the new King of France, was on the ship with us.

He sat on his father's throne beneath an awning, surrounded by men in black robes with long faces. Deep lines of sorrow dove from his nose to his chin and marred his forehead. His skin was fair, though burnt by the fierce African sun. The same sun burnished his hair bright gold and his eyes were chips of blue sapphires beneath tanned brows. He sat still and seemed to take no heed of anyone around him.

Later I heard rumours that he'd run from the fortress out of fear after the battle that had taken Jean's life, rumours that he'd fled from cowardice. I can tell you now that none of that is true. I was there. During the battle, while fighting the infidel, he was valiant. He fought in the thick of it. Then, when his soldiers and the crusaders started dying of the pest, he did what he thought best. Should his country lose two kings, or more? He left the miasma of the marshy lands around the forest and headed to the caves. Unfortunately, the dusty caves didn't stave off the rats, which followed the grain, and on the rats were the deadly fleas.

After less than a week, the death toll was stupendous. Weakened by malaria and lack of proper food, the crusaders were decimated by the quickly spreading sickness. It was a miracle that the queen and king survived.

The queen clutched at her skirt, raised her thin pale face to the sky, and asked me if I knew how long it would take to sail to France.

'I wish I knew,' I answered.

She sighed and got to her feet. 'I shall see you soon, angel,' she said, in her high, quavering voice.

'Where are you going?'

'To my quarters to pray. The sight of Tunis makes me weep.' She gave a little choking sob and motioned at her ladies-in-waiting to accompany her below deck.

I looked for Charles, but he was gone. He must have put our belongings away, for I no longer saw the bundles we'd carried on board the ship. I peered down the trapdoor where a ladder disappeared into the darkness. Sighing, I wrapped my robe tightly around my legs and climbed down.

The wood was rough, and I got two splinters before I reached our level. I couldn't walk upright as the ceiling was too low, so I had to hunch over as I searched for Charles and our room. The rooms were separated by planks knotted together with hemp rope, so the word 'wall' didn't quite describe them, and they had no doors. I looked into each one, trying to find mine.

In one room stood a flock of priests, crowded together and arguing about who was to sleep on the only bunk. In another huddled the queen's two ladies-in-waiting and the nurse, Carolina, their pale faces glowing like moons in the penumbra. I bade them good evening, but they were petrified with fear. Their only reaction was a sort of shiver that ran over their bodies and set their pointed caps knocking together like branches on a tree in a high wind.

Our tiny cabin was just behind the mainmast, two storeys below deck. It was perhaps six feet square and damp. It was cramped, especially as we'd brought our tent, our rug, and all our belongings with us. A narrow plank fastened to the wall boasted a peg upon which to hang our cloaks. We rolled everything into tight sausages and wedged them wherever there was space. Fortunately, our donkey had been loaded onto a ship carrying livestock.

After sailing for months, then being docked in a bay where it had baked in the sun, the tar and pitch that sealed the planks of the ship had begun to give. The ship was still seaworthy, but repairs were in order. I touched the rough wood that separated me from the deep water and my hand felt the damp.

'It's better than nothing,' said Charles stoically.

'And it could be worse,' I said. 'Most of the crusaders are bedded on dirty straw in the hold of ships carrying livestock.'

He didn't answer, too occupied with shoving the rug as far as it could go beneath the wooden shelf that was the bed.

'Let me help,' I said.

'No, you have to take care of yourself,' he said.

I smiled. He had appointed himself my guardian angel, and there was nothing I could do to dissuade him that I didn't need one. He was sure I was as fragile as porcelain, now that I was *'enceinte'* as he put it.

Above us came the sounds of footsteps walking across the wooden floor. A thump was heard, and loud voices started arguing about who was going to sleep where and on which bunk. 'The nobles,' Charles said succinctly. 'They're all on the first level.'

'Where is the king's room and where do the sailors sleep?' I knew Charles had likely explored the entire ship. He was always curious.

'The sailors share a room at the bow – they take turns sleeping in hammocks. The supplies are in their room, and one floor below us are the water kegs. They're heavy enough to use as ballast, I suppose. King Philip and Queen Isabella have the biggest room, at the stern. The nobles are all packed in small cabins to the left and right of a narrow corridor, and there is a steep staircase leading to their quarters.' He grinned. 'The stairs are always jammed with nobility trying to go above deck for fresh air or back to their cabins to fetch something.'

'We have a ladder to get to our deck,' I said. 'It will be crowded too, I imagine.'

'Yes, full of maids, priests, sailors and uncertainties, such as us.'

'Uncertainties?' I raised my eyebrows. 'Well, that would describe us. Shall we uncertainties go eat? I just heard the dinner bell.'

That evening, after we'd eaten a few bites of the cold lentil stew the cooks offered to everyone, we huddled into the small space left by our baggage and braced ourselves against the rise and fall of the waves. Since we'd left sight of land, the waves had grown steadily bigger. The wind picked up, whipping the tops of the waves into white foam, and the mast creaked with the strain. The ship bobbed like a cork, rising to the top of the swell and then sliding down into a trough with a sickening lurch. From neighbouring rooms came sharp cries, thuds and moans as people were tossed about. Through the wide cracks in the walls I saw the four priests huddled together like a murder of crows in their black cloaks as they knelt and chanted in prayer. The maidens on the other side of our room squealed and shrieked each time the ship shuddered with the onslaught of the waves.

The swells deepened. The ship pointed her nose at the sky and climbed up another wave, her timbers groaning and masts creaking, before plunging downwards again. I huddled closer to Charles and hoped my poor little donkey wasn't suffering too much.

'Stop worrying about the donkey and pray for us,' Charles said.

'Oh, Lord . . . I think my stomach is somewhere in my throat,' I moaned.

'That's not a prayer.'

'Then I pray I don't throw up on you. Pass me the bowl, quick!'

'Oh no! Not again!'

I retched miserably into the tin bowl clutched in my hands. The sour smell of vomit filled the stuffy cabin, and Charles wrenched the bowl out of my hands and bent over it, his sides heaving.

When he had nothing left in his stomach, he raised his pale, crumpled face and looked at me. 'The waves are getting bigger,' he said. 'I hope there's not a storm coming.'

'Don't be silly,' I said weakly. Just then there came the sound of trapdoors slamming shut and darkness enveloped us.

We looked at each other, but all I saw of Charles were the whites of his eyes. We clutched at the walls as the ship keeled once more. I heard the rush of water on deck and imagined the sailors, what they must be suffering as they attempted to hold the tiller straight.

I heard shouting. 'Lower the sails! Quickly, men, quickly!'

Another gust of wind came and the sound of tearing cloth silenced our cabin, as well as those around us. After a moment, the ship rolled again, and the maidens screamed in unison. The scent of urine was mixed with that of vomit. I buried my face in my sleeve and wished for perhaps the hundred thousandth time I was still in my own century.

The ship struggled gamely up another wave, tottered for a moment, then swooped downwards. I gave a strangled cry and gasped as the sound of the wind and waves rose above the sailors' shouts and the handmaidens' cries. The priests started chanting again, but it sounded more like crying.

'Our Father, who art in heaven,' recited Charles feverishly. 'Are you there, Isobel?'

'I am. Lord, it's dark. I wish we had some light,' I said. There was no light. Some usually filtered in through cracks, but the sky had darkened and the only thing coming through was tiny sprays of seawater. I couldn't see them, but I could feel them, sometimes on my back or face. The waves forced water through the ship's sides, and the timber moaned like a living beast.

A bolt of lightning showed for a split second through one of the seams, and a clap of thunder followed soon after. Charles prayed under his breath, but I was too terrified to remember any of the words. The only thing I could keep thinking of was Philip, King of France.

'He doesn't die,' I muttered. 'He doesn't die, he doesn't die, he doesn't die.'

'Who?' shouted Charles, raising his voice above the wind.

'King Philip. He reigns over France,' I cried.

'How do you . . .' His voice was lost in a huge roar of thunder and the ship pitched with renewed violence.

'I just know.' I clutched his arm to keep from rolling across the floor. The tin bowl clattered across the ground, and the reek of spilled vomit added to our discomfort, but at that moment it was the least of our worries.

We held each other as the storm mounted in fury and the thunder deafened us. Rain battered the ship and hit the water with a sound like an avalanche. The mast cracked so loudly I figured it had split in two, and I screamed, my voice joining the chorus of screams from neighbouring cabins.

'Does it hurt when we drown?' Charles asked, his whole body shaking.

'I don't know.' I bit my tongue as the ship slid into another trough. We were jarred as it ploughed bow first into the waves. It

120

righted itself, shuddering like a wounded hound, and staggered back up while the wind howled all around us and the thunder cracked the sky in two. My head spun, and I felt faint prickles all over my body. But it was just the static electricity from the storm, raising our hair and sparking whenever we touched something woollen.

Charles propped himself against the rug, and he shrieked when the greenish light ran up and down his arms. He leapt up to flee but lost his footing and fell. In the eerie light his face was a mask of terror.

The thunder boomed, the ship plunged and I grabbed Charles and tried to calm him the best I could, although I was half mad with fright myself. 'It's nothing, just St Elmo's fire. Don't worry, it can't burn!' I pointed, but the ethereal light had already vanished and we were once more in inky darkness. We tried to clamber onto the tiny bunk, but the tossing ship made that impossible. Clutched together, we rolled about on the floor.

Gradually, the storm blew itself out, thunder fading into the night. Above deck, the sailors shouted to each other as they rushed to repair the damage the sails and masts sustained. The sea calmed, the waves subsiding to choppy swells. The storm had lasted for many hours and we were exhausted. In the ensuing silence, Charles and I fell asleep, tangled in a heap on the soggy floor.

I woke first. My mouth was dry and filled with a bitter, acrid taste. My head hurt, my tongue was swollen where I'd bitten it, and my eyelids stuck together when I tried to open them. Charles was curled up, wedged beneath the rug. Faint snores came out of his open mouth. His little face looked battered, and great lavender circles around his eyes made him look nearly dead. But he'd always looked pale, thin and ill. I hoped to remedy that once we reached Paris and I could feed him some decent food.

A grey light filtered in through the doorway, which meant the trapdoor was open.

I hauled myself stiffly to my feet and stood, whacking my head on the ceiling. Stars danced in front of my eyes and tears of pain ran down my cheeks. I used them to clean my face. Then I rubbed my poor head, trying not to mind how greasy and lank my hair was. With shaking hands, I braided it the best I could, smoothed my stained dress over my hips, and made my way up on deck.

Watery sunlight blinded me and I stood for a moment just blinking. When I could see through the dazzle, I went towards the bow where the cooks had set up a large cast-iron pot.

'Ah, lentils,' I said.

I wasn't a noble, so I was given a small bowl but otherwise ignored. The smiles and fawning were for those with power and prestige. I knew from both my studies and my observations that the hierarchy of French courtly politics was merciless and rigid. Well, at least I was being fed.

I said thank you with my best finishing school courtesy and got a flicker of a glance from the assistant cook. I wandered over to a clear space on deck. Most of the passengers had come out of the bowels of the ship to get some air. Coils of ropes and great lengths of sail were spread out everywhere, and the sailors were busy painting cracked planks with pitch, tarring weakened joints and checking the masts and rigging.

Charles appeared, a bowl of lentils in hand, and sat next to me. We found a place out of the way of the sailors and nibbled our breakfast.

The air was perfectly clear, scrubbed clean by the storm. I wished I felt the same. My robe was stiff with grime and smelled atrocious. I finished my tasteless, overcooked lentils and waited a few minutes to see if I was going to be sick. Happily, my stomach seemed to have quieted.

My next concern was using the bathroom, always an adventure on board the ship. Toilet facilities were buckets standing near the sides. One used them, emptied them over the side and set them back in place. Stuffed into a crack, usually, was a piece of indescribably filthy cloth, the use of which can be surmised. I carried my own rags, which I used once and tossed over the side or washed if I was running low. I had got more or less used to availing myself of the toilets in plain sight of everyone, though I preferred the out-of-the-way buckets. No one else gave it a second's thought.

Nudity bothered no one, though a woman's modesty was considered a virtue. In this time, bodies and their functions were considered natural and healthy. Puritan notions of propriety hadn't been dreamed up yet.

King Philip clambered onto the deck, was greeted by deep bows by everyone, and went to the closest bucket and sat down. As he was sitting there, others who hadn't bowed to him a first time came and greeted him. He inclined his head graciously to everyone.

Then he stood up, adjusted his royal robes, and ate lentil stew for breakfast. A servant emptied his bucket over the side. Afterwards the priests led us in prayer, and we gave hearty thanks to God for sparing us from a watery grave.

After the meal, King Philip gave orders to his sailors to search for the other ships, for we were alone on the shimmering sea that morning. We had been scattered like chaff by the storm, and the other ships could be anywhere by now.

All day long, we searched. People climbed the rigging, strained their eyes towards the horizon and peered through spy-tubes for a glimpse of white sails. When someone spotted one, he'd give a hoarse cry and we'd all pile onto the railing and wave frantically, our voices shrill in the vast sea.

Slowly, the other ships drifted towards us. Some limped badly, their masts splintered, sails tattered, and half the crew vanished in the tempest. Some were nearly intact, as our ship was. That evening there were fifteen ships bobbing alongside of us.

Fifteen out of a hundred. At night, sailors lit lanterns and hung them on the tops of the masts so that the remaining ships would see us. Sails were reefed, anchors lowered, and we waited, water slapping against the wooden hulls, for the rest of the fleet to arrive.

That night was strangely silent, almost soothing. Perhaps we all knew where the other ships were, but nobody would say it aloud. The priests chanted from sunset to sunrise while King Philip sat immobile on his throne. At his side, like a dark shadow, huddled his wife. She'd fallen during the storm and injured her face. Purple bruises bloomed on nearly everyone. We were all battered and worn out, beaten by the storm.

Charles and I elected to sleep on deck. I couldn't bear to go down into our stuffy, stinking cabin. Urine, faeces and vomit made below deck a sort of preview of hell, especially since there were no windows and water had leaked in to soak everything. I salvaged an almost dry robe and wrapped myself in it, propping my back against Charles'. We both dropped immediately into a deep slumber.

Because of my exhaustion, compounded by the pregnancy, neither footsteps nor waves woke me the next morning, nor even the sun as it crept over the horizon. Quiet, shocked whispers stirred me out of my slumber. I raised my head and groped for Charles. He hunkered next to me, but his back was stiff, and when he took my hand, his own hand was icy.

'What is it?' I asked, my voice coming out raspy with thirst.

'Another ship has been spotted.'

'That's good, isn't it?' I struggled to arrange my clothing into some sort of order.

'The ship was upside down.' There was a silence as we stared at each other. 'One hundred ships are lost,' he said. His blue eyes were bleak in his face. 'More than four thousand people died in that storm. Some are saying that the infidels put a curse on us with their black magic.'

I licked my dry lips. 'What happens now?'

'We raise anchor and head for the nearest port.' Charles wrapped his arms around his knees and hugged them to his chest. 'We'll be in Sicily in another week, if the wind holds.'

I looked over at the pavilion, beneath which was Philip's throne. He still sat upon it, motionless. How could he not turn into stone? To lose his brother, his father, and now over half of his followers in the space of a couple of weeks was beyond terrible. Isabella, on the other hand, wrung her hands continuously, her face a white mask of terror. When the anchor was hoisted, she crossed herself, and with each pull of the ropes to raise the sails she flinched.

With black oriflammes cracking in the wind and the mainsail billowing, the ship heeled slowly around and headed towards the Kingdom of Sicily.

Chapter Ten

Gold coins were first copied from dinars and bore Kufic script, but after 1250, Christian symbols were added following Papal complaints. Correctors will be given three gold coins (called bezants). Do not spend them all at once.

Tempus University Corrector's Handbook

In November, we landed. I'd been terrified, thinking we were going to land on another island, and would have to get on board the ship again, but the Kingdom of Sicily also included part of the mainland on the toe of the boot of Italy. It was ruled by Philip's uncle, Charles I, who had stayed in Tunis to negotiate an extremely profitable deal (for himself, of course) with the emir. But he'd given his palace to his nephew, Philip, to stay in before he set off to France.

The sky mocked us, blue and limpid as if the world was fair and just. A soft breeze blew the ships to the docks, where hundreds of people were gathered to hear the news. Because the ships wore the black of mourning, they must have known something terrible had happened. The crowd stood, silent, shifting, watching the ships carefully. Perhaps they counted them too. As one ship then another cast anchor their bewilderment grew. When all the ships were anchored, there was a stir in the crowd. Banners were raised, timidly, and a man stepped onto the docks.

I stood at the rail, Charles at my side. 'Do you recognize that man?' I asked.

'From the banner his page holds, I would say it is one of the dukes of Sicily, come to welcome the King of France back home.'

'He doesn't know?'

'I don't believe so.' Charles sighed. 'Shall we prepare to leave the ship? We need to buy another donkey – ours drowned in the storm.'

I gave him some coins. I still had some left, and I'd taken Jean's purse, though it had been nearly empty. 'You take the money and go buy one. I'll wait here.'

Charles nodded and tucked the money I handed him into his belt. 'I'll be back as soon as possible.' Then he surprised me with a quick peck on the cheek. 'Don't worry, I'll take care of you.'

I blinked several times, rapidly, as I watched him make his way down the crowded gangplank and into the crowd. In a moment, he disappeared. He was still small for his age, but his eyes were ancient.

The king held his wife's elbow as they made their way down the main gangplank. Isabella leaned heavily on her husband, and even from my perch I could see her hands trembling. Her belly was round now, accentuated by the dress she wore. The style was close to the body, with a tight belt just below the breasts and a narrow skirt. Her clothes were filthy, her tightly braided hair was greasy, and her face was pallid.

King Philip wasn't in much better shape. We were all filthy, lousy and smelly. The duke wrinkled his nose as he stepped forward to greet Philip.

A low wailing grew in the crowd, and I guessed that news of King Louis' death had been announced. Soon everyone was beating their breasts, crying and sobbing his name like a chant. The dirge followed us as we made our way to the campgrounds, where the Sicilians had built fires and the smell of roasting meat tickled our nostrils. This was our welcoming feast.

As we watched, the meats cooking on the fires were heaped upon platters and carted around to individual tents. Two men held the poles that supported the platters while a third man handed out pieces of meat. Other men passed huge pitchers of mead around as well,

127

and there was even wine for the nobles. We were all famished, but there was no jostling, shouting or reaching, even from the peasant crusaders. We stood, apathetic, while the food was passed around, and then we simply ate where we were.

During the days that followed, the crowds dispersed as crusaders made their way back to their homes. Silently, banners drooping, groups of tattered pilgrims took to the road once more. Their progress was hurried – winter nipped at their heels.

After a week's rest and recuperation Charles and I followed the court, headed for a castle lent to the king for the occasion. The king wanted to head immediately for Paris, but his advisers considered it prudent to wait. The season was unusually cold. Ice fell in showers, breaking tree branches and making roads impossible to travel. Then cold winds swept down from the north along with deep snow, even as far south as Venice. The court made a temporary home in the castle while the snowflakes whirled and ice glittered on every branch. So it was decided we would wait until winter eased its grip. Time went by slowly.

My stomach swelled, as did the queen's, and we often stood side by side and compared bumps. She hadn't forgotten me, and an invitation had arrived as soon as we left the campground for us to come to the queen's quarters. There, she'd asked me to replace one of her ladies-in-waiting, and I would be given room and board. And that included Charles, of course.

We were staying near the coast, and the room Charles and I shared was spacious. It overlooked the courtyard and the front gate, and there was always something to see from my window. I spent hours leaning against the stone casement, a warm shawl over my shoulders, watching the comings and goings of diplomats, peasants and merchants. Dinners were eaten in the great hall, where everyone sat according to a strict hierarchy. Only I was somehow exempt. I was the widow of Prince Jean-Tristan's dearest friend, said the queen to anyone who asked.

'You must miss your husband dreadfully,' she said to me one evening, patting my hand gently.

'Yes, I do.' I was surprised, as always, by the stab of sorrow I felt when I thought of Jean.

'We will try and find you another husband as soon as you birth your babe,' she said.

'I think I'll wait a while. Perhaps Jean's father will let me stay with them.' Actually, I had no idea what would happen to me. I'd received a letter saying that Jean's mother had died. But Jean's father didn't know yet that his son was dead. The letter I'd written telling the family about Jean's death, and the one Jean's father had sent must have crossed each other en route. A message had arrived from Jean's father nearly two months after we arrived in Italy. It was brief, but explicit.

'From the Count de Bourbon-Dampierre,

'My son, a misfortune has befallen us. Your mother is dead. Your departure left her grieving while the message you sent from Tunis only hurt her more. That the king wants you near him is flattering. King Louis is a brave man and I am sure you will learn much from him. It is unfortunate you couldn't have waited for another crusade before running away like a villain. The news of Prince Jean-Tristan's death reached me only yesterday, along with your latest letter. Alas for your mother that she wasn't alive to read it. She suffered a cold that went to her chest. Never very strong, she succumbed as so many others did in the palace. I have decided to take your sister to Tours.

'Now I arrive at the heart of the matter. You said that you have married and that your wife, Isobel, is carrying your child. I shall look forward to meeting you both in Tours. Make haste.

'Your father, the Count.'

I knew Jean hadn't been an only child. Sometimes he talked about his younger sister, the one who wanted him to marry a wealthy woman. He hadn't known that his mother had died soon after he'd left. He would have been crushed. The reason was given as a chest cold, but the allusion was, from a broken heart. Now I had to write for Jean's father to come and fetch me.

Perhaps, I thought wryly, I'd break the news of Jean's death to him gently, along the lines of 'A misfortune has befallen us'. It took me three days to compose a suitable message telling him of Jean's demise. Charles helped me, looking over my shoulder, and trying to sound out the letters as I wrote.

'That's an F, not a T,' I said to Charles. 'I've written, "Sire de Bourbon-Dampierre, it grieves me to write this letter, but I see no other way to break the terrible news. Your son Jean died in battle. His body rests in Tunis, beneath an olive tree. He died bravely, fighting alongside Prince Philip."'

'King Philip,' corrected Charles. 'Is that how you spell Tunis?'

'Yes. Lord, where was I? "I had hoped to reach Paris in the spring, but as you are now in Tours, perhaps you can meet me halfway, as I will be travelling with Queen Isabella. I am now her lady-in-waiting. I await your reply and look forward to meeting you. Sincerely yours, Isobel, wife of Jean de Bourbon-Dampierre".'

Charles made a face. 'That sounds terribly awkward.'

'What does?'

'That you're the queen's lady-in-waiting, awaiting his reply.'

'You're right. Oh, Charles . . .' My voice broke. 'I hate writing letters. Especially this one. But I can't start another one. I haven't any vellum left, and the ink is nearly gone. Take this to the queen's messenger and have him put it in the bag with the rest of the mail.'

Thus November passed. In December, we celebrated a sad Christmas, and I received another curt message from Jean's father addressed to Jean. He'd received word that the king was dead. He was on his way to Italy and would arrive as soon as possible. There was no mention of my letter.

In January, the weather was bitter, and I huddled in a multitude of cloaks, my feet practically inside the fireplace.

When the warm winds of an early spring finally broke winter's grip, we made plans to leave. Isabella was eight months pregnant, and I was seven months along. When we stood side by side, my stomach stuck out much further than hers did, and she teased me.

'Look, you're fatter than I am,' she said. The months we'd passed resting had put weight on both of us. Her cheeks were smooth and the wings of hair peeping from beneath her pointed hat were sleek and shiny.

'It only means my baby is bigger than yours.' I ran my hand over my dress, thankful each time I did that the cloth was warm and clean. 'Perhaps you're to have a girl and I'm to have a boy.'

'No, you're carrying him higher than I am. Look, your belly is still pointing straight out. Mine has dropped. It means the child is getting into the birthing position.'

'Aren't you afraid of travelling now?' I asked. 'Won't it be better to wait until the baby is born?'

Isobel shook her head. 'I want to leave when my husband does. I've stayed with him since we were married, and I'll leave him only when death separates us.' She crossed herself. 'That reminds me. Would you please send my confessor to me? I need to speak with him before vespers.'

'Very well.' I curtsied and left her room to seek her priest, Père Sebastian. Since nearly all her ladies-in-waiting had perished, I did many of her errands. Mostly I fetched her shawl, recited a poem or a story, or looked for her confessor. She confessed at least three times a day, sometimes more if any impure thoughts flitted through her head.

As I'd discovered, being pregnant makes a woman's hormones go rather mad. Impure thoughts were easy to come by in a castle filled with males. I even found myself eyeing one of the grooms one day as he took off his shift to bathe in the watering trough. The shock was so great I nearly rushed off in search of Père Sebastian that minute.

If a bandy-legged groom, sixty years old and scrawny, could spark an interest, you can imagine what a handsome knight in a short tunic and tights could do. There were a few around. They spent their days polishing their armour, riding, or fixing their helmets, which always seemed to break. Several of the queen's younger

131

ladies-in-waiting found many excuses to go to the blacksmith, stop by the armoury or stroll through the courtyard as the knights supervised their grooms. If, through my open window, I heard a chorus of giggles, I knew there was a knight in sight. I'll admit, it usually gave me an excuse to put down my lamentable embroidery and lean out of the window.

I made no effort to go beyond that. It was nothing but the tug of war of hormones in my body. My breasts swelled, I grew languorous, my appetite was ferocious, and Charles remarked that I had grown as big as a warhorse, which was the largest animal he'd ever seen.

I tucked the last of my tunics into the leather bag on my bed and brushed a strand of hair out of my eyes. 'I am not enormous,' I said, fingering my braid. My hair was nearly to my waist now, and I wondered when it would stop growing.

'You are bigger than Sire Quentin's horse, and his is the biggest in the stables,' said Charles.

I was no horse, but I was huge and ungainly. A thought crossed my mind. 'I hope I won't be a nuisance. We're leaving tomorrow, and the trip will last nearly a month.'

'Luckily we're not going all the way to Paris,' said Charles.

'Where is Jean's father? What if we leave before he gets here?'

'We'll surely meet him en route,' Charles said with a shrug. 'We can't miss him. There's only one road.'

'That right. I forgot.' I sighed and put a hand behind my back to support it. 'How lucky that I'll be riding in a litter. I couldn't imagine how I was going to sit on that poor little donkey that you bought.'

'She'll carry our belongings.' Charles held a pair of stockings up. 'Did you really mend these?'

I blushed. 'I tried. Didn't the hole disappear?'

'The hole is gone, but now one leg is shorter than the other.'

'Perhaps your tunic will hide that.' I'd quickly discovered that the mending I'd taught myself in prison was limited, but I persevered.

Charles shrugged. 'It's of no importance, Isobel.'

When everything was packed, he shouldered the bag and made his way to the stables to load the donkey. I stood at the window and watched the bustle as everyone prepared to leave.

Despite the effervescence, the caravan that left Italy was not gay. Jean-Tristan and King Louis' bones accompanied us to Paris. Mourning flags hung low on the standards, and voices were muted. Even after two full months' rest, we were still shaky. The tragic crusade had weakened everyone who'd managed to escape the war, the plague, or the shipwrecks. Mostly we were silent; only the snorts of the horses and the steady clop, clop, clop of their hooves could be heard. The weather was dismal, wet and foggy. Winter left the roads deeply gutted and muddy, and progress was slow.

Barely a week after we left, five horsemen were spotted galloping towards us.

The guards rode out to intercept them, and then standards were raised and Charles grabbed my leg. 'It's Jean's father,' he said. 'I recognize the flag. Jean had the same insignia on his cloak.' His eyes sparkled. 'When he sees you and recognizes you, he's going to have a royal fit.'

I swallowed as I realized I was going to have to level with Charles. I lowered my voice so only he could hear. 'Charles, he won't recognize me. He's never seen me before.' I spoke in a very low voice. My throat was so tight I could hardly breathe.

'Of course he will! Why, you told us he made you promise to bring Jean back . . .' he stopped chattering and stared at me. 'He never saw you? But you said that, that . . .'

'I know what I said. It was all a lie. I needed to convince Jean to go home. I've never met Jean's father.'

Charles stopped smiling. 'There is some mysterious force at work here,' he whispered. 'You swore you weren't a witch, so what are you, Isobel? Are you a seraph, as Jean said? I'm starting to believe he was right. You're one of the fallen ones, condemned to suffer on Earth for the sins you committed in time.' He crossed himself.

133

His words hit close to home, and they hurt. 'I'm not a witch, nor am I a seraph. I simply had a mission.'

'You promised you'd tell me of your mission and the magicians. Can you tell me about it now?'

'You already know most of it. I had to make sure Jean founded a dynasty. Now, please, hush. If anyone else finds out, they will have us burned.'

Charles looked undecided. 'I hope someday you'll tell me everything.'

'When the time is right, I will.' I watched as the rider trotted nearer. As he passed, people turned and pointed towards my litter. I arranged my robes the best I could with hands that shook. In a quiet voice I said, 'Charles, I need you. Don't fail me now.'

He gave a little start and said, aggrieved, 'I will never fail you, my lady. No matter what you are, you're my friend.' He reached for my hand and helped me out of the litter. Shoulder pressing against shoulder, we waited together for Jean's father.

He clattered up on a great warhorse. He didn't dismount. His head was bare, his face an older, harder copy of Jean's, with deep-set green eyes. A long scar ran from his cheek to his throat. Seeing it, my hand strayed towards my own scar. I checked myself and managed a clumsy curtsey.

'My lord,' I said.

'Are you Jean's wife, Isobel?' He leaned down and frowned at me.

'I am.' I turned away from his piercing gaze, too tired, too frightened to confront anyone. Head bowed, I waited for his verdict.

'I received your letter, telling me about my son's death, two weeks ago.' His voice was dry, with barely any inflection.

'I'm very sorry,' I said. I waited for some sign of emotion, but he simply sighed.

'You will accompany me to Tours.' He tugged on his horse's reins, turned him around, and left at a heavy gallop. He positioned himself right behind King Philip.

'There goes a man who knows his place in the world and isn't afraid to show it,' Charles said to me.

I climbed back onto my litter and Charles took the donkey's bridle. Since our route would be the same for several weeks at least, we didn't leave the king's company. Then the king and his court would go north to Paris, and we would cut across the great swamp and lake region of Sologne towards Tours.

That night, Jean's father sent one of his guards to help set up our tent. Charles, who had been doing everything by himself, was relieved. The guard was a tall, sturdy, red-haired man called Lucien. He bowed to me and said that his services had been offered to me by the Lord de Bourbon-Dampierre. I nodded and thanked him.

We all gathered for dinner. Travelling was a slow business with the court. We left after the morning prayers, stopped for lunch at noon, had a short nap and more prayers, travelled until the shadows grew long, then stopped for vespers. After the prayers were done, we pitched our tents and the cooks started dinner. Servants set up the long benches and trellis tables and covered them with thick cloth. The table was set with pewter plates and jugs of wine and water. After the king and queen said a short prayer, we ate. Servants cleared the table and everything was put away again.

After dinner, I usually tried to find a stream to wash in or, failing that, begged a basin of warm water from the cooks. The grooms cared for the horses and donkeys, although Charles took care of our donkey and my litter, which was carried by two docile ponies the queen had given me.

That evening was no different. We ate dinner while a troubadour sang a mournful song. Afterwards, the women were excused and readied themselves for bed. Charles obtained a basin of water for me, and I bathed in the privacy of my tent after lighting a small brazier for warmth. I put on my sleeping gown and lay on my hard pallet. The tent flap was open to let out the smoke from my brazier, and I could see the stars and hear the faint sounds of men talking.

Charles unrolled his pallet next to mine and we huddled together for warmth. He rested his hand on my belly, as he did so often. He

135

loved to feel the baby moving, bumps sliding under the skin like a dolphin, he said.

'A dolphin?' I was amused.

'He has a pointy head,' said Charles in a whisper.

'Perhaps that's his elbow.' The night grew deeper and my eyes slid shut.

'Tell me how you knew the king would die,' Charles said.

I sighed. 'We need to go to sleep.'

'You can't sleep anyway when the baby is moving so much. Oh, he just turned over! Did you feel that?'

I gave a tired chuckle. 'Of course. Now let me sleep.'

'You promised. When you were ill you raved about the world ending.' His voice was a mere whisper, but it was tense. 'Will the world truly end? I'm frightened.'

I sighed and propped my head on my arms. 'No, it goes on and on. I come from a time far in the future, and the world has not ended yet.'

'How far?'

'How far can you count?' I asked Charles.

'I know a few sums, perhaps to one hundred.'

'The years that separate my time from this are as many as the leaves on ten mighty oaks. I was sent back to save Jean's life, and I failed. I should have been punished, but I think the baby gave me a second chance. He must take Jean's place as the founder of a dynasty. One day, his descendants will inherit the crown of France.'

'How will he do that?'

'I don't know. Or rather, I know who will found the dynasty, but I don't know how my baby and that person are related. In three hundred years, there will be a bloody war in France. Two religions will confront each other, the Catholics and the Protestants. The war will also involve two families, one headed by the Catholic king of France and the other by the king of Navarre, a Protestant called Henry.'

'Go on!'

'Henry will marry the king's daughter in a vain attempt to pacify the kingdom. Right after his wedding, on the night of St Bartholomew, the people of Paris will massacre the Protestants, killing more than six thousand men, women, and children.'

'Six thousand!' Charles gagged. 'That's horrible!'

'More horrible than you can imagine. Rivers of blood will run in Paris that night, and stain it for all of history. Henry manages to flee to Navarre and hide in a fortress. After several years, the king dies, his sons die with no heirs, and Henry, by right of marriage and blood, becomes King of France. He is obliged to give up his religion and becomes Catholic. He is the first of the Bourbons to rule France.'

Charles digested all this. 'So your child must somehow rule Navarre,' he said.

'No, I don't think so. Perhaps he will marry a princess of Navarre. Who knows?'

Charles swallowed. His hand tightened on my belly, then relaxed. 'What a terrifying story,' he whispered.

'Hush, I need to sleep now.'

'I can't sleep. I'll have nightmares for sure. Can't you tell me anything cheerful? Do the time magicians send people back in time every day? How does it work? Will time run amok if you make a mistake?' His voice trembled.

'Don't be frightened,' I said. 'Time is like a river. It flows in one direction. We're but tiny minnows in that river. We can swim upstream a-ways, and it won't change anything. You and I are just minnows, our actions won't change the flow of the river. It takes something terribly drastic to change the course of time. With Jean, a small portion of the river was diverted. I was the minnow sent back to put a twig in place and dam it up. The time magicians are there to make sure the river flows on and on. But we cannot tell anybody where I'm from.'

'We're just little minnows then,' murmured Charles, his words ending in a huge yawn. 'I'm glad you're the minnow they chose, Isobel. Otherwise, I'd never have got to meet you.'

I was strangely touched and smiled in the darkness. 'I didn't have much of a choice,' I said. 'But thank you, Charles.'

His only reply was a soft snore.

I was left staring at the glowing brazier, wondering what sort of man Jean's father was. For some reason, when I closed my eyes, I saw his face. His green eyes seemed to mock me, and the cruel scar on his cheek made my own scar ache.

Chapter Eleven

Voyaging in this time should be kept at a minimum. Roads are barely existent and a fall from a horse can be fatal. This said, learning the art of equitation may be a good idea. See Chapters 8 and 9 'Animals and their uses' and 'Identifying and caring for farm animals in the thirteenth century'.

Tempus University *Corrector's Handbook*

Each morning, the encampment woke and stretched its myriad arms and legs. Cooks hurried to fetch water. Grooms led the horses to drink then harnessed them. Priests intoned their morning prayers. Smoke rose in lazy spirals as fires were lit and meat was grilled for breakfast. The king and queen were greeted by the court. Chamber pots were filled and emptied. I wrinkled my nose and dressed while Charles folded our tent. Lucien, the guard assigned to us, rode up and offered to help.

Charles showed him where my ponies and litter were, and soon I sat more or less comfortably in my narrow, curtained litter as we moved off. The whole procession was lengthy, clumsy and slow, but we were advancing, even if it was sometimes no more than ten kilometres a day.

That day, a white mist covered the sun. Fog lay in soft swaths in the road, and sound was muted. Water droplets sparkled on spiderwebs and decorated the manes and tails of the horses. It was colder than usual. At noon, we stopped and the cooks built a huge fire to warm everyone.

I stood on the periphery of the fire and searched for Jean's father. Except for demanding to know if I was, indeed, Isobel, he hadn't made the slightest attempt to speak to me. I didn't catch more than a glimpse of him.

The queen was by herself, so I went to see her. She stood hip-deep in the mist, wrapped in a thick blue cloak. Her face was very pale.

'Are you feeling well?' I asked.

'My travail will start soon. I lost a drop of blood this morning. That's a sure sign. You will need to look for it yourself soon, my angel.' She smiled at me. 'I'm always anxious before it starts. Then, when it finally gets underway, I put myself in the hands of God and pray. It's easier to accept.'

I shifted my feet. An ache had begun low in my back that morning. 'Should you journey today? Would it be better to stay here?'

'It could be days before it gets underway. The full moon isn't for another two days. Usually it happens then. The pull of the moon works on birthing, as well as the tides,' she said, glancing at the sky. 'It's lovely when the fog covers the ground like a silver cloud. Philip says I suffer from flights of fancy, but he says it so kindly. I truly believe he loves me.'

Her comment surprised me. 'Of course he does. Do you doubt it?'

'After what happened in Tunis, I've begun to doubt everything.' She raised her eyes to mine. 'Some nights I can't sleep. I lie awake and remember.'

I nodded awkwardly. 'I'm sure time will erase those memories.'

Her eyes glittered and her mouth trembled. I thought she would cry, but instead, she darted off on to another subject. 'The trees are starting to bud already, did you notice? The willows are always first, then the hazel.' Her voice was high, nerves making her laughter brittle.

I patted her shoulder gently. 'I'm sure everything will be all right now.' The look in her eyes frightened me. In prison, sometimes, I'd seen looks like that. Usually the woman was taken to the infirmary and given a strong dose of tranquilizers. Here, I wasn't sure what to do besides keep her talking. 'Tell me about your childhood,' I said.

She gave me a startled look and her dark eyes softened a bit. 'It was nearly always sunny, and orange trees grew in our garden. Sometimes I dream I'm back home, and when I wake up the scent of orange blossoms is in my nostrils. My mother was a very small woman, only up to here.' She held her hand chest high to show me. 'So very tiny, yet she ruled the entire palace, and even my father jumped when she called his name.' The queen laughed, and I was relieved to hear her sound almost normal. She took a deep breath and smiled at me. 'When I was twelve my marriage was announced, and the whole kingdom had a fête in my honour. For three days the people feasted, and we invited musicians from all over the country. When I saw Philip, I fell in love. He'd sent me a miniature, but the painting did him no justice. Don't you think he's handsome? He is so tall, his shoulders so broad, and his eyes so keen—'

'Your highness!' One of the priests stepped up behind us.

We jumped, and the queen blushed. 'Père Denis, you frightened me!'

'Your litter awaits.' He eyed me frostily. Perhaps he thought I'd started the conversation about his king's physical attributes.

'Tell the grooms I want to ride next to my husband this afternoon,' said the queen.

The priest looked as if he wanted to refuse. He was a priest, not a messenger or a groom. Nevertheless, after a second's hesitation, he bowed very low and trotted away, his black robes flapping in the mist. To avoid tripping, he held them high and displayed his muddy shoes and thin white shanks.

'Will you ride with me?' asked the queen.

I shook my head. 'I'm a poor rider, and in my condition I'd roll off my pony's back like a ball.'

The queen, who was proud of her equestrian prowess, smiled kindly. 'I'll teach you how to ride once your baby is born.' She cocked her head. 'The trumpets blow. We're off now. 'Til tonight, my melancholy angel.' She pecked me on the cheek and waded through the soft mist.

Although the air had warmed, the fog had grown even thicker. It took me a while to locate Charles. He held my lead pony with a look of worry on his face. When I appeared, he crossed himself and helped me into my litter.

'You mustn't fret about me,' I said, parting the curtains and leaning out to see him.

'Hush, it's not that. Jean's father came while you were gone and asked me many questions. I don't know what to make of the man.'

The blanket of fog made it seem we were alone, though I knew we weren't. I could just barely see the rump of the pack mule in front of me, and behind us, the head of a white horse poked out of the mist like a phantom.

'What did he want to know?'

'How long I'd been in your service. Where you'd come from, who your people were and when Jean married you.'

'What did you say?' I wasn't worried. That day, for some reason, a strange, relaxed glow enveloped me.

'I told him I was born on your family's property and that you were from a village just north of Montpellier. I said we met Jean en route, and he fell in love with you. Your parents went on the crusade with us, by the way, and they both perished.'

'Charles!' I clapped my hand over my mouth, then took it off. 'What if he asks someone else?'

'Who can he ask? Your family is dead, and the only other person who knows you is the queen. The bigger the lie, the better it sounds.' Charles shrugged. 'Perhaps I should have added a few more family members who died in the storm.'

'Stop killing off all my family.' I laughed. 'What else did he ask?'

'He wanted to know if you had lands or any money. I replied that your family had sold everything to pay for the crusade and that your father, a wine merchant, had been buried with his armour in Tunis.'

'A wine merchant? Go on.' I was smiling broadly now. I hadn't felt so relaxed in ages.

Charles and I grinned at each other, enjoying our joke.

'Well . . .'

At that moment, the pack mule in front of us skidded to a halt and threw its head up, braying loudly. The man holding its reins cursed, and we heard shouting. Whatever was causing the ruckus was hidden by the fog, so we couldn't see what had happened.

'What is it?' I peered into the thick mist. 'Is the trouble in front of us, or behind?'

Charles pulled the ponies to the side of the road, for the sounds of clattering hooves could clearly be heard now. My ponies tossed their heads and whickered nervously as Charles swatted their sides, urging them into the tall grass. The litter swayed alarmingly as the ponies edged away from the road.

The sound of galloping hoofbeats grew louder, although with the dense fog it was hard to pinpoint where they came from. Louder and louder they grew, and as they got closer, frantic yells and shouts accompanied them. Hoarse cries of fright echoed through the fog, and shrill screams as well. All around us, we could make out people and horses moving out of the way. Fear made my heart pound as I peered into the greyness.

Suddenly, a horse surged into sight. It was a runaway, careening out of the mist, its head high, its eyes rolling. At first I thought it had broken free from a cart and that part of its load dragged behind it.

When the horse slalomed by, I realized otherwise. A human body hung by the foot from the ornate harness. I caught a glimpse of the horse's white-rimmed eyes, its lathered flanks, and the body trailing behind it, and then it was gone. I froze, shock washing over me like an icy, prickly shower. I'd recognized the person trapped by the stirrup. It had been the queen.

We jumped further back as more horses galloped out of the mist the king and his guards racing after the queen. I saw Jean's father among the white-faced men. Then I heard the sound of a heavy

143

crash and panicked voices shouting they'd caught the horse and to get help, quickly!

I threw my furs off my lap and struggled out of my litter. Sharp sobs escaped my throat as I hastened down the road, Charles at my heels. Other people joined us, all hurrying towards the sound of heart-wrenching screams that had no trouble penetrating the fog.

The mist clogged my nostrils as I ran, pearled on my hair and made the stones underfoot slick as glass. Charles grabbed my elbow when I staggered, and we hurried through the greyness. Dark shadows slowly revealed themselves as a crowd huddled in a circle around the queen.

I elbowed my way to the middle. My pregnancy made most people move out of my way. No one stopped me. If only someone had.

The queen, freed from the harness, lay crumpled in the road. She screamed as she writhed on the stony ground, wet with a dark stain I realized was her blood. Her cries horrified me, chilled me, and raised the hair on my head. I clenched my teeth together.

'She's giving birth,' cried someone. 'Hurry! Get the priest! Fetch a midwife! Hurry, man!'

I stood at her side, frozen in horror. There was nothing anyone could do except put her out of her misery, but she wasn't a dog. She was a woman, and she was dying.

Slowly, heavily, I knelt by her side. I wanted to touch her, but where could I place my hand? She was broken, shattered, everywhere I looked there was the scarlet of blood or the white of bone. As I watched, her body convulsed and steam rose from between her legs.

She gave birth to her baby in the middle of the road. The pain must have been indescribable. Her spine, legs and arms were broken and folded at impossible angles. Her scalp flapped back with the skull bared, and her nose was torn clear off her face. Her robes had been shredded by the horse's hooves and the stones.

She gave another gurgling scream and arched her back. There was the sound of something ripping, and the baby surged out of its mother's womb into the waiting hands of a priest. The child was dead, its head limp, and the king, kneeling just behind the priest, toppled over in a faint. Other people swooned as well, hitting the ground with loud thumps, but I knelt at the queen's head and touched her cheek.

She opened one eye. The other was gone. I saw the pain, the question, and the white veil of death slowly obscuring her view, like the fog. Little shrieks were torn out of her throat with each breath she drew. Her hand scrabbled on the rocks, digging into the bloody ground.

I leaned over until my mouth was near her ear. 'The baby is well. It's a perfect little girl. She is tiny, beautiful, and strong, just like you. Just like your mother.'

She closed her eye. Her teeth were bared in pain, ribbons of blood seeping between them, and a rattle sounded deep in her throat. Her hand scraped madly in the mud. A strange quivering seized her body, and a priest took a hold of the back of my robe and pulled me up. It was time for the Last Rites.

Someone took my arm and led me away. I followed blindly, not seeing where I was going. Bile welled in my throat. 'Charles, stop, I'm going to vomit,' I gasped.

The man holding my elbow tightened his grip. 'Go ahead,' he said. It was Jean's father, the Count de Bourbon-Dampierre.

Startled, I whirled around. I clapped a hand over my mouth, but it was too late. I threw up on his feet.

With an oath, he leapt backwards. I lost my balance and would have fallen, but he was quick, I'll grant him that. He caught me neatly under the arms and set me onto a nearby boulder.

'I'm sorry,' I said. The shock caught up with me and I shook uncontrollably. I screwed my eyes shut to block out the image I still saw in my mind, but it didn't work.

'I can't,' I gasped. 'I just can't.'

'Can't what?' His voice was neither harsh nor gentle, but it was strong. As was his hand. I winced as his fingers dug into my arm.

'I can't bear to see any more,' I said, and then I was sick again. I retched miserably while he held my head and shoulders. After, he hefted me into his arms and walked back to my litter, where he set me gently inside.

'We go now,' he said.

'Where?'

'Tours. We're leaving. A dead king, a dead prince, a dead queen, and a stillborn child. A funeral cortege is what Philip is bringing to Paris. I won't accompany him any longer.'

He slapped my pony on the rump and we started to move.

'Charles!' I cried, but Jean's father only grunted and took my pony's bridle.

'Charles!' I sobbed, leaning precariously out the litter.

The Count glared at me, his green eyes uncannily resembling Jean's. 'Get back inside and close the drapes. I'll send Lucien after your page and your pack mule.'

I dared protest no longer. All the strength drained out of my trembling limbs and I sank back onto the furs. I was suddenly grateful for them, and I snuggled into their warmth like a child. The day had been too much for me. My mind switched itself off and I fell asleep.

I awoke the next day after dozing on and off for twenty hours. Horror had clenched my teeth so tightly together I could hardly breathe. The muscles in my neck and back ached, and my chest hurt. Stabbing pains made me wonder if I was having a heart attack, but it was just stress.

The worst part was, I'd known. I'd known that Isabella died young, but I'd forgotten. I'd refused to think about it. Life and friendship had got in the way of my history lessons, and the two lines I'd read had escaped me. Only two lines were written in a history book about a lovely, fanciful Spanish princess with a fondness for poetry and oranges. Two lines that I'd chosen deliberately to forget. *'Isabella became Queen of France after the death of King Louis in Tunis. She died soon after, falling off a horse.'*

I pounded my litter in impotent fury. What good would it have done? Would I have changed time, changed the future, if I'd been able to, or would I have let events take their course to save myself from erasure?

We camped near a path, a dirt track really, which Lucien assured us led to Tours through the charcoal makers' forest. Lucien had caught a rabbit and built a fire to cook it. Jean's father was not around, and I didn't ask where he'd gone, but Charles had no such qualms.

'Where is the Sire Dampierre?' he asked.

'He went to get fresh water. The forest is a tricky place, and many have got lost there, but Sire Dampierre knows his way around,' Lucien said. He took a piece of rabbit from the carcass and chewed it hungrily.

Charles and I looked at each other. My throat was still locked too tightly to speak, eat or even drink. The sight of food made me shudder. Charles nibbled on a crust of bread, but I could tell his heart wasn't in it. 'How long until we arrive?' he asked.

'That depends on the weather, our pace, and the lady here,' said Lucien, nodding at me.

Stiffly, I made my way to the ditch to relieve myself. The fog hadn't lifted, and the evening was as grey and cheerless as could be. Memories of yesterday's drama kept flitting through my mind, and every time I closed my eyes the sight of Isabella's ruined face intruded.

I finished my business and stood up slowly. If only that ache in my back would disappear! I put my hands behind me and winced. At that moment a queer feeling swept over me. It was like something fragile tearing painlessly inside of me. Sweat sprang out on my forehead and upper lip. I hurried to lift my skirt again and squatted over the ditch. Hot liquid splashed onto the ground, and a strange odour assailed me. It was soon finished, and I actually felt better after.

I wondered what had happened. I counted backwards, frowning. Was it my waters breaking? Isabella, poor Isabella, had mentioned that although she hadn't said what it was like. Damn the Time Senders! Since I was supposed to be sterile, I'd never given any thought to childbirth. In my time, it was all done by machines. Test tubes and incubators were so much more reliable than human bodies. What was natural childbirth like? I tried to dredge up memories of history books, but nothing occurred to me.

I lay down on my pallet, Charles at my side, and prepared to sleep. Instead, strange cramps in my abdomen kept me awake. They grew stronger and stronger, and my whole belly shuddered and tightened with them. It felt almost like food poisoning.

Around midnight, after three or four hours of this, I woke Charles. 'Something is wrong,' I whispered, then groaned as another pain swept over me. If only I'd questioned Isabella more!

'I'll get Lucien.' In the short time Charles had known the guard, he'd grown to think of him as the answer to all questions. While Lucien was handy with setting up tents and skinning rabbits, I had no idea what good he could do as a midwife, for by now I'd realized this must be childbirth. Before I could protest, Charles had gone, the tent flap fluttered and I was alone and gasping with another pain.

Within minutes, the tent flap opened again, but it was Jean's father, a peculiar look on his face. 'Is it starting already?' he asked.

'I don't know,' I moaned. 'I've never done this before.'

He almost smiled. 'Neither have I, but I've seen it done.'

'You have?' I gasped.

He shrugged. 'When my wife gave birth to her children I helped. Don't worry. You'll be fine.'

'No, I won't,' I said stubbornly.

Lucien and Charles came in with their arms loaded with wood. Soon the brazier glowed brightly. Charles fetched clean linens from my trunk, and Lucien disappeared into the night. I heard the sound of galloping hooves, and Charles said, 'He's gone to the charcoal makers to fetch a nursemaid. Don't worry, Isobel, we'll take care of you.'

His small hand found mine, and I took it for comfort.

While Jean's father tended the fire and fashioned a makeshift cradle with supple willow branches, Charles sat at my side. I was fascinated to watch the tiny cradle grow before my eyes.

'How lovely,' I breathed, then grunted as a cramp shook me.

Charles whimpered as well, for I'd crushed his hand in my grip.

'Sorry,' I gasped. 'I'll hold a stick. Oh, Lord.' Another pain came, this time nearly submerging me. I didn't understand them. Sometimes they were painless, and only the muscles across my huge belly tightened, and sometimes they wrenched me from the inside out. The pain of the forceful ones left me panting and bewildered. To add to my discomfort, the aching feeling was back, and heaviness seemed to grow between my legs.

I felt the baby then, moving downwards. It surprised me, and more than that, it frightened me. I hauled myself to my elbows and stared at the mound that was my stomach. My knees parted by themselves. I had only one urge, to push as hard as I could. I gave a sharp scream.

Charles echoed my cry, and Jean's father dropped the cradle and sat down at my side. He placed a hand on my shoulder. 'The child comes. I shall have to catch him. Don't look. Close your eyes and push.'

I thought that it was an odd command, but I was used to taking orders. I gritted my teeth, closed my eyes and bore down. Two strong hands pushed my thighs apart and lifted my robe to my waist, but I kept my eyes shut. While I shuddered and strained, iron hands stilled my trembling legs. After one huge push, a sharp, tearing sensation made me squeal.

It was the baby crowning. Someone – not me – uttered an excited gasp. Pain flowered and subsided as soon as a slippery, heavy weight left my body. It happened so quickly I thought my insides had come undone, and I fainted.

The next time I opened my eyes, a warm glow bathed the tent and a tiny baby nestled in my arms. I peered at the crumpled face, a dusky, dark red colour, and felt absurdly proud of myself. Tears pricked my eyes and I laughed softly. The infant stirred, opened the tiniest mouth imaginable, and yawned with the same mewing sound a kitten makes.

'What a precious little boy,' I whispered.

Charles cleared his throat. 'It's a girl, actually.'

149

I stared at him. 'Wh-*what*?'

'A girl. A fine, healthy girl.' His tone was apologetic. He knew, as well as I did, that I had to have a boy, or my mission was a failure.

I held my breath and listened for thunder. All I heard was the sound of branches crackling in the fire and the wind in the trees. 'A girl,' I said dully.

'She's a fine, healthy g—'

'I know, you said that.' Exhaustion kept my voice level. Otherwise, I think I would have screamed. Would I be erased now? What of my child? Panic, pain and exhaustion warred within me. The result was a curious numbness and buzzing in my head.

Jean's father stood from his corner and held up a small cradle made of woven willow branches. He eyed it critically and set it down by the fire. He stretched and lifted the tent flap to peer at the sky. 'It's dawn,' he said.

'Dawn,' I echoed. I looked at the peaceful creature in my arms and sighed. 'We'll call her Aurore,' I said, the French word for dawn.

'That's a nice name. Lucien's coming back. I hope he's found someone decent.' Jean's father spoke absently, still looking outside.

'Found someone for what?' I heard hoofbeats now, quite clearly, but I was amazed that Jean's father had heard them before I did. My ears were usually the keenest.

'For the babe. She'll need a nurse.' He still didn't look at me when he spoke. Instead he drew on his cloak and went into the grey dawn without a backward glance at me or his new grandchild. I think I clutched the baby to my breast. I vaguely remember someone taking her from my arms, and I tried to protest, but nothing I could do kept me from falling deeply asleep.

I met the woman Lucien had fetched the next morning when I awoke. The nurse was a stout peasant woman with a thatch of black hair so dense it looked at first like a felt hat. Her round face was small, her mouth constantly pursed, and for a very long time she never uttered a single word. She was nimble and did everything with an efficiency of movement that was almost poetical to see.

No one told me her name she was called 'Nurse'. When I asked her what her name was, she ducked her head and turned beet red. Perhaps she was mute and couldn't speak, I thought, although she crooned in a rough voice to the child as she nursed her or held her on her shoulder to burp.

I noticed almost immediately Nurse was only as clean as peasants went in that time, and thought to myself I might have to do something about that if she were to tend my baby. She did wash her hands and face, but the rest of her body stayed unwashed until spring thaws. I was slowly getting used to odours, thankfully, for she was to share the litter with me as we travelled.

The first two days we spent at the campsite and I learned how to hold my baby and how to nurse her. I wanted to feed my own baby, but my breasts were sore and I couldn't sit up without wincing. Mothers in my time didn't give birth and didn't nurse, so I had no idea if anything I was doing was correct. I had to put my entire trust in an uneducated peasant woman. It was both frustrating and frightening.

As for my other ills, I knew that salt was an antiseptic, so I sat in a shallow tub filled with hot salt water for a few hours. To my relief, this seemed to help and I started to feel better.

Nurse assisted me a great deal and I was deeply grateful. She cleaned my bed linens and clothes and took care of Aurore. She approved of my salt baths and produced a cream for my sore breasts. The cream was in a wooden vial and smelled like herbs, garlic, and lanolin. After three days, I felt almost human again, except for my sore breasts, my sorer nipples, and having to change the thick pad between my legs every hour or so. Nurse was a wonder in efficiency, and I never went without a clean pad of cloth.

Jean's father spoke to Charles and even to the nurse, but not to directly me. I'd wondered if Aurore's birth would make him friendlier to me, but I was the vessel into which Jean had poured his seed. I'd carried the progeny, and now I was simply an extra mouth to feed at dinnertime. Nothing was asked of me, nor was I supposed to take any initiative. A woman of my rank was expected to follow meekly whatever orders were given to her, to raise her children, and to sew, mind the house and hearth, and to dabble in the stewpot or gardens every now and then.

One day as I lay in my bed contemplating the tiny infant in my arms, Jean's father entered the tent, ducking through the heavy tent flap, and looked down at the baby with sharp eyes. His expression was so bleak I felt a quick stab of pity. It welled up out of my emotional state and my exhaustion, and made me bold.

'She's a lovely baby, sire,' I ventured. 'Sire. It seems odd to name my husband's father so. Is there nothing I may call you except sire?'

'You may call me François,' he said. Then he closed his mouth, turned on his heel and left the tent, as if he'd already said too much.

François? I turned the name over in my mouth, but it seemed too soft for him. I'd have thought that he'd have a harder name, something with more bite. 'François.' But the name didn't soften his attitude towards me. He hardly addressed a word to me, except to say, 'We're off now,' or, 'No, we can't stop here. You'll have to wait to relieve yourself later'.

I rode in the litter, I ate, I nursed, and I sewed three little vests for my baby out of an old skirt I'd torn apart. My strength slowly returned, and my breasts grew less sensitive, but Nurse had more milk than I did and nursed Aurore more often. It didn't bother me. I was content to hold my baby and cuddle with her. She hardly slept anywhere but in my arms, and I was completely besotted with the tiny creature. Since she had two women nursing her, Aurore was never hungry and she thrived, growing rosy with good health.

The voyage was slow. I was weaker than I thought and couldn't sit for any length of time. The litter was uncomfortable as it rose and dropped with each of the two ponies' footsteps. Once the lead pony shied and jumped sideways. The litter rocked violently, and I nearly fell out of it.

Nurse grabbed my dress and hauled me back inside. Her other arm was firmly locked around Aurore, and the baby didn't even stir.

I thanked her for saving me from a nasty fall, but she only flushed again, the blood rushing to her cheeks and staining them violet. She shook her head, wordlessly, but a timid smile darted across her face. She was strong, silent, and smelled like ripe cheese, but she'd acted swiftly to save me and my daughter. Any reservations about trusting her with Aurore faded that moment.

Chapter Twelve

In case you succeed in your mission, you will want to find a place to live out the rest of your life in relative comfort. Founding a small shop in a village and selling eggs, or fruit and vegetables, may be an option. See Chapter 3 'Business plans for the Thirteenth Century'. Pay special attention to the section 'How to blend in with peasants and poor people without arousing suspicion'.

Tempus University *Corrector's Handbook*

We arrived in Tours at dusk on the ninth day of our voyage. Night was falling, and I didn't get a good look at the castle. I saw a stone foundation and tall wooden walls. We climbed a small hill and entered a large gate. Suddenly valets and grooms crowded the cobblestone courtyard, some taking hold of baggage, others grabbing the ponies and leading them away. Torches had been lit outside, and I saw windows overlooking the courtyard, though they were dark. Was anyone home?

The bustle made me feel faint, though more likely it was fatigue. I was so stiff I could hardly move as Lucien helped me out of the litter. He turned to take Aurore from Nurse while she clambered down and I stretched, rubbed my back and neck, and sought Charles with my eyes. He was just disappearing around the corner, taking our donkey to the stables.

François' voice rose over the chatter and clattering hooves. 'Elaine! Come and meet Jean's wife, Isobel, and your new niece.'

I turned to see a hooded figure move gracefully forward and stand beside her father, not far from me. He pointed towards me, and I smiled, intending to greet her.

Without throwing back her hood, she curtsied abruptly, like a puppet whose strings have suddenly been jerked. Then she whirled and left, her cape swooping outwards like huge, dark wings. Soon thereafter, Nurse and I were installed in a small room in the north tower, reserved for unwanted guests, I'm sure.

That night at dinner, I finally saw Elaine's face and her clear, emerald-green eyes. The meal was informal, and Charles ate with us. I was thankful François had suggested Charles sit next to me. At the table as well was an elderly woman called Dame Blanche who was introduced to me as François' aunt, and who had been Elaine and Jean's old nurse.

Elaine was a lovely, pale girl with dark hair. Her resemblance to Jean troubled me. It seemed that François had placed his stamp upon his children, and I suddenly wondered what his wife had looked like.

'Pass the water, Elaine,' her father said.

She reached her arm towards the pitcher and dragged her velvet sleeve across her dinner plate. *'Merde,'* she swore, which caused Blanche to drop her spoon with a clatter and her father to thump his pewter tankard on the wooden table.

'I'll not have that word at my table,' said François.

'And I'll not have a whore at my table,' Elaine snapped right back at him. 'That woman can't be Jean's wife. She's nothing but a whore he met on the crusade.'

I raised my eyes, shocked. Nothing had prepared me for *that* onslaught. Elaine had been quiet, but polite. She had enquired as to the voyage, speaking only to her father, but I thought that normal. She hadn't seen him in nearly three months.

Perhaps she was troubled because of her mother's recent death, so I gave a tiny shrug and continued to eat.

Silence caused me to raise my head again. Everyone, I suddenly realized, was staring at me. Elaine with spite, Charles with something like terror, and François with the first spark of interest I'd seen in his eyes.

'I'm not a whore,' I commented mildly. Keeping my temper under control was easy when I was numb with exhaustion. 'Pass the salt, please, François.'

He did, and Elaine rose suddenly, nearly overturning her chair. Before she left, she turned and stared hard at me. She opened her mouth, then shut it. I watched her go and realized that my hand gripped my spoon so tight that my knuckles cracked. I tried to dredge up some emotions, but it was too much of an effort. Besides, I had no idea how to react.

Dame Blanche leaned towards me over the table and smiled, showing a wide gap between her two front teeth. 'Elaine is usually very friendly,' she said. Dame Blanche, I learned, was from Paris and had soft white hands that fluttered at her breast when she spoke. She had grey hair that she covered with a white kerchief and she wore a kirtle made of fine, pale grey wool.

Not knowing what to say, I shrugged again. She sank back in her chair with a loud sigh. 'It's a pity, Sir François, that your daughter accuses her own sister-in-law of being a whore. Perhaps you should reprimand her.'

'Why? She's just speaking her mind.' François sounded amused.

I choked on my watery soup. I raised my head and met his eyes. 'And what, pray tell, can your mind be on the matter?' I was surprised to hear my voice come out of my throat in such an even tone. It sounded almost light, as if I was bantering. His words had shocked me out of my apathy, though. What would happen if he found out I'd never married Jean? What would happen to my new baby? Panic made my heart thump painfully.

He matched my tone, although his eyes were icy. 'I have no thoughts at all on the matter. Jean wrote, then you wrote, and Queen Isabella, God rest her soul, wrote as well. What would you have me do? Berate my daughter for being rude? I'm sure she realizes it by now, or she'd never have left the table. Shall I call her back?'

'No!' I lowered my eyes. I was so tired. My shoulders slumped and the energy I'd mustered for the dinner left me in a rush. The news that Queen Isabella had written to Jean's father bewildered me. Why had she written? What had she said? I wanted to ask, but I didn't dare.

'Will you excuse me? I want to go to bed now. Thank you for the meal.' I stood up without waiting for a reply and made my way to my room. The narrow, wooden corridors seemed endless, poorly lit with sputtering torches. It was bitterly cold, and I was glad to reach my room. Heavy tapestries hung on the walls, and the fire was lit, although it burned low. Nurse sat on a cushioned stool by the chimney, Aurore in her arms. I shut the door and leaned on it.

'I'm so tired,' I said to Nurse. 'I hate it here. I wish I could go home.' The enormity of my words sank in, and I dug my nails into the wooden door at my back. I felt depression settle over me like heavy water. I could hardly breathe. My melancholy was coming back, and I was too weak to resist.

'You can't go home.' The voice came from behind the door, muffled by thick wood. 'Let me enter.'

It was an order, and I backed away. The door swung open and let in a gust of cold air. Jean's father stepped in, which made me realize just how tiny the room was. I shivered. His body filled the whole room. In two strides, he was at the chimney. He tossed another three logs on the fire and stirred the flames with a poker.

'Put the child to bed,' he said to Nurse and she complied, placing the sleeping infant in her willow crib. She curtsied and left the room, shutting the door behind her.

'What do you want?' I sat heavily on my bed and started to unbraid my hair, but my hands slid down the tress and landed on my lap. It was an effort to sit upright. I drew a deep breath and raised my eyes, expecting to see François staring into the fire, or anywhere other than my own face. But he was looking at me with a queer expression.

'You can't go home,' he repeated. 'Your family is dead, and I'm all you have left.'

'I have Charles and Aurore.' I smiled thinly. 'I don't have *you* at all. You don't care for me or for your granddaughter. According to Jean, you didn't care for him either.' I spoke rashly, but exhaustion and hopelessness made me short-tempered.

'My son and I never got along. It was my wife's fault she spoiled him.' He spoke absently, his eyes still locked with mine. Before I realized it he'd come to my side and lifted my heavy braid. 'Here, let me.' He deftly unplaited it and smoothed it on my shoulders. Jean had sometimes done that at night.

'You have lovely hair, Isobel,' he said. 'It looks like wheat just before the harvest.'

'Thank you,' I said dully. Tears seeped from my eyes and trickled down my cheeks. Why did he have to look so much like his son? In the firelight, in the darkness, I could imagine it was Jean. 'Go away, please.'

'No.' His hand found my cheek and wiped the tears away with his thumb. 'You may think I don't care, but I do. Jean was my only son and I loved him, although I never told him. It's not my way to speak of such things as love or hate. I prefer to speak of hunting. Perhaps you know something of stag hunting?' His voice was low, almost teasing.

I jerked back. 'No. I never hunted.'

'Tell me, Isobel, about your family.' He sat down beside me. His arm, next to mine, felt as strong as steel. Behind his words I thought I heard a hidden threat and I trembled.

'My family?' My mouth dried with nervousness and I licked my lips. I knew what Charles had said about my history and what we had agreed upon should anyone question us, a mixture of fact and fancy that none could, hopefully, disprove.

I thought of my parents. How could I describe them? I saw my mother's face clearly. She sat on a folding chair in the hospital when I awoke from the coma after the accident, so straight and stiff it looked painful. Her frozen face stared at the screen in the corner of my room. When the judge on the portable television screen pronounced me guilty, she swallowed once, very hard. Then her shoulders slumped and she leaned against my father.

158

My father never looked at me again. As soon as the verdict was given, I'd ceased to be his daughter. They'd left the room before the television had been turned off. The door locked behind them with a sharp click. I was alone in the prison hospital, alone and without family. The calls, the holo-mails – all bounced back with the message 'Return to sender person or persons unknown'.

I didn't tell these things to François, of course. Instead I said, 'They were good, honest, hard-working people, and I was their only daughter.'

'Did you sail with them to Tunis? Where, exactly, did you meet Jean?'

'I met him in a shelter, with the other crusaders. He was so different from anyone else around him. He glowed. I saw him . . .' My voice trailed off.

'You met him before you sailed then? Is that it?'

'Yes. My family left on one ship, and I sailed with Jean on another ship. Charles came with me because he's been in my service since he was a lad.'

'He's not much older than a lad.' His voice was dry.

'He's devoted to me.' The fire cast tall shadows on the walls, and Aurore whimpered in her sleep.

'You've told me nothing.' Jean's father took my chin in his hand and tipped my face to his. 'You have a fearsome scar.'

'Stop. Stop, please,' I begged. The voice, the eyes, it was all too much. Even the words were the same. My composure was breaking, and I could feel the cracks like sharp pains in my chest.

'What happened?' His fingers traced it, ignoring my feeble attempts to turn my face away.

'I fell through a window.' I stopped struggling. He was too strong, and I was too exhausted.

'Glass cut your face?'

'Yes. And your scar?' I spoke without looking at him, but I could still picture his scar, a jagged silver stripe on one cheek.

'A sword cut me.' His voice was soft. 'Did your parents leave you any money?'

159

'No. They sold everything to pay for the crusade. My father wanted to buy goods in Tunis and bring them back to sell, so he had a large sum of money with him. But it disappeared when their ship sank.'

'I thought they perished of a plague.'

I gave a small start and remembered Charles' words. The bigger the lie, the better it sounds. 'No, just my mother died of illness. When their ship ran aground, my parents were rescued from the water, but their money was gone. All that remained was my father's armour. When he died in battle, my mother buried him with his horse and his armour. Then she died of the plague within the week.'

'It must have been terrible for you.'

'Jean was there. He gave me comfort.'

'How did he die?' Suddenly I realized why he was with me. The anguish in his voice couldn't be hidden.

I faltered as the painful memories flashed before my eyes. But François deserved to know. 'The battle was short, but terrible. So many died. I walked across the battlefield, looking for him. I called and called . . .' My voice cracked. 'There was an arrow in his side. He didn't suffer. His face was peaceful. He bled to death.' There was no stopping my tears now. I leaned against him, and I sobbed.

He held me until I fell asleep, although I have no recollection. I woke the next morning still dressed, but my hair was carefully arranged on my pillow. Nurse sat at the fireplace rocking Aurore in her arms, and weak sunlight made the tapestries hanging on the walls glow with jewel-like colours.

My head was clear; my depression had passed, or more likely it had simply been stress and fatigue. A good sleep often put things right and my bed had been comfortable for the first time in weeks.

I wondered if François would be different with me now, but when I made my way downstairs I learned that he had gone to Paris and wouldn't be back until late spring.

'He's gone to see about business matters,' said Elaine. She'd decided to like me, or at least to act as if she did. Sometimes I caught glimpses of anger, but I was beginning to understand why. Jean had spoken to me of his sister, and sometimes he'd mention the fact that she hadn't wanted to marry. I thought I knew what angered her now. She'd been expecting a rich, titled heiress. I was a penniless commoner, and her family's fortune, which I quickly realized had been dilapidated, was, in her mind at least, now hers to save.

'It's hopeless.' I set a linen square down on my lap and tried vainly to smooth the stitches.

'If you tug on them like that, you'll tear the cloth,' said Elaine. With impatient hands, she plucked it away from me. 'Look, you must try and make all the stitches go in the same direction. If you cross over this way, it will make the fabric pull. It's very fine linen, and you're ruining it. Didn't anyone teach you to sew?' Her tone was scornful.

'I'm sorry.' I rubbed a weary hand over my eyes. 'I can hardly see anymore. The sun is dipping below the battlements. Do you think we could light a lamp?'

'Heavens, no! Do you think we're rich?' She laughed, but it was a brittle sound. 'What a pity that Jean didn't marry a wealthy woman so we could afford to light lamps all day and all night. We also wouldn't be obliged to live in this dreary castle, in the middle of the swamps and forest. We could return to Paris where there are fêtes every night and lights on every street. I'd be able to see my friends, instead of being shut up like a nun in this horrid, cold, damp ruin.' She finished her tirade and poked her needle savagely through the linen.

'I was wealthy once, I suppose, although not by your high standards.' I thought back on all my conversations with Jean about his sister. 'Is your father going to bargain for your husband in Paris? Is that why he left so suddenly?'

The white spots around her nostrils showed how close I'd come to the target. 'I am engaged to be married, if that's what you insinuate.'

'I insinuate nothing. Who is it? Do you know him well?'

'He's Réné, Count of Artois.' She sounded almost smug.

I peered closely at her face. She turned away quickly to look out the window. It was an unfortunate choice if she wanted to hide her

161

fear, because the remaining daylight only emphasized the sudden pallor of her cheeks and the twitch of compressed lips.

'Who is he?' I asked.

Now surprise lifted her eyebrows. 'You don't know Réné d'Artois?'

'Not unless he was on the crusade, then I would have seen him in the court. Perhaps my memory fails me. Was he there?'

'No.' Her fingers plucked restlessly at the stitches. I was afraid she'd undo all my work, so I tapped her gently on the arm. She jumped, startled. 'What?'

'Do you love him?' I asked.

'It doesn't matter whether I love him or not. He's wealthy, and he asked for me in marriage. He saw me in Paris, just before Jean left.'

I nodded slowly. My suspicions had been right, and there was something else as well. 'Your brother didn't leave because he hated your father. He left to gain fortune and spare you this marriage,' I said. 'You helped him get away, didn't you?'

She bowed her head and tears sparkled on her lashes.

I thought, then spoke slowly. 'You and Jean must have been very close to each other. He didn't betray you. I was rich at the time he met me.' I stuck to the story Charles had woven. 'My father's fortune sank with the ship.'

'So he did try.' She spoke quietly. 'Before I saw you, I hoped you'd be rich. But when you came and I saw how poor your valet looked, and the state of your thin ponies and wretched donkey . . .'

'The ponies were a gift from her majesty, Isabella, may God rest her soul.' I paused, and we both made the sign of the cross over our breasts. 'Is your betrothed so dreadful?'

'He's rich,' she said sullenly. The needle flashed.

'Is he nice?'

'He's been married three times. I'll be his fourth wife.'

With that admission it was as if the floodgates on Elaine's fears burst, and words tumbled out in a rush. She took my hands, her embroidery sliding to a heap on the floor. Tears sparkled on her long lashes.

'I *do* wish you had money! His first wife was unfaithful and he sent her to a tower, where some say she was strangled and others say

162

she starved to death.' In those times, an adulterous woman was usually punished by her husband, but I couldn't tell if Elaine thought she'd deserved her fate. 'His second wife died in childbirth, and the third one died in a fall. She tumbled off the battlements while walking with her baby son in her arms. They both perished. Some say she was the only woman he ever loved, and now his heart is as cold as stone.'

'Do you want to marry him?' I asked.

'No. Yes. Oh, I don't know,' she said. 'If only Father would find a wealthy wife so I wouldn't have to marry d'Artois. Then I could wait awhile. I'm afraid to marry and have children.'

I nodded, understanding. Childbirth was the main cause of death among women at that time, with one-third of the deaths of adult women due to complications. Thankfully, that statistic had slipped my mind when I was in the middle of birthing Aurore. 'Does your father search for a new wife?'

'I believe so.' She sat back, sniffed and wiped her cheeks. 'He wants to see me married and secure, but I'd never feel safe if I had to bear a child every year. René only wants an heir, I'm sure. Then Father said we were nearly ruined, and the lands are fallow. There are no more serfs to work for us – they've all left, gone to the crusades or into the forest to be freemen. We've no money to pay the taxes, so Father has gone to speak to King Philip and beg for an extension. I don't know how long we'll be able to hold on to the castle. Already Father has sold his horses, and the gold cups that belonged to our grandfather.'

'I'm sorry.' I thought of the gold coins still sewn in the hem of my robe. I'd save them for an emergency – they were my only insurance if I were cast adrift, and if, of course, I wasn't erased by the Time Correctors. 'How will we feed everyone?'

'Lucien and Father hunt nearly every week. Luckily, we have hunting rights to the forest around us. Some vegetables grow in the kitchen courtyard, and the chestnuts were abundant this year. We dry them and grind chestnut flour. Without those, we'd starve.'

'Don't you have any chickens?' I asked.

'No, a fox got into the coop and killed them all. We haven't had any for months and we'll have to wait for spring to buy some pullets. The rabbits died of fright during a lighting storm, and the milk goat died of old age.' She ticked off the dead animals on her fingers.

'Can't we get a chicken now and use the eggs?' I asked. 'Some farmer must have one or two for sale.'

'Chickens don't lay in the winter. You city folk know nothing at all.'

I stood and pulled Elaine to her feet. 'Show me the larder. I might not be rich, and I may not know anything about farming, but maybe I can make myself useful.'

I hadn't studied those history books for nothing. I hoped I could use my knowledge to find something to do to help. One of my books claimed that dandelions, among other common plants, were rich in vitamins, and that peasants of the times often used them for food. I imagined myself bringing baskets of fresh greens to the kitchen to go with venison steaks.

We left the sitting room and crossed the courtyard to the kitchen, which was a separate building made of stone with a thick thatched roof. There were two small doors and two large casement windows covered in dust. Though it was nearly empty now, I saw traces of the kitchen's past splendour in the rusting spit, the long chains that could hold a whole ox over the fire, and in the fireplace itself, big enough to hold the ox with room to spare. A black kettle in which I could have bathed sat unused off to the side, and a functioning well, though just a hole in the stone floor, was in the corner of the room. I peered down its mossy sides but could see only blackness. A bucket dangled on a long rope from a beam on the ceiling, and a dipper hung from a nail on the wall above.

Turning, I surveyed the room. The main fireplace was no longer used as such. Instead, a small brick oven had been built at its centre. The servants baked bread there, and meat, when it was available, was cooked on a grill on the top, the drippings falling onto the bread beneath. Beside the fireplace was a three-legged pot for cooking vegetables and a flat iron stovetop for the chestnut-flour pancakes.

The reed torches were burnt to stubs, and small beeswax candles were piled in a corner, for use at night. Pale sunlight lit the room, though not the dark corners, where cobwebs covered massive wooden platters, a legacy from the castle's prosperous era.

The cook stood, hands on his skinny hips, and stared at me. He was an old man by those times, toothless and gaunt. 'Sad thing that young master Jean didn't come home,' he muttered in a gummy voice.

'Yes,' I agreed.

He scratched his head, examined his nails for signs of lice, and motioned us towards the pantry. 'There's not much left,' he said. 'We'll have to make do with that until Lucien gets back from the forest.' He opened a creaking door and took a lit candle from its place on the table.

'Each time he must go further afield,' said Elaine.

'Game is getting scarce.' The old man shrugged. 'But Lucien can follow a scent as well as any hound.'

I peered into the darkness, then took the candle and held it above my head. A set of spiral stairs was dug out of the bedrock. I sneezed, lifted my skirts, and descended into the cellar pantry. Cook and Elaine followed, chatting together about Lucien, whom I gathered was Cook's grandson.

There were more spiders in that room than food. A wooden crate held some old cabbages, a half-full bag of carrots hung on a nail and the bin of chestnuts was nearly empty.

I pointed to the chestnuts. 'Shouldn't we get more of these?'

'It's not their season any longer,' said the cook. 'But there's bound to be mushrooms in the forest. I'm not as spry as I used to be. Perhaps you could ask your valet, the little chap, Charles, to get some.'

'I'll ask him.' I continued with the inventory. 'Is there any dried meat?'

'No, and no salt left either. No honey, no nuts, no buckwheat . . .' The cook ticked off the absent food on his fingers.

'What is there besides shrivelled carrots and chestnuts?' Elaine asked, worry in her voice.

'Mushrooms if we're lucky, fresh water, some shrivelled parsnips, two ponies in the stable and a donkey.' He didn't lack humour. His eyes sparkled though the tone was serious.

Elaine didn't smile. 'Don't be frivolous.' Then she sighed. 'I'm sure Lucien will be back soon. Shall we get Charles? If we all go, perhaps we'll find thrice as many mushrooms.'

'Thrice nothing is nothing,' I said, wiping my muddy hands on my skirt. 'There isn't a mushroom within a hundred leagues of here.' My books had shown loads of pictures of edible mushrooms, but had given no indication of where to find them.

Elaine didn't know much more about mushrooms than I did, and even Charles had had no luck. He stood from picking around the base of an oak tree and nodded. 'I think you're right. I looked for field roses, oyster mushrooms, death trumpets, and spring porcini. There are none around. The wild boars must have got to them sooner than we did.'

'Death trumpets?' I asked. 'Are they poisonous?'

'No, they're quite good. They're also called horns of plenty, and they're pitch black, thus the name "death trumpet". I find them in autumn, but sometimes you can get some in the spring.' Charles, as I'd noticed on the crusade, knew all the edible plants. He knew more than my books could ever have taught me. He'd already dug up handfuls of dog-tooth violet roots and stuffed them in his pockets. I'd found a few miserable dandelions and dug them up, roots, leaves, and all, but there were hardly enough. My élan of helpfulness was rapidly turning into the familiar feeling of uselessness.

'Who lives in the castle now?' I asked Elaine. 'Besides you and your father, the cook, Lucien, and Dame Blanche?'

'There are three farmhands, but they don't live in the castle. They have houses nearby and their families live on and farm their own plots of land. Over the gatehouse lives old Marthe who used to be Father's nurse. She can hardly walk and we take food to her in the evenings.' Elaine scratched her head and frowned. 'Father still has his groom, Richard, who has three sons. They live in the dwelling over the stables and do odd jobs around the castle. Last month they drained the moat and we had fish for a week.'

'Any fish left?' Charles asked.

'We buried the last ones in the vegetable plot just before you arrived. They'd started stinking.'

'What about ducks?'

'We ate the last duck a year ago, it seems. The canny birds used to come to the moat every evening, but they stopped when we started snaring them. Father wanted to net the whole lot of them, but they got away. A pity – we could have smoked some.' Elaine grimaced. 'We would have starved if Lucien hadn't caught the deer at Christmas. Mother was already dead then. I think her heart simply gave up.'

'I'm sorry about your mother,' I said.

She glanced at me sideways. 'She loved Jean the best. I was used to it, but when he left, it was as if he'd betrayed her. I thought she'd go mad. For three days and nights she didn't do anything but scream.'

'It seems a bit much. After all, he planned to come back.' Charles made a face.

'She knew he wouldn't. She always said she had fairy blood and could see the future. When Jean left, she mourned him as if he'd died. She knew it, you see, just as she knew about her own death. She told me she'd die of a broken heart.'

'Elaine!' I exclaimed.

'It's true. She was proud of her fairy blood. She said her family came from Brocilande forest, and Morgaine la Fée was her ancestor.'

'What does your father think?'

'He hated it when she spoke of things he couldn't understand. When she died, I heard him talking to her body.' She clamped her mouth shut.

'What did he say?' Charles asked.

Elaine thought for a minute then admitted, 'I'm not sure. I was crossing the hall and I heard him murmuring. The words were indistinct, but I think he was talking about Jean. He'd just received the letter telling him about Prince Jean-Tristan's death and Jean's marriage to you.'

167

'Oh.' I looked askance at Charles, who shrugged. 'I suppose it was a great disappointment to your father that Jean ran away and married someone like me.'

'Yes.' Elaine was no diplomat.

Charles bristled, but a sharp glance from me shut his mouth. I examined my dirty nails then looked at my two companions. Charles brushed the dirt off the roots he'd gathered, his peaked face a study in concentration. Elaine stood quite still, her face turned towards the castle, just visible in the distance. The setting sun cast a coppery light over the fallow fields. Shadows grew long, and the trees, just beginning to bud, were tipped with ruby light.

We gave up any notion of having mushrooms for dinner and made our way home.

My breasts were leaking milk by the time we arrived. It was past nursing hour. However, Aurore wasn't hungry. Her wet nurse had plenty of milk, and I was simply a between-meals snack for the tiny girl. My milk was slowly drying up, and soon I'd have none left. Even now, the pale drops were fewer on the tips of my nipples. I squeezed the rest out as the nurse had shown me. Aurore slept peacefully in her crib. It seemed that all she did was sleep, but when I worried the nurse assured me it was normal.

I bent over the infant. In sleep, her little face was as pure as an angel's. I touched my scar, running my fingers down it, my heart aching so I could hardly breathe. A mother had loved her child as fiercely as I loved mine, and I had killed him. Tears trickled down my cheeks as I breathed in the sweet, milky scent of my baby and watched her sleep.

Dinner was frugal again that evening. The staple meal for those times was soup, and when there was no meat, they made soup with wild herbs. Sorrel, onion, dandelion, and what looked like grass floated in the broth along with a thin layer of grease. Lucien hadn't returned.

At the table, Elaine sat at her father's place, and I was at her right. Also with us was the priest, whom Elaine had neglected to count in her tally of castle residents.

168

Père Martin was a short, swarthy man with whiskers so dark his face looked navy blue even when closely shaved. His eyes were black and very sharp, his fingers were fat sausages and his face was as round as the full moon. He was unused to fasting, and when he said the blessing for our meal, he could hardly hide his disdain. Apparently, he too missed the luxury of Paris life.

The cook shuffled around the table, serving us. The first course was boiled herb soup with no salt. For the next course we had chestnut flatbread, and I was grateful for the dog violet roots that Charles had found. Cook had mashed them and added cloves of garlic to cover the insipid, starchy taste.

We spoke little until the end of dinner. Then Père Martin leaned back, fixed me with his obsidian stare and asked, 'How long has it been since you confessed, my lady?'

I gaped at him, but as usual, Charles came to my rescue. 'My lady confessed with the queen's own confessor, the Père Denis.' He blinked, looking as innocent as a choirboy.

'Oh.' The priest looked decidedly put out. 'You'll have to choose another confessor, my lady, as that good man has gone to Paris to accompany his queen's body.'

'I'm sure I will,' I said.

Elaine said, 'Père Martin is the only priest within ten leagues, but I'm sure he'll be able to find time for you, Isobel. Don't forget the new edict about confessing every day.'

I looked at her sharply, but she could look as bland as Charles when she wanted. I wished I knew what mischief she was brewing. I had got the impression that the only things that interested her were money and going to Paris to escape this 'dreadful countryside', and here she was, suddenly concerned with my immortal soul.

'Thank you,' I said, and left it at that. If Père Martin wanted to hear my confession, he'd have to come and get it. I was certainly not going to trot after him.

After dinner, we all went to our rooms. Candles were scarce, and there were only rush torches to burn. They burned so quickly that by dinner's end we were practically in pitch darkness.

Nurse had eaten with the farmhands in the kitchen. There was no difference in the food between the kitchen table and the dining-room table, except that in the kitchen the food was served hot. After being carried through chilly hallways by the shuffling cook, our food was stone cold when it arrived.

I undressed and crawled hastily into bed. Nurse sat in her usual spot by the fireplace on her low, cushioned stool, with Aurore in her arms. Aurore nursed with little suckling sounds, her little hand opening and closing in the air. When she finished, Nurse burped her, changed her diaper, wrapped her up in cloth so tightly she couldn't move, and laid her in her cradle. I winced, but babies at that time were swaddled like little mummies, their arms pinned to their sides.

I supposed it was all right because it didn't bother Aurore, who cooed for a moment before falling asleep. Nurse rocked the little cradle with her foot as she stared at the flames. I had no idea what she was thinking. Any attempt at conversation was usually met with silence and flushed cheeks. I'd given up trying to pose questions, but it didn't stop me from talking. After so many years in prison, with no one to speak to and no one around, I tended towards silence myself. But when someone was in the same room as I, it was hard to ignore them.

'It's getting warmer,' I began, propping myself up on one elbow and leaning down so I could watch Aurore. 'Soon spring will be here, and we'll be able to take the baby for walks in the fields. I hope that Lucien comes back with some meat. I'm sick of cabbage soup, cabbage salad, and cabbage sauté. It gives us all gas, and we smell badly enough as it is. Thank goodness we don't have any cabbages left now.'

This elicited a tiny grin from Nurse. Encouraged, I went on. 'I don't know about you, but I think this castle is dreary. Not that I've seen many others, but the one in Italy was nicer. We stayed there two months. Our room was warm.' I sighed. 'The food was better too. Queen Isabella had oranges brought by courier from Sardinia. I used to think oranges were of no importance, but now I find myself longing for them.'

'I n'er seen un,' said Nurse, in an almost inaudible mutter.

I gaped at her, then closed my mouth and nodded. 'I'll have to find one for you, somehow. They are as orange as the sun when it sets, and they are full of sweet juice. You peel the skin off, and it's so oily and fragrant your hands stay scented for hours. The flesh is divided into sections, not like an apple with a core. Each section has its own seeds. They're white and round. Charles made a game of spitting the seeds out the window, trying for the knights' helmets. When his aim was good, the knight would think it was a bird shitting on his helmet.'

I laughed, and Nurse joined me. 'In Tunis, oranges were sold by the basket. The crusaders used to eat them all day long. Even during mass there would be the sound of people spitting orange seeds into their hands; and it almost covered the smell of garlic.'

'Soundzgud,' she said, her voice rusty and creaking. 'Was z'Holy Lan' gud?'

'We weren't in the Holy Land, not really. We were in Tunis.'

She looked confused. 'Thought you wen' cruzade?'

I realized she had no idea where Tunis was. To her, there was France, Italy, Spain, and the Holy Land. I nodded. 'There were good things in the Holy Land,' I said. 'The people, although you call them infidels, are very kind and love life and God as much as any human being. They would come to sell their goods at the fort, and I used to buy oranges and dates from them. It's funny. They call *us* the infidels and wonder why we come to kill and plunder.

'The forts that the crusaders built are marvellous to see, but so are the cities and the countryside. It's so warm that figs grow all year round, and there are dates too, much sweeter than honey.'

'Ztop talkin' 'bout fud,' said Nurse, shaking her head.

'I'm sorry.' I laughed again. 'I wasn't thinking. You must be hungry all the time, like I am. The queen, God rest her soul, warned me that nursing a baby does that to you.'

'Mine died,' she said, quite clearly.

I felt as if I'd been hit very hard. The woman's expression didn't alter. She sat as still as stone next to the fire. 'How?' I asked, after the silence had stretched to its limit.

She shrugged. 'Dunno. Fever.'

'Was it a girl or a boy? What was its name?'

'Girl, Jan.'

'Where is your husband?'

'Works forest making charcoal.' As she spoke, her voice limbered as if she'd not spoken in years. After each phrase she'd snap her mouth shut and frown, embarrassed by her speech. Yet each phrase was clearer than the last.

'Whenever you want, I'll send you home,' I said to her.

'No. I prefer here.' She nodded once, emphatically, then turned her back to me to stir the fire. The conversation was finished.

Chapter Thirteen

The poor people often had nothing but soup to eat. The soup could be made with leftover meat, withered vegetables, grass, or even mushrooms. However hungry you may be, avoid eating mushrooms as they can be poisonous. Ask if the soup has mushrooms in it, and if it does, refuse to eat it as a precaution.

Tempus University *Corrector's Handbook*

The next day and for days after, rain fell in sheets. The countryside was soon flooded as we were in the lowlands, and shining ponds grew all around the castle and covered the fields. The swamps left their boundaries and encircled us, and a warm spell brought forth a burst of creation from plants and trees. Buds popped open and each tree laced itself with pale green. Primroses bloomed on each patch of dry ground, along with wild cabbage and purple crocus.

With the rains, frogs emerged. Cook was so excited he could hardly wait until the rain stopped to catch them, and we ate them grilled, boiled, or stewed for weeks.

Along with the frogs, the ducks came back, and we snared four. We held a feast in honour of Lucien, who returned from the hunt one rainy day with two wet stags slung over his tired pony's back.

The rest of the meat was smoked to preserve it. Elaine and I took great satisfaction one day in cleaning out the meat pantry and whitewashing the walls. The lye we used stung my nose for days and my hands turned grey, but after the house-cleaning, three haunches of smoked meat replaced the millions of cobwebs in the room.

I stood in the pantry, hands on hips, and laughed in delight. The walls were still damp and the lye fumes brought tears to our eyes, but the sight of so much meat was like a gift. Elaine had a sneezing fit, and Charles counted her sneezes to see if they came to an even or an odd number.

'Five! That's good luck,' he crowed.

'I hope so. I hate to think it's a cold coming on. Quick, tell me, do I have a fever?'

She turned to me and stuck her wrist out.

I took her wrist and frowned. 'How can I tell from your wrist? I need to touch your forehead.'

'You feel my wrist to see if my humours are balanced. Everyone knows that.' She rolled her eyes. 'Honestly, Isobel, sometimes I think you're so strange.'

Charles came to my rescue. 'In the south we feel the forehead to check humours,' he said loftily. 'You can tell by the heat it gives off if you have a fever or not. If it's damp, you must be careful, as the humours are out of balance.'

Elaine raised her eyebrows. 'What shall I learn next from you, Charles? For one so young, you're certainly erudite!'

Charles bristled, unsure about the word 'erudite', but I heard the faint sound of hoofbeats and shushed him. 'Someone is coming,' I said.

'It's Father!' Elaine shrieked and bolted towards the steps.

'How do you know?' I lifted my skirt and trotted after her. 'Slow down, you'll trip on these blasted stairs.' We climbed the spiral stairs out of the basement pantry and dashed through the kitchen, now brightly lit by spring sunlight streaming through the casement windows. Cook was at the stone sink, muttering at a plate, and didn't turn as we rushed by.

'He's deaf as a post,' said Charles with a laugh.

Our pace increased as we reached the long main hallway and turned into an impromptu race. Charles, unhampered by skirts, was in the lead with Elaine bounding at his heels. I was unused to running, but my legs were longer than theirs, and I soon caught up.

The end of the hallway was in sight, and we were gasping with pent-up laughter when the door flew open. A dark shadow blocked the sunlight, and a knight in full armour stepped through the door. Elaine was going too fast to stop – she ran into Charles and sent him headlong into the man's legs.

There was a huge clang, a crash as the man fell, and a cry from Elaine as she tripped over the uneven flagstones. She landed on top of Charles, and the three of them lay in a heap on the floor.

'Get off me!' came the muffled command from the bottom of the pile.

Elaine scrambled to her feet, and Charles stood up slowly, his hands pressed to his forehead where a bruise already bloomed like a purple flower. The knight, face down, rolled over with the sound of falling pots and pans, and I started to laugh. It began as a snort, but it bubbled out of my throat and ended in a roar. I held my stomach, doubled over with mirth, tears pouring down my cheeks. Elaine started to giggle, then laugh, and the sound bounced around the hallway as gay as spring sunlight.

The knight lifted his visor, and François stared at us. His green eyes were at first angry, then a spark of humour lit their emerald depths and he chuckled warmly. 'That was some welcome,' he said. He got to his feet and examined the armour. The breastplate, which he unbuckled, had a fresh dent.

'Let me help,' said Elaine. She sprang forward and tackled the stiff leather straps.

'I'm so glad you're back. We've been terribly worried about you.' This was news to me, but I hastened to nod when Elaine said, 'Haven't we worried?'

'Yes, terribly. How is everything in Paris?' I tried to smooth my hair. My cheeks were hot, and I couldn't seem to get my breath back from the run. My kirtle was laced too tightly – it hurt to breathe.

Charles rubbed his fingers across his bruised forehead, looked at his hands, saw there was no blood, and sighed. 'You have fine armour, sir, but why are you wearing it? Are there brigands in the area?'

François gave him a sharp glance. 'As a matter of fact, yes. I met them three days ago, and they've been following me ever since. I hardly dared sleep, and if I hadn't taken Richard with me, I probably would have been robbed, or worse. Don't worry now. I sent Richard and his sons to the village to warn the mayor.'

Elaine gave a cry and threw her arms around her father's metal-plated shoulders.

'I'm so glad you're all right. You must come and sit down and tell us all the news of Paris. Were there any parties? Has it changed much since we left? Did you see any of my friends?'

'Don't you want to hear about the Count of Artois?' François asked, his voice stern.

'I suppose you'll tell me of him anyway. How is he, the old fart?' Elaine shrugged sulkily. Her eyes lost their sparkle.

'He's dead.'

Elaine's hands slid off the buckle she was unfastening. 'What? How?'

'Hunting accident.' François sounded weary. 'The stupid man went chasing wolves in the middle of winter and fell off his horse while fording a frozen stream. The ice broke and he drowned.'

'Wolves?' I gasped.

'Wolves.' He shook his head and grimaced. 'You can't even eat the beasts, so what's the use chasing them? Poor sport, if you ask me.'

'Wolves.' I rubbed my face and looked at Elaine. She was trying very hard to find a suitable expression.

'Well, I won't have to be in such a rush to finish my trousseau,' she said. She didn't seem sure whether to be upset or relieved. She wrung her hands together. 'Now what shall we do?'

'We're going to Navarre,' said François. He shrugged out of his thigh guards and tossed his gloves to the floor.

'What about the castle?' Elaine asked.

'Sold. We're free of this pile of sticks and stones. My niece is marrying the Count of Tours, and she wants a place of her own. I reminded her about our grandfather's glorious castle, the rich, outlying farmland, and the lovely chapel, and she bought it.' He shrugged.

'Did you include Père Martin in the deal?' I whispered, forgetting how sharp François's ears were.

He chuckled again. 'No, he's coming with us. We can't travel without a priest, especially now. The Church has declared it a sin not to confess, and now even the priests outside of Paris have started selling pardons.' He snorted. 'As if you could buy God's pardon. It's the Inquisition. They're a bunch a fanatics.'

'The Inquisition?' Charles asked, still rubbing his head.

'That's what I said. Let me see that.' François bent down and peered at the egg-sized bruise. 'You'd better see Cook and ask him to put some arnica on that.' He swatted the boy on the shoulder and sent him scurrying down the hall.

He and Elaine grinned at each other, but I shivered. Père Martin had been sniffing around me like a hunting hound scenting its prey. I confessed every once in a while, but had refused to buy pardons, and lately he'd taken to pointing his fat finger at me during mass and saying, 'Beware the sinners among us, who refuse God's pardon and even His Word!' He didn't dare say my name, but I assumed that he was simply biding his time. I had no idea what he wanted of me – I'd made it clear from the beginning that I wasn't wealthy and wouldn't buy the pardons he offered. As the family had recently dwelt in Paris, Père Martin had known about this new trend and taken it up, especially with François gone these months. I hoped François would put a stop to it now that he was back.

Père Martin had asked me, of course, as he asked everyone in the castle and outlying villages. Nurse had given him a part of her wages, and I'd scolded her roundly. Even Dame Blanche paid him. I saw her slip him a coin after mass one day. Of course, Père Martin made a great show of pardoning all her sins right there, on the chapel steps. Impressed, some of the poorer peasants asked if he'd accept fresh eggs or cream as payment.

I was of two minds about that. The wages of sin ended up in our kitchen since Père Martin lived with us, and it was hard to fault him when he gave a clutch of eggs to Cook. On the other hand, the peasants needed food just as badly as we did, and I hated the thought of taking a dinner away from a hungry child.

The day was too lovely to waste worrying about the priest, though. While Elaine and François gossiped about the court, I slipped away for some fresh air, first fetching Aurore to take her outside. The sun warmed the grass, and the flowers scented the air.

Honeybees droned in the apple blossoms, and Aurore opened her slate blue eyes wide and looked at the vast world. Actually, it was simply the walled orchard. We sat on a thick rug that Nurse carried outside for us. She darned stockings while I taught Aurore a little song about puppets.

'Ainsi font, font, font, les petites marionnettes!

'Ainsi font, font, font, trois petits tours et puis s'en vont!'

The baby gave a wide, toothless smile, and I clapped delightedly. 'She's smiling, did you see?'

Nurse nodded, intent on her knitting. Her mouth moved silently as she counted the stitches.

We were perfectly content, with the soft grass waving gently in the spring breeze and the white apple blossoms drifting like snowflakes through the balmy air. Aurore yawned and fell asleep as suddenly as only babies can do. Her pale eyelashes rested gently on her round cheeks. I lay down beside her and watched her. She was still brand-new, a miracle to me. Her little nose was so tiny, the wings of her nostrils translucent in the light. Her cheeks were rosy, her mouth a perfect, tiny replica of my own. Her hands were small yet strong when she grasped my fingers. As she slept she dreamed, and her mouth worked softly. Her breath was as sweet as honey, and her hair as fine as gossamer, shining in the bright sun.

I hadn't realized how strongly a baby affects emotions. Whenever I looked at Aurore, I felt a joy so sharp it was painful, and I knew that if I had to, I'd defend her with my life. My own self faded to nothing when I was near her. I was simply a link in the chain, and the newest link was all that mattered. It was strange and powerful.

I leaned over and kissed her perfect cheek. She uttered a faint snore, and I laughed.

Footsteps sounded, and I turned to see who intruded in our haven of tranquillity. To my astonishment, it was François. I shut my gaping mouth and scrambled to my feet, brushing strands of grass from my skirt. I gave a little curtsey, my eyes fastened on his tall form.

He hardly glanced at me. He was looking at Aurore. He tilted his head, a faint smile on his lips. 'She's grown,' he said.

I let my breath out. 'Won't you sit down a while?' I motioned with my hand.

He settled in the grass near Aurore. Nurse had fallen asleep as well, slumped against an apple tree, her chin on her ample chest, and now and then a faint snore escaped her. François glanced her way. 'She's a good woman.'

'I can't thank you enough for getting her,' I said.

'Thank Lucien, not me.' His voice was mellow.

'Will you be sad to leave this place?'

'Perhaps. It's been my home all my life, yet I can't honestly say I love it. There are other places that are grander, or smaller and more comfortable.'

I smiled sadly. 'Often places are loved for the memories they shelter.'

'My children were born here . . .' His voice trailed off. He looked at me with a strange expression in his eyes. I turned away. 'Do I make you so uncomfortable?' he asked.

'No!' Surprise made me face him again. 'No, that's not it. You were staring at me, that's all.'

'I was just thinking that Aurore was born in a tent. I wondered what sort of memories you would have.' His hand was close to mine, and when he shifted in the grass, we touched.

I drew a quick breath. 'You were there. I'll always remember how you wove the cradle and how strong you were when you brought Aurore into the world. I didn't know what to do.'

He laughed. 'You don't have to know anything. Nature takes care of itself.'

His hand crept over mine, and my heart pounded. There was a sort of tingling sensation where our skin met. Flower blossoms floated in the air between us, along with motes of golden pollen and the silver thread of a spider's web. All that I saw clearly, but what most impressed me was the steady regard of the man in front of me. He sat in silence, his hand covering mine, and both the silence and the touch were more intimate than any moment I'd shared with Jean.

We held hands, watching as Aurore slept. François asked no questions of me, and every now and then, he reached over and gently touched my cheek, as if to reassure himself I was real, and sitting next to him.

I didn't want to talk. To speak would break the spell cast by the sun, the fragrant apple blossoms and the sweetly sleeping baby. Instead I leaned against François' shoulder and let myself relax into a tranquil bliss that lasted all that afternoon.

The day went by too quickly. It was the last peaceful day I'd have in a very long time. How fortunate we cannot see ahead in time, and how ironic it is that I should be the one to say those words.

We packed the contents of the castle into crates, cramming as much as we could into wooden chests and rolling tapestries into long sausages. There was bustle everywhere as wall hangings were unhooked, and shrieks as huge spiders and mice skittered out of every nook and cranny. Fragile items were packed in sawdust. Whatever torches could be salvaged were laid in rows in the hallway. The rushes that had cushioned our feet all winter and insulated the stone floor from the bitter cold were raked out of the manor and burned.

Elaine and Dame Blanche oversaw the chambers while Charles and I were appointed Cook's aids. We lugged the huge iron spit outside after dropping it twice on the stairs only to be told crossly to take it back to the kitchen.

'Iron doesn't travel,' said Cook, narrowing his rheumy eyes at us. 'Do you want us all to drown the first time we cross a river?'

I didn't know that. All the iron stayed in the castle. The gardener dug up the rose bushes and packed them in jute sacks. Roses travelled, then, and it amused me to see them wrapped so carefully in preparation for their journey.

The beehives were carefully emptied and the honey added to our baggage. The bees themselves were left behind, to Lucien's regret, as he doubled as beekeeper.

The moat was emptied one last time and scoured with rush brooms. The fish we hoped to find were not forthcoming, except for three skinny minnows that were quickly snapped up by a tall grey heron stalking the banks.

'Shoo! Shoo! Damn him!' screeched Cook. 'He's taken a frog too!'

I hid my relief. We'd had frog's legs so often I was beginning to think I'd turn green. I held my hands to the light and examined them critically. They weren't green they were red, my knuckles raw from scrubbing. There were two new cuts on my thumb from the sharp copper kettle. My wrists stuck out like white twigs from my work dress's sleeves, and my nails were broken to the quick. I'd bunched my hair into a snarly braid and shoved it under a worn cap that tied under my chin. The linen was rough and chafed my throat. My legs ached, my back hurt, and I hadn't taken a decent bath since François had got back from Paris a week earlier.

I was glad that the packing was nearly done. The few people working for us had performed a titan's job. Stacked beneath the eaves of the hay barn were twenty numbered crates and chests. Elaine had a list somewhere of every item packed away and its exact location. We expected the muleteer with his mule train to come any day now. Lucien had gone into the forest to hire the animals from the charcoal makers, who used them for transporting their wares all over the kingdom. We were ready to leave.

I let my weary shoulders sag. Soon the bells for vespers would ring from the chapel then dinner would be served in the stable yard. We'd set up makeshift tables and benches with boards and hay bales. I could hear arguing from the stables, Richard's sons, no doubt, squabbling about who would lead the livestock to drink that evening.

181

They could never decide whose turn it was. Water trickled into the moat from the stream and its gurgle was hypnotizing.

I let myself slide down into the long grass beneath the gate I leaned on. The water bubbled merrily, the argument quieted as Richard came around the corner, and I fell into a deep sleep.

The bells for vespers failed to awaken me, so Charles was sent to look for me and found me sleeping soundly. He shook me awake and made a face.

'Père Martin ranted hellfire and brimstone this evening. You were right to miss mass.'

I yawned. 'I'm sorry, I was watching the brook one moment and the next I was having the most marvellous dream.'

'Dinner is ready.' For Charles, marvellous dreams and food were closely linked. 'Richard's sons caught some pigeons.'

'I'll wash up here and join you in a minute.' This was a polite euphemism for 'I'd like to pee in the stream, could you leave me alone?'

Charles disappeared and I hitched up my skirts and waded into a sheltered spot beneath the willow branches. In the castle, the bathrooms consisted of metal buckets or porcelain bowls, which were emptied into the stream or into the fertilizer heap, depending on the nature of the contents. I was just skipping a step.

When I finished, I walked upstream and washed my face and hands at the spring. I tried to smooth some semblance of order into my hair. It didn't work. I stuffed my cap back on, tied it beneath my chin, wincing at the rough cloth, and strode off to the stables. I was starving.

We ate dinner beneath a calico sky. The sun was setting, and the clouds were gilded with deep orange and rose. In the east, the night sky was indigo, and the first stars twinkled in it. Lucien lit smudge torches, supposedly to keep the mosquitoes away, although it never seemed to work. Luckily, there weren't too many insects. All the birds, bats, frogs, and spiders around kept the horseflies and mosquitoes in check. As we ate, bats swooped into the flickering torchlight, so close that their wings glowed transparently red. Huge pale moths blundered about, landing in our hair and food. Their soft wings shed powder when we touched them. Two half-wild cats slunk around the edges of the light, waiting to pounce on any bit of food that fell upon the ground.

François had a dog, the last of his once-mighty hunting pack. The dog was old now and stiff-jointed. His muzzle was white and his eyes opaque. He sat with his bony head resting on François' knee. François slipped him tender morsels when he thought no one was looking. Once or twice, beneath the table, our knees or our hands collided. Each time we both froze, as if trying to make the most of the brief contacts. When our hands strayed apart, François' eyes twinkled, although he said nothing.

Elaine, with her bird-sharp eyes, sometimes caught these glances, and each time she did, her lips thinned and the skin around her nose whitened.

Did she suspect something of the growing emotion between François and me? We were never alone, and with the bustle of packing, François was so busy he sometimes literally fell asleep standing up. He hadn't courted me, except that one day in the apple orchard. All that happened was, if we met, he found an excuse to touch me. Sometimes the touch was fleeting, sometimes it was a caress. Each time I felt a shock, as if electricity flowed from his hands to my skin. Each time, his face reflected a little of what I felt. His mouth grew softer, and his eyes deepened. I started to dream about him at night, and I would wake up, prey to a longing so sharp that I wanted to cry aloud.

That evening, during dinner, I propped Aurore in a cradle right on the table. Her little face glowed in the candlelight. Her wide eyes followed everyone's movements avidly. She was beginning to take interest in the world around her, and I was absurdly proud whenever someone leaned over and chucked her under the chin or addressed kind words to her.

Richard's sons carried old Marthe down. She had the only chair while the rest of us sat on prickly hay bales. Her supper was a bowl of broth, and she sucked noisily on boiled onions. Her teeth were gone, but her mind was sharp, and she loved reminiscing.

183

'Jean was a good baby, never fussy or difficult. He ate everything you put in his mouth. Just like this little sweetheart.' Marthe leaned over to peer at Aurore. 'I can't believe I'm seeing Jean's baby, and him cold in his grave.'

A silence fell over us, and then Elaine said in a mournful voice, 'I wish he'd never left.' She'd admitted to me that she'd felt pangs of guilt ever since she discovered Réné d'Artois had drowned. All her planning to convince Jean to go on the crusade (though in truth he didn't need much prodding) had gone for naught. Her brother was dead, and now she didn't have to marry anyone anyway.

Before she could speak further, one of the cats leapt up on the table and snatched a whole pigeon. The resulting hue and cry as two of Richard's sons jumped to their feet, overturning the ale jug, distracted everyone from the gloom that had threatened to overwhelm us at the mention of Jean.

I felt my shoulders relax, and I took a rather shaky breath. Any talk about Jean made me uneasy. I darted a glance at François. He sat perfectly still, his hand resting on his dog's head. His face was halfway in shadow, but the bones seemed to show right through the skin. He gazed unseeingly at the table and his mouth drew into a thin line.

Gently, I reached under the table and took his hand. It was the first time I dared do so. He jumped, and the look he gave me was sharp, but I hung on, tightening my fingers when he made to pull away. His mouth curved in a smile, a real smile that lit up his eyes. He gave my hand a squeeze and nodded. 'Thank you,' he said softly.

'I don't understand,' I said, puzzled.

The smile stayed, though his eyes grew bleak. 'I hope to God you never have to,' he said. He took a deep breath, as if he'd been holding it, and nodded toward Aurore. 'I think she takes after you, more than Jean. She has your pure features.' With his free hand, he traced the line of my scar. 'If it wasn't for this, you'd look like an angel.'

There was a loud crack as Elaine set her knife down hard enough to break the bone handle.

I hastily pulled away from François. He bent over to pat his dog, but I could see a smile dancing at the corners of his mouth, and so I didn't pay the slightest attention to Elaine's venomous looks.

Dinner finished soon after that. Light bantering punctuated with guffaws gave way to yawns and remarks about rising early in the morning. The torches were doused, the food gathered up and taken into the kitchen, and we all made our way to our rooms to collapse fully dressed on fresh rushes covered with linen sheets, having packed the beds and bedding already.

Chapter Fourteen

*Most of what you will encounter in the past will be strange and even
frightening. Try not to show your fear. Practise looking calm in front of
a mirror.*

Tempus University *Corrector's Handbook*

'HEEEhaawww HEEEEhaawwww!'

The noise woke us before dawn. The sky was steely grey, a light
frost covered the ground, and the muleteer trotted into the courtyard with thirty mules and called out in a huge, bellowing voice. 'Is
anyone here? I say, is anyone about?' He brayed as loudly as his
charges. The mules milled about, hooves clattering on stone. They
hee-hawed shrilly and unceasingly. Steam rose from their backs in
white clouds, and sparks flew from their iron-shod hooves hitting
the cobblestones. The muleteer stood in the centre of the milling
beasts, his huge fists on his hips and a long whip wrapped around his
broad shoulders.

We stumbled to the windows and leaned out. We must have
made a comical sight, our sleep-crumpled faces peering out of nearly
every window on the courtyard side of the castle.

'Richard!' François cried. 'Get the man settled in the stables!'

There were more cries as Richard woke his sons, and then a
flurry of shrieks and more yells as he apparently found one of them
in the hay with a girl.

'Damn your rutting, boy! I've told you to stay away from that

186

wench!' A figure scurried from the barn clutching a dress and cap. She halted in front of Richard and waggled her naked buttocks saucily in his direction. Then she stuck her tongue out at him, adroitly dodged his foot as he kicked at her, and ran down the path into the darkness, crying at the top of her lungs, 'I'm tellin' my dadda, an' he'll make ye pay, ye ol' fool!'

'You stupid clod!' Richard yanked his naked son into the courtyard by his hair. He swung his fist at the boy but missed as his son darted away.

We all stayed at the windows to watch, of course. Charles and the cook erupted in gales of laughter while the women – Elaine, Dame Blanche, Nurse, and I – hooted and whistled. The young man ran around the dark courtyard, trying to escape his father's flailing fists and the mules' hooves.

'What's this? What's this?' The hoarse cry came from the priest's window. Père Martin held a lantern outside, which cast a yellow glow on the commotion below. The priest uttered an outraged shriek. *Par tous les saints!* he cried. 'A naked imp in our midst!'

The young man gaped up at the priest and quickly hid his privates with a handful of hay, but it was soon scattered as he ran about. Finally the muleteer collared him, booted him in the rear, and sent him sprawling.

'Listen to yer father next time, boy!' he bellowed. 'Now help me with these mules!'

The spectacle finished, we withdrew into our rooms to gather our belongings and leave the castle for the last time.

The castle disappeared as if it was sinking into the ground. As we rode further and further away, the stone buttresses shrank, the walls were swallowed by the fields and, last, the pointed tops of the wooden turrets vanished. I heard a sigh and turned towards my travelling companion, the Lady Elaine, late of Castle Touraine, soon to be resident in the court of Navarre. What I knew of Navarre was that it was now ruled by a French branch of King Louis's family, and that its king, Theobald II, had gone on the same Crusade I'd been

187

on, though I'd only rarely seen him. King Theobald II had survived the Crusade but had died in Sicily from illness on the return journey. His brother, called King Henry the Fat, ruled Navarre now. I also knew that Henry's daughter, Joan, would marry King Philip's son, and the small kingdom of Navarre would remain under French rule for many years.

'Are you sad to be leaving?' I asked.

She shrugged, and her face twisted as if she were trying not to cry. A smile tugged at her mouth, though, and the look she gave me was droll. 'I was thinking of my brother,' she admitted, 'not about the castle at all. When I was eight, he dared me to walk across the moat one winter. I stepped on the ice and there was a cracking sound. I hesitated, Jean gave me a shove, and I slipped and fell on my rear, sliding right out into the moat. At that moment, Richard came running through the snow, yelling at me not to move and for Jean to grab my cloak. The ice gave away just as Jean took my arm, and I pulled him in with me.

'Richard fished us out and ran with us to the kitchen where we undressed and sat right in the chimney. Cook gave us broth and Dame Blanche was fetched from her chambers and got scolded for not watching us. She fluttered and flapped around the kitchen like a chicken and finally went to get us our dry clothes.

'Everyone treated Jean like a hero. Richard saw him grab for me and thought he dove in after me. I was the fool who tried to walk on thin ice. Mother, of course, covered Jean with kisses for being so brave and saving his little sister. I was made to sit in the corner of the chimney all day.'

Her voice faded and she gave a little laugh. 'The strange thing is, it never occurred to me to tell anyone that Jean pushed me out on the ice. It seemed normal to me that Jean was a hero. He was always mine. People loved him and fussed over him, and I was never jealous because I was sure he deserved it.' Her mouth quirked and tears sparkled on her lashes. 'I miss him terribly. Will you tell me about him? You were with him this past year, what did he do? What did he say when you first met him? Will you tell me?'

I nodded slowly. 'I saw Jean for the first time in the middle of a barn. He stood with a group of lads, but it seemed he stood alone. He was taller than they were and stood straight. He looked like a young eagle. His green eyes were the first things I loved about him.' I smiled and shook my head. 'You and your father have those same eyes. It disconcerts me. Especially when you gaze at me from beneath your lashes, as if you're weighing each of my words and finding them wanting.'

Elaine gave a short laugh. 'It's a family trait, I'm afraid. We all seem terribly critical, but I think it's only nearsightedness. Now you know our darkest secret.'

I smiled. 'Another thing you share with your brother is your lightness of spirit. Nothing could keep Jean down for long. He bounced back from each misfortune with a smile and a joke. The only other person I met like that was Prince Jean-Tristan. His death was a terrible blow for Jean. He grieved a long time for his friend.'

Our mules were tied together. We sat on a sort of wooden platform lashed across their backs and cushioned with a thick carpet. A wooden frame could be inserted into its four corners to make a covered litter, but the weather was fair and we enjoyed the sun.

'Why did he say he'd gone on the crusade?' asked Elaine in a low voice. Her hand plucked nervously at the rug.

I answered honestly. 'He never really told me why, but he did say he was at odds with your father. Whenever I begged him to turn around and go back, he replied that he wouldn't until he could prove to his father that he was a man.'

'You begged him to go back home?' Elaine frowned. 'I didn't know you wanted to turn back.'

I cleared my throat. 'I never wanted to leave, and I desperately wanted to go back because I was afraid he would die.'

'You knew he would die?' Elaine leaned forward, and her eyes narrowed. 'Was it a premonition?'

Her words made me nervous. 'No, nothing like that. The whole voyage seemed unlucky. First, the ship with my family foundered, and our fortune was lost. Then there was the fever, and Jean-Tristan died so suddenly. King Louis, too. All I wanted to do was go back to France.'

'Then your parents died as well. The crusade *was* ill-fated. Perhaps you're clairvoyant.' Elaine stuck her palm at me. 'Can you read my future?'

'No!' I pushed her hand away. 'Don't let Père Martin see you do that. He'll think I'm a witch.' I shuddered. 'Tell me more about Jean. I hardly knew him at all. He never told me about his childhood or where he grew up.'

Elaine looked troubled. 'Mother gave him so much attention no one could compete. Father was always away, hunting or at the court. Then Jean was sent to school.' She shook her head. 'Jean hated school, he wanted to become a knight. He begged for a horse and armour, but all Father did was give him his grandfather's armour and told him to joust with Richard's sons. It was a blow to Jean's ego, because Jean-Tristan was training to be a knight and he wrote letters telling about his fights. Jean wanted more than anything to be able to take part in a tournament. He dreamed of winning a joust or fighting in battle.'

'He got his wish,' I said sadly. 'He fought in a battle. Two, actually.'

'He fought two battles? Tell me!' cried Elaine.

'The first was at Jean-Tristan's side. They won easily, and Jean came back that evening looking as if the sun shone out of his eyes.' I smiled, remembering the scrap of underwear on his helmet. 'He was so happy that day, and I found out I was pregnant.'

Elaine gave a small start. 'It's so strange. I see you, yet I can't imagine you with Jean, and I have the hardest time imagining that Aurore is truly his baby. When Father got Jean's letter informing us you were expecting a child, he was livid!' She laughed, then sobered. 'No one was angrier than I was, though. I'd gone out of my way to help Jean run away so he could marry a wealthy woman, and he married a nobody.'

'Thank you,' I said dryly.

She had the grace to blush. 'Sometimes I feel Jean is dead by my fault because I helped him run away, and other times I feel it's

Father's fault for betrothing me to Réné d'Artois. If that hadn't happened, Jean would still be here, and so would Mother.' Her voice turned venomous. 'Father loved Mother, you know. You're just a pretty diversion for him. He wouldn't dream of marrying someone with no fortune. If he does marry you, I'll hate him for ever.'

Her comment caught me by surprise and I felt my cheeks grow hot. At that moment, I glanced behind us and saw François.

Our eyes met. What my face looked like, I don't know, but his face was drawn so tightly the bones showed white beneath his skin. I spun around, facing frontward again, and my breath came fast.

'What is it?' Elaine looked back. 'Oh! Father . . .' but her words died in her throat as François kicked his horse and galloped by us.

The litter pitched as our mules shied sideways. I slipped off the edge. Elaine grabbed at my arm. It wasn't a long drop, but my kirtle had wrapped around my legs, and Elaine, by grasping my sleeve, hindered rather than helped me. I couldn't put both hands out to save myself, and I landed on my head. There was a flash of light, the breath was knocked out of me, and the day grew strangely dark.

I opened my eyes. Sharp pain chased itself around my skull, and I moaned.

Immediately someone took my hand. 'Are you awake?' Charles asked.

I blinked, but the darkness was so deep and inky I could see nothing. 'What happened?' Then I remembered. 'I fell off the litter, didn't I? Have I been unconscious long?'

'A few hours. Do you remember falling?'

'Yes.' I spoke quietly. 'I'm sorry. Did I wake you?'

There was a confused silence, and Charles said, 'No,' rather hesitantly. Then he said, 'Would you like some water?'

I was parched. 'Yes, please.' I struggled to a sitting position, my head aching horribly. White points of light danced in front of my eyes and I blinked hard to clear my vision, which remained black. Where was the glow of embers in the fireplace or glimmer of stars in the sky? I squinted towards the sky.

'Here.' It was Charles.

191

I turned towards the sound of his voice and frowned. 'Where are you?' My head hurt so much that tears leaked down my cheeks. I could feel each heartbeat in my skull like a blow. I heard more footsteps and the swishing sound of a tent flap being opened.

'I'm right here.' Charles sounded anxious.

I reached my hand out, blundering into the goblet he held. Liquid spilled over my hands and I gave a little cry. 'Perhaps you should light tinder. It's so dark in here that I can't see anything. What time is it?'

'It's just past vespers.' Charles' voice was high with fright.

I turned my head towards the sound of his breathing. 'What did you say?'

'It's sunset,' said Charles.

Fear iced my blood. I felt as if I'd just been dropped into a well. I lay back down, slowly, for the pain was dire, and reached a hand to my head. A bandage swathed my forehead, but my eyes were uncovered. I opened and shut my fingers, right in front of my eyes. Nothing. I moved my hand over my face, strangely numb, and dried blood flaked beneath my fingers. I traced a line from my forehead to chin and noted that my cheekbones felt as if they'd been shot with anaesthesia. So did the bridge of my nose.

My skin prickled. 'I can't see,' I whispered.

A choking cry sounded behind Charles, and I recognized Elaine's voice.

'Elaine?'

'I'm here.' She swallowed hard. I heard her.

'Where is François?' I was afraid to ask, but I had to.

'I'm here.' His voice came from next to me, and his hand took mine. It was large and warm. I felt some of the ice thaw.

I used François' hand to pull myself to a seated position. 'It's just a nerve,' I said, trying to ignore the sharp pain every movement cost me. 'I fell on my forehead and damaged the optic nerve. Perhaps there's a small bruise in my brain, and the pressure is causing blindness. It could go away when the bleeding is absorbed.' I babbled from sheer fright.

There was a rather uncomfortable silence, and François said, 'It was my fault.' His voice was raw.

Elaine started to speak, but he shushed her. 'I'll look after you, Isobel, and you shall want for nothing, I promise.' His hand trembled. I could picture his face. His eyes would be downcast, their emerald green hidden by long lashes. His mouth would be drawn in that thin line I'd come to know so well. That line of frustration, of simmering anger against life in general. François was not one to accept anything gracefully. I think discovering his beloved Elaine had helped Jean run away had shocked him. Our words had wounded him.

I put my hand out to search for his face. He caught it before I could touch him.

'No,' he said. 'I don't want your pity.' His words were so low I doubt anyone in the tent heard them except me. His face was close to mine, and I felt his warm breath on my neck.

My hand tightened on his. 'I don't want your pity, either,' I whispered. My headache reached a crescendo, and I thought I'd probably pass out in another minute, or die, but I had to do something first. I turned my head, guided by instinct more than anything else, and pulled him to me. My lips brushed against his, and I pressed closer.

Our kiss deepened, but only for a moment.

Elaine's sharp cry knifed between us. 'What are you doing?' she shrieked. 'Isobel is Jean's wife!'

François pulled away from me as if he was burned. I didn't care. I fainted, I think.

I would have loved to have seen Navarre in the summertime. All I could do was hear it and smell it. I knew from maps that the kingdom was small, niched between Spain and France, and reached from the mountains to the Atlantic. It was a powerful little kingdom, affiliated to France through blood and marriage but independent by religion and government. Even without sight I could measure the gentle climate, with orchards and vineyards on the mountain slopes. Hot springs dotted the countryside.

On one side was France, and on the other was Spain and then, further south, the Moorish Kingdom of Cordova. Navarre contained a mixture of culture and learning that existed nowhere else on Earth at that time. The city of Pamplona was one of the biggest capitals in the world, and traders and minstrels roamed through both the city and the kingdom. It was the passageway from north to south, east to west. A cool breeze greeted me, redolent of rain, orange blossoms, spices and mountain snows. The first moment my feet crossed the border, I felt as if I was coming home.

At first, we stayed in the city of Pamplona, at the court. The King of Navarre was in his northern holds when we arrived, so we didn't meet him. We spent a few days at the court while François searched for suitable lodgings. He found us a small manor, and we moved in the first week of July.

I was in severe pain most of the time and stayed bedridden. Noise hurt my head, and I begged Nurse to take Aurore away when she cried. She was teething, so the poor baby whimpered frequently. Charles was my constant companion in those days. He would sit by my side so silently I would fear he'd left, and my hand would grope for him. He was always there, though, and he brought me food and small tidbits of gossip of those I knew from the crusade. Everyone who had accompanied King Philip was now in Paris with his court. The rumour was he would remarry in the autumn.

Charles was silent while I thought about this bit of news. After a moment, I sighed.

'It's better for him. He must be so lonely.'

'Are you thinking about the king?' Charles asked quietly.

'Who else would I be thinking about?' I asked, but he wouldn't answer.

I wanted to explore the manor and experience the countryside, but my pain was such that I stayed in a room with my head swathed in heavy cloth to keep it still. When I think back on that time, it seems as if everything is coloured by that pain. It was dark, of course, and it was darkness made heavier by suffering. Movement brought stabbing pains, so I lay still even when I felt I might go mad from restiveness. I was afraid of damaging my eyes, so I had Nurse keep the curtains drawn. The resulting stuffiness made me feel trapped in some terrible nightmare. I slept fitfully, never sure what time it was. My sense of time shifted so much I was often wide awake while the household slept. Only in those quiet hours could I imagine that my pain grew fainter, and I could think about other things.

Other things being François.

When had I fallen in love with him? The first time I'd seen him, astride his restless horse and looking down upon me, his face had been cold, hard. I hadn't loved him then. Nor had it been when he'd questioned me, gazing into the distance, as if what I said interested him not in the least.

Perhaps it was when he'd bent over Aurore that first morning of her existence. For a minute his guard had fallen, and I'd seen something glow in his eyes. He'd turned to me and his face held some of the wonder he'd felt. It stirred something in my breast that no one had touched, not Jean, not my former fiancé. No one. I knew, suddenly, that he was vulnerable, that his frown was his shield and that his icy stare was a sham. It was only a matter of time before those thoughts crystallized in my mind, and I recognized what I felt to be love.

It was easier for me to recognize love now that I had Aurore. She had opened the gates to my heart. I felt silly, sometimes, with these thoughts mingling with the pain in my skull, but they kept me from sliding into the depths of melancholy. I'd found something to cling to – perhaps, someday, François could learn to love me too.

A week before he left for Bruges, François visited my room. I still remember each word he said, each nuance of his voice, and even the faint air currents his movements stirred as he moved around my room.

He was a pacer. He could rarely stay still. His hands moved and he leaned forward when he spoke. He would often get up in the middle of a phrase and walk around. He'd go to the window or the chimney to prod the embers.

When he came to my room, he first knocked softly, and then

leaned in to see if I was awake. Charles had been sitting by my side, as usual. 'I'll go now,' he said. His voice was carefully neutral. He had guessed what I felt but had no idea what François wanted. Neither did I, so with his entrance my heart pounded and my face warmed. I hoped that the curtains were drawn so that shadow would hide my flushed cheeks.

François sat on the stool Charles had vacated. I heard it creak and he took my hand.

'How are you feeling?'

I tried to guess what he was about by the grip of his hand. It was firm, yet gentle.

His skin was warm and slightly rough. I felt the strongest tingling in my hand and wondered how he could miss it. Perhaps he felt it too, because his hand tightened. 'I'm feeling much better,' I said.

'You say that each time I ask.'

I smiled. 'It's true, though. If there were more light, I could see a bit. My vision is slowly returning. And I can move my head without much pain.'

'Is your vision truly returning?' He sounded doubtful.

'I promise.'

'I still feel dreadful about the accident.'

'I wish you wouldn't.' I was trembling now. The mere feel of his hand in mine was so intense it was as if my whole being was condensed in our simple touch. I had the strongest longing to run my hand up his arm, over his broad shoulders, and trace the firm lines of his neck and chin. I couldn't see him anymore, but I knew the tilt of his head, each swooping line that drew his face, and the soft curve of his lips.

'François,' I whispered.

He touched my cheek. His fingers tickled over my own face. He took a ragged breath and leaned towards me. Our lips touched for just a second, so lightly that I'm still not sure if I imagined it. Then he gently disengaged his hand from mine and stood up.

'I'll see you in a few weeks, Isobel.' My name was a caress when he said it.

196

'Where are you going?'

'I have some business to look into.' I could hear him walk across the room. Then his footsteps stopped near the doorway. 'Don't worry about Elaine. I'll be back as soon as I can.' he said.

That evening, when everyone was asleep, I crept out of my bed and walked on bare feet across my chamber. In the dark, my eyes could pick out dim places where moonlight shone through the window. I pressed my forehead to the glass and stared at the sky. I saw a faint, fuzzy circle that I took to be the moon. From Nurse's side of the room, I heard her snores muffled behind thick curtains. I glided to Aurore's bed and leaned down, but I could see nothing. I could hear her soft breathing, and I touched her rose-petal cheek with one finger. Then I straightened, drew a deep breath and eased my door open.

The hallway was dark, and I had to feel my way along, hands outstretched, groping carefully as I walked, counting the doorways. One, two, three. I hesitated then lifted the wooden latch. It made a little sighing sound, and the person in the bed stirred. I closed the door behind me and made my way towards the broad expanse of white I could just make out with my ruined eyes. Sliding my hands along the linen sheets, I encountered a warm shoulder.

Quick as a snake, a hand grabbed my wrist and pinned me down. Then I heard a rapid intake of breath. I thought he would say something, but he didn't. My heart hammered in my chest. Would he push me away?

No. Gently, he drew me into the bed with him and smoothed my hair from my face. I saw a shadow loom as he reared over me, then the shadow blotted out the faint light.

We sighed as we came together. He buried his face in my neck and I heard his breathing deepen and quicken. He was tender. Each touch was featherlight, each kiss was a whisper. I urged him on in the end, a little cry escaping my lips. He chuckled softly and pulled me to him, curling around me and holding me close. 'Isobel?'

'Yes, François?' My voice was a whisper.

'Why did you come tonight?' His hands tightened around my waist.

197

'You're leaving tomorrow. I'll miss you.'

'I'll miss you too, Isobel.' There was a definite chuckle in his voice now.

'I wish I'd come sooner,' I said. Then I turned around and kissed him. I waited until he'd fallen asleep again, and I crept out of his warm bed and made my blind way back to my room.

The next day François left before dawn. He took Lucien with him. No one was up to see him off. For no reason I understood, Elaine was in a foul mood after her father left. She made everyone in the manor miserable for a week by changing all the furniture around ten times a day to her liking. Eventually she calmed, and life went back to normal.

Chapter Fifteen

War and Peace in the Middle Ages: you won't be able to tell the difference. As a time-traveller, your job is to remain anonymous and not create any diplomatic incidences that could lead to an un authorized war. If anything like that happens, you will be erased.*

Tempus University *Corrector's Handbook*

The month of August arrived with the first rumours of war, which I knew King Philip would soon quell.

For years, France had managed to keep her neighbours at bay, first with Philip Augustus' careful politics, then by force, as he won decisive victories against Spain and Burgundy. King Louis had had a peaceful reign, except for the two forays into the Holy Land and Tunis that cost France so much money and so many lives. War was just a whisper yet, so the people tilled their fields, went to church, and prayed for peace and prosperity.

I was lucky, or unlucky enough, to be there to witness some of the first signs of the changes that would shape the country over the next centuries. Some changes were good, like our larder stocked with fresh produce that the farmers, taking advantage of the new-found peace, sold at the markets. And some changes were hints of conflicts to come, as the Church sought more power.

In cold weather, the peasants often brought their animals to church

---

* Erasure cannot be explained to the layman.

with them. They held them on their laps to keep warm. Services could last three or four hours and the churches were built of stone, and freezing cold. Holes in the roofs leaked rain and snow, and cracks in walls meant draughts. As at Chartres, peasants held their chickens tightly in their arms, rested their feet on the backs of pigs, or sat with a goat firmly wedged between them. After mass, we'd often find the pigs or chickens for sale in the Sunday market, which was where I was when the messenger came, announcing one of the coming changes.

'No more animals allowed in church,' cried the messenger. According to Charles, standing at my elbow, the messenger had a hole in his stocking above his knee, wore a blue woollen cape, and held a rolled parchment which he didn't even glance at as he shouted to everyone in the marketplace.

The babble in the market quieted as the people mulled over that command. It was part of a longer edict issued by the Church and backed by the government. Part of it dealt with taxes, and the other half contained new policies relating to the Church.

The messenger repeated the new rule. 'No animals in church, and by order of the University of Paris, anyone caught reading pamphlets or reciting prose by Thomas Aquinas will be prosecuted by the Church's Inquisition.'

I turned to Charles. 'And so the Dark Ages were ushered in with a rule against chickens in church.'

He didn't laugh. Instead, his husky voice was pensive as he said, 'The Dark Ages? Is that what they call this time period?'

'I'm afraid so,' I answered. 'But next is the Age of Enlightenment. Things will get better.'

He nodded and sighed. 'I would have liked to see the world you lived in.'

'It wasn't much different from this one,' I lied. 'People still live and die, and the world still revolves around the sun.'

'The world turns around the sun?'

'Yes, it does. The idea you have now of everything revolving around the Earth came from the ancient Greeks, but in a few hundred years people will learn the true nature of the universe.'

Charles gave a ghost of a laugh. 'Don't let Père Martin hear you speaking thus, or he'll cry heresy. The Earth is the centre of the universe, and it is quite flat, don't forget.' He spoke wryly.

Charles frequently questioned me when we were alone, but never when there was a chance of being overheard by anyone. Even so, sometimes I wasn't as cautious as I should have been. Luckily he was my shadow and gave me a sharp jab with his elbow if I started to sound outlandish. Like today, when we chanced to be in the market and heard the messenger. I suppose I was giddy with relief that I could leave the house now. My vision was slowly creeping back, although light was painful and I could only see vague, shadowy forms. Migraines were constant companions. The only thing that helped was when I wrapped a linen bandage around my eyes and let Charles lead me about.

The villagers got used to seeing me blind, and they all shifted over when I got to church and made room for me at the front. The old priest had died two days after we arrived in the village and to my relief, Père Martin had become the new priest and was no longer underfoot at the house all day.

When he was at the house, Père Martin always managed to be at my side, taking my hand to pray, and I hated hearing his heavy breathing. It annoyed me, but who could I complain to? Even with him gone most of the time, I didn't dare arouse his ire by avoiding him. Confession was now an obligation, and every day, it seemed, new edicts from the Church arrived. So, one by one, Elaine, Nurse, Dame Blanche and I confessed every day, kneeling on the hard floor while Père Martin breathed loudly through his mouth.

I didn't have much to say, so I usually invented some minor sin, just to get it over with.

'Forgive me, my Father, for I have sinned,' I said.

'What was it?' His voice gave me the chills. I hated not being able to see him as he sat by my side. Some days his cassock rustled so much that I wondered if he had fleas.

'I was angry at Elaine. I felt that she had a finer robe than I.' The sin of envy was a handy sin. Père Martin would be able to concentrate on one thing, and his sermon would be over sooner. I settled myself as comfortably as I could on the stones and gritted my teeth. I had to be careful of my expressions. I couldn't see, but Père Martin could.

Today, though, his sermon was briefer than usual. After the absolving of my sin, he muttered, 'Your sins are forgiven, my daughter. Try not to envy those placed above you, and be charitable to those below you on the great wheel of life.'

I nodded, stifled a yawn and began to rise to my feet. Père Martin put his hand on my arm, ostensibly to help me rise.

'Thank you,' I said, stepping away. I hoped Charles would come and lead me to my room, as I wanted to lie down a bit.

'Isobel.' Père Martin's voice was oily. 'Your blindness is a terrible handicap. In the future, you'll want a protector, someone to look after you in your need.' His hands closed around my arms and he drew me near. 'I'd like you to think of me as a friend, Dame Isobel. A very intimate friend who will take you in when you have nowhere to turn.'

'Pardon me?' Blind, I whipped my head around. My mouth must have been open in shock, but I managed not to cringe as he pawed at me.

'Sir François cannot keep you for ever. He is seeking a new wife, and she'll be the head of the household. She won't want you around, will she?'

'Who told you that?'

'Lady Elaine.' He sounded smug. He probably knew Elaine was furious with me, especially if he heard her confessions. She hadn't spoken a word to me since she'd seen her father kiss me. What she would have done if she'd seen me creeping out of his room didn't bear thinking about.

'I don't know what to say.' A man of the cloth, making a pass at me? Did the clergy at this time have kept women? I knew they didn't marry, but had my history books mentioned whether or not they kept mistresses? I was too stunned to recall.

His hand ran up my arm. 'You need someone to take care of you, Isobel.'

'I . . . I'll think about it.' To my relief, I heard Charles's light footsteps. 'Good day, Père Martin.'

'Good day to you, Lady Isobel.' His fat fingers brushed across my breasts, and I jerked backwards. 'A shy creature, aren't you?' He spoke in a thick whisper, and his breath came fast. Charles came in and took my arm, and I left without replying.

'What was that all about?' Charles asked me, when we were safely out of earshot.

'He wants me as his mistress,' I said. I shivered in disgust. 'I think I'm about to be sick.'

There was a stunned silence from Charles, then, 'What did you say?'

'Oh, God, Charles, I'd rather die.'

'You didn't tell him that, did you?' Humour crept into his voice and I smiled.

'No, of course not. Is it true François is looking for a new wife?'

Another silence, then, 'I don't know. Elaine won't speak to me either.'

'What can I do?' I sighed. 'I love him, you know.'

'I know.' I could practically hear Charles shrug. 'You must miss him.'

'I do. I wish he'd come back. He left so soon after we settled here and there's been no news from him, or none Elaine will share. I wish she weren't so angry with me.' I bit my lip and put my hand out as Charles warned me of the doorway. 'Will she ever forgive me?'

'Ask me something I know,' he said.

'Is it rainy today?'

'No, it's sunny.'

'Will you take me to town later?'

'We'll go after you rest. Lie down, Isobel. Your face is so white it looks transparent. You look more and more like the marble angels carved in the churches. It frightens me, sometimes, to see you.'

'How is Aurore?'

'She's fine. Nurse says she'll bring her to you this evening. Now sleep, please.' Charles stroked my forehead. 'I'll try and find out what François has said to Elaine. Perhaps Dame Blanche will know something.'

He left and shut the door quietly behind him.

I lay awake for a long while, thinking about what Père Martin's proposal meant and what it would mean if François did find a new wife. I wouldn't be able to stay if he came back with someone else. Elaine, I thought, was counting on that fact.

Worry kept me from sleeping. I tried to think about something more pleasant until I drifted off. What was good about this time? Aurore, obviously, and Charles, and my feelings for François. I also loved to go to the village. It was a prosperous place, directly beneath the fortress being built on the hills. We weren't far from Pamplona. The mountains soared above us, their shoulders sometimes frosted with snow even in the summer. To the west was the Atlantic Ocean, the great sea. No one knew what lay beyond it. We were still in the in-between times, caught between the demise of the Roman Empire and the beginning of the Renaissance. The Middle Ages, also referred to as the Dark Ages, was in full swing, and the Inquisition was an ominous whisper on the horizon.

'Do I hear a chicken?'

The congregation suddenly became very still. Père Martin had taken the animal edict very seriously. Now anyone bringing an animal into the church was liable to pay a fine to the priest. In the tiny church, a faint clucking could clearly be heard. Someone shifted, then everyone turned about and craned their heads to see who the offender was.

I choked back a nervous giggle. Charles, at my side, dug his elbow into my ribs.

'He's looking at you,' he hissed out of the corner of his mouth.

'I don't see why. I don't have a chicken,' I whispered back. I didn't have to ask who 'he' was. Since Père Martin had made his intentions clear, he was almost always present, either in my room or at my side when we dined. In church, he often referred obliquely to a woman's obligations. His sermons shifted from fire and brimstone to the importance of duty and obedience. Especially a woman's obedience towards men.

'Who has the chicken?' Père Martin lowered his voice dramatically. 'Bring him forth!'

I shook in a desperate effort not to giggle. But the 'Bring him forth!' was too much. I exploded in a peal of laughter.

There was a second of stunned silence before some of the congregation, restless from a two-hour sermon about duty, tittered as well. Charles tugged on my sleeve.

'Hush, Isobel, please!' His voice was strained.

I pressed my hands to my mouth and leaned over to stifle the laughter bubbling out of my throat. In front of us, I heard Elaine whisper, 'Really!' in an aggrieved voice.

Père Martin thumped his fist on the pulpit. 'Be quiet!' he thundered.

All tittering ceased, and all giggles were hastily choked.

'That's better,' he said.

Then the chicken let out a loud cackle, and the entire congregation burst into gales of laughter.

The sermon was over. Père Martin never found the chicken, and everyone surged out of the church at once without waiting for the benediction, which was not forthcoming since the priest was too angry. Charles pulled me out of the church and pushed his way through the crowd. I followed blindly, tripped and hastily grasped at my skirt.

'Slow down,' I said.

'We'd better get back to the manor before Père Martin sees you. He kept looking at you all through the sermon. It was very queer. He had one hand in his pocket the whole time as if he had something there.'

I giggled nervously. 'Something in his pocket?'

'He's on the far side of the market now.' Charles stopped and I crashed into him. 'Damn, he's headed this way. Quick, into the marketplace. Hopefully we'll get away from him.'

'Why bother?' I tripped again on a cobblestone. 'Damn these

streets! Why don't they fix the holes? I can't see well enough to avoid them.'

'His face is so red it looks like a boiled beet,' said Charles, tugging on my arm.

'I can't run away for ever. I'll just tell him I have a cold.'

'He's seen us.' Charles said mournfully. Then he stiffened. 'He has some sort of letter in his hand that he's waving at us.'

'Maybe it's from François!' I cried.

'Elaine is at his heels.' Charles' hand tightened on my arm. 'I don't like the look of this.'

'Isobel!' Père Martin's voice rose above the bustle in the market-place. 'Isobel! Stay right where you are! I have here a letter from the queen's confessor, Père Denis.' He arrived in front of us, puffing like bellows, and he fanned the paper at my face. I blinked. 'It says you were exempted from the year of mourning. The queen, Isabella, expressed her wishes to her confessor that you should marry as soon as your child was born. It's been over a year since your husband died.'

'The queen, God rest her soul, meant to choose the suitor herself,' Charles retorted in his dry, rasping voice.

'Unfortunately she died before she could,' I said.

'It still means you can marry right away.' Elaine's voice had a note of triumph in it, and a note of spite. I wished I could see her face, so that I could slap it.

'And if not marry, you can open your heart to other things,' Père Martin added. I could hear the gloating in his words. 'No need to mourn for your deceased husband for ever.'

'I prefer to wait, thank you,' I said stiffly. I gathered my skirt in one hand and nudged Charles with the other. 'If you'll excuse me, I wish to go back to the house and see my child.'

'You can't *see* anything.' Elaine's voice was bright with anger. 'You're blind. You're simply another mouth to feed. We've no more money, and I've decided to get rid of excess expenses. Like you.'

I was stunned. 'You can't do this. François won't let you throw me out of his home.'

206

'My father sent me a letter giving me power to do whatever I liked with the household. He's looking for another wife in Paris, and he won't be back until he finds someone.'

'I'd like to see that letter,' I said, keeping my voice steady.

'See it?' She laughed. 'Look all you want.'

A piece of paper was thrust into my hand. I pushed the linen bandage off my eyes and peered at the blur in front of me. I could vaguely make out a glow where the sunlight hit the paper and darkness where shadows fell from my fingers, but the words were totally lost to me. I'd never be able to read it, and I doubted they'd let Charles read it to me. I lowered my hand. The paper was snatched away.

'If you don't want to marry, that's fine,' Elaine said. 'You can leave any time you wish, the sooner the better. Just know that you're no longer welcome in my household.'

I heard the wooden heels of Elaine's shoes tapping a staccato on the stone street as she left.

Père Martin cleared his throat. 'I believe that, under the circumstances, we should discuss your plans.' I heard the sound of his palms rubbing together. 'I can get an apartment for you in town.'

'What shall I do?' I asked Charles, when the swish of the priest's robes vanished into the busy marketplace.

'I saw the letter,' he said. 'Elaine held it towards me. She doesn't know I can read.'

'Was it from François?'

'Yes.' My heart sank, but Charles patted my arm. 'I didn't see the word "wife" written anywhere, but one thing was clear. The king refused to extend his credit, and he sold the last of their land in Tours. He told her to do what she could with the money he left her and get rid of useless and frivolous expenses.'

'To Elaine, I am useless,' I said.

'Don't sound so bitter.' Charles and I wandered through the market. On my left, I heard hens cackling and I grinned briefly. Charles cleared his throat. 'Do you suppose she means to keep Aurore?'

That was something that hadn't occurred to me, but it was

entirely possible. Legally, in those times the family of the father would have the right to the child, especially if the wife were cast out.

'I don't know! François won't take it lightly if Elaine sends away his granddaughter. I'd like to think he'd mind if I were sent away, but perhaps not, if he plans to find a wife.' I shivered and cold despair settled over me. How could I leave Aurore? Simply put, I couldn't. I couldn't possibly. If I married Père Martin, I might be allowed to keep her, but he hadn't offered marriage. And if Elaine cast me out, I'd have to leave her behind. My heart pounded with a sudden onset of panic. 'Maybe you're right. Maybe François doesn't care for me.'

'I didn't say that,' Charles protested.

'I know. I wish I knew where he was so I could go to him.' I said. Then I stopped walking. 'That's it! We'll go to Paris!'

'Isobel!'

'Please, we'll go to Paris and find François.'

'You think we can?' Charles sounded wry. 'I'll lead you all the way to Paris, tripping and stumbling on your skirt?'

I jerked angrily upright. 'I didn't say that. I'll ride.'

Charles heaved a great sigh. 'Isobel, I think you'd better speak to Elaine. She holds the only chance you have of staying at the house until François comes home. I didn't see the end of the letter, so I don't know if he said he'd return soon.'

'If you didn't see the end of the letter, how do you know he didn't write of getting a new wife?' My voice wavered. 'Perhaps I'll be obliged to move into an apartment and be Père Martin's kept woman. Otherwise I'll be cast out of the house, and I'll never see Aurore again.'

It was too much. My legs were trembling so hard I had to stop walking. I still had two gold pieces sewed into my skirt, and the silver. I could live for at least a year on that, but still, without Aurore . . . A little sob surprised me by creeping out of my throat.

Charles sighed again and tugged my hand. 'Come, we'd best go home and see what Elaine has in mind. Then we can make plans.'

It sounded like a sensible idea, so I followed him quietly. Inwardly

208

I seethed with anger at Elaine. Fear that I'd be separated from my daughter and despair that I'd never see François again nearly paralyzed me.

A few paces further I stopped again and sniffed the air. 'Charles, what is that heavenly smell?' I turned my head this way and that to locate the scent I'd caught on the breeze.

He gave a loud sniff. 'Linden blossoms, if I'm not mistaken.'

'How wonderful! They smell like the sweetest honey and the deepest rose. Are they for sale in the marketplace?'

'No, they are blooming on a linden tree, not far from here. I think I saw one as we came up the crest of the hill. They're very easy to spot, as tall as they are wide.'

'Tell me what they look like.'

Charles sighed with impatience, but he humoured me. 'The leaves are heart-shaped. The flowers small, pale green, and are dried and used as infusions. Dame Blanche always has an infusion of them at night, before she sleeps. I take them to her.'

I bit my lip, frowning. 'Do they make you work very hard?'

I felt his shrug. His raspy voice was resigned. 'No, not very hard. Less so than Madame Latrainée made me work when I was in Chartres. But I tire of forever running errands, and it seems as though I can't sit still two minutes without someone having a chore for me to do.'

'At least you're useful,' I said.

'At least you still have your sense of humour,' he replied.

'Please take me to the tree. The scent is marvellous, even borne on the wind.' I wanted to take some flowers back to Aurore and Nurse.

'From close it will be overpowering, but I'll take you. Come on, and watch your step. We're heading into the meadow now. There's a path, but it's narrow. Take my belt and follow me.'

I did as he said, and he led me into a meadow where a great linden tree spread its fragrant shade over a burbling brook.

I took the bandage off my eyes and peered up at the tree. The dappled light filtered through its branches, turning my white apron green. I smiled then, tears leaking from my weakened eyes. 'It's beautiful. I can see better here in the shade.'

Charles' face was a white blur, and a darker blur was the tree trunk behind him. I put my hand out and caught a branch. Drawing it towards me, I saw two pale, narrow leaves framing a double flower. It looked like a fuzzy miniature cherry with its stems and pompoms. The leaves of the linden tree were larger than my hand, and, as Charles said, nearly heart-shaped. The scent of the blossoms was intoxicating and the whole tree sang with the heady buzzing of bees.

'What part do they dry for tea?' I asked.

'The little round flowers and their stems. The narrow leaves are discarded.'

Charles' finger poked the bloom in my hand.

'Will you ask Dame Blanche if I can try some tonight?'

'Of course. Here, if we pick some, we can dry it. It's easy to do, and Dame Blanche told me it can be used for years if you keep it in a covered jar.'

We filled my apron with the blossoms, and I carried them back to the manor. I kept the bandage off my eyes because I wanted to exercise them and because I wanted Elaine to know my sight was nigh on restored. I paid for my vanity with a violent headache that evening, but the linden blossom tea soothed me.

Chapter Sixteen

A woman's place in the past can be summed up in three words: mother, nun, prostitute. A woman was either married and respectable, a nun, or a fallen woman. Women could take shelter in nunneries, and female Correctors are encouraged to choose this option for survival. See Chapter 14, 'How to buy your way into a nunnery'. Note the paragraph about Hildegard of Bingen in that chapter.

Tempus University *Corrector's Handbook*

I tried to speak to Elaine soon thereafter. The fear of losing my daughter spurred me on. I couldn't imagine becoming Père Martin's mistress. I made my way to her room, my hand on the wall for guidance and balance, my heart pounding in my chest. I rapped on her door, and she called out, 'Come in, Dame Blanche!'

'It's Isobel,' I said, opening her door. My voice was husky with nerves so I cleared my throat a bit.

I couldn't see her, but I heard her swift intake of breath. 'Why are you here?'

'I want to talk to you.' I wasn't sure where to start. 'You've been avoiding me, and I thought perhaps you were angry with me for some reason.' I knew why she was angry, but I wanted to hear it from her lips.

'I want you to leave,' she said, her voice angry. If only I could see her face clearly!

She rose from her bed to stand stiffly in front of the window, blocking the light.

'I don't want to leave, and I won't leave Aurore,' I said.

'You'd best stay in Père Martin's good graces then.' Spite turned her voice into a jab of hate.

'I don't want to be with him, I'm not in love with him and you know it. I love your father.'

'Get out,' she spat. 'Get out! I know what you're about. I realize now what kind of viper you are. Get out of my room, you scheming whore.'

I wasn't prepared for her venom. I reeled backwards but caught myself on the doorway. My shock made me forget myself. 'No, I love him!' I cried. I suppose I wasn't brave enough to stand up to her. I'd misjudged her anger and my strength.

'You don't love him, you're using him, just as you used my brother. When your parents lost their fortune, you saw Jean as a way to hoist yourself back to riches. When he died, you decided to seduce my father. You're nothing but a leech, a parasite – of course you need him! You're blind! If we cast you away, you'll be nothing but a beggar!'

'I'm not blind.' I tried to steady my voice. 'It will pass.'

'There you go with your prophesying again. Beware . . . if Père Martin hears you, he'll think you're a witch. Then not even he will stand by you.' She gave a bitter laugh. 'I knew you were trouble the minute I saw you. How much older than Jean are you? That didn't stop you from seducing him, did it?'

I took a wavering breath then let it out slowly. She was right, in a way. I never should have been involved with Jean. That had been a weakness on my part, and a mistake. 'I'm sorry he's dead,' I said. 'I wish he hadn't died.' There wasn't a day gone by that I didn't wish Jean still alive and back home. The image of François' face came to me, and I realized, not for the first time, that whatever I'd felt about Jean, it paled to nothing next to my feelings for François. But I still wished Jean were alive.

'Get out,' Elaine said. Her blurred figure grew larger as she walked towards me, and her hands pushed me off the door. When I was in the hallway, she slammed it in my face.

I stood there for a long while, trying to sort out my feelings. I was too confused to understand why I'd fallen in love with a man I barely knew. Suppose he didn't care for me? I put my hands over my face and shuddered. I almost wished the sky would crack open and the TCF would erase me and my pain from the face of the earth. If I were gone, I wouldn't care anymore about François or agonize about my baby.

The day after I'd gathered linden blossoms and had the disastrous talk with Elaine, I decided to sort laundry. I suppose I wanted to prove I was 'useful'. The laundry room was vast and dark, perfect for my tired eyes. Charles came to see if he could help, and I put the sheet I was folding carefully into a basket and nodded. I had a question to ask him, and in this private place, I could speak without worrying about anyone overhearing.

'Charles, will you do something for me?' I had debated with myself for hours before making up my mind. It wouldn't be easy, and his life would be in danger if he were caught.

'Yes, I'd do anything for you.' He looked up at me, and I caught a hint of a question in his eyes. My sight was coming back and each day I saw more clearly. I could make out faces when they were as close as Charles' was.

'I know that, but weigh what I ask you carefully. I want you to go to Elaine's room and get the letter that François sent her. If there are several, take them all. We won't steal them,' I hastened to add. 'We'll simply borrow them. I need to read them and find out what I must do.'

Charles pondered my words. 'I will,' he decided. 'I'll take them just after she leaves her room for breakfast. If I can, I'll bring the letters to your room. Then, when she goes to vespers, I'll put them back.'

'We must hope she won't spot the missing letters.'

'Then perhaps we'd better do it today, before she gets more mail to tuck into her box,' said Charles. He was quiet again, helping me fold and sort the clean laundry.

When the baskets were full, we carried them to their respective owners. Elaine had the most laundry because she insisted on changing her sheets once a week. Dame Blanche had a multitude of shifts, and

Aurore had two dozen linen diapers that I washed endlessly. Père Martin still lived with us, and he had several smocks and vests to wash. That was no problem, though. It was feeding him that cost Elaine the most.

I knocked on his door and then set his basket just outside of it. He was probably out visiting the poor and comforting the sick. He wasn't a bad man, and I knew that he took his priestly duties far more seriously than many village priests did at that time. Plus he was honest. Most of the money from the pardons he sold went to the church coffers, which were collected twice a year by the king's own men. Père Martin was fond of jewellery, though, and I often caught sight of a new bauble glinting from his fingers or strung around his neck.

I returned to the laundry room. My eyes were tired, and by the time I made the second trip with Dame Blanche's laundry, my head ached and I knew I must put my linen bandage back on or suffer sharper pain.

Dame Blanche was gone as well, and I wondered where everyone was that afternoon. The sun was bright and fine, so perhaps they were in the orchards or in the village.

In my room, the window was open, and the sweet scents of summer, along with the ripe odour of the manure pile, floated on the breeze. I knew I was lucky to live in such luxury in this age. Most people lived in single-roomed houses, rife with fleas and diseases. Even the wealthy often slept all massed together in the main dining room, everyone curled in the rushes along with the dogs, cats and geese.

The manor we lived in was new and had a stone foundation and first floor, with a stucco and beam second storey. There were fireplaces in the main rooms, and the bedrooms were built just above them, sharing the heat from the brick chimney conduit.

The kitchen was in a separate building, as wont in a century with wooden houses and no fire department. The stables and barn were the north and east walls of the courtyard, and the main house was an 'L' shape facing south and west. Everyone had his own

214

room except the cook and Charles, who shared a room over the kitchen. Richard and his family slept in rooms over the stables. They had no fireplace, but the animals kept the building warm. The north-facing walls were twice as thick as the other walls and had no windows.

Windows were a luxury at that time, yet our manor had beautiful windows set with round glass panes thick enough to keep the cold at bay and let in floods of warm sunlight. My room was small, and a curtain separated it from Nurse's half of the room, where she shared a bed with Aurore now that she'd grown out of her little cradle. They were out too, most likely taking advantage of the balmy weather.

As I wrapped my eyes with linen, I thought I should be proud to have survived so far, but what was the use of surviving if I couldn't live happily? Why struggle and half-starve simply to live a miserable life? If I couldn't have my daughter or be near the man I loved, why bother to live? Or was this my punishment for killing someone else's child? I recognized the dark feelings of depression settling on my shoulders, pushing me down into the depths of my own mind. Stress, like a bitter taste in my throat, rose to seize me around the chest. My breathing quickened. I struggled to the window where I leaned out to get some fresh air. My eyes strained towards the light, and my hands clenched the sill as the blur brightened, like headlights swinging around the bend in the road.

A child stared up at me. His face was white in the light, white against the shining black top, white and frozen with shock. He held a filmy net in one hand and a glass jar flashed in the other. All those things I saw so clearly and so slowly. Time is not arbitrary. It follows rules of its own making. It can slow down, or speed up. That night, it had been as slow as molasses. Right now, it was even slower.

There was no sound. When time is warped, sound escapes, or is erased, it seems. I wrenched the steering wheel around, swerving away from the small, pale form caught in the headlights. There was a shock as the car hit the child. A jolt that I felt through my hands, feet, skull . . . Oh Lord. The tree loomed huge and black and swallowed the car. I didn't care. All I could think about was the shock and its implications, and the sight of the child's pale face turned towards me, mouth open.

The jar shattered, sparkling, or maybe it was the windshield. I flew, but not for long. When the sound came back, I heard a scream, a mother's scream for her child, and for the first time, millennia away, I knew exactly how she felt.

Depression always hit me too fast for me to ward it off. One minute I would be fine, and the next, I would be incapable of speech, locked in a world where my own heartbeat frightened me, where all I could think about was death and the blessed silence it could bring.

I leaned further out the window.

'Isobel!'

Charles dragged me back from doom. I didn't struggle. I longed for death, but it was a rabbit's longing, weak, quivering, and incapable of decisive movement. My hands were nerveless. I lay on my bed and trembled. Charles felt my pulse, touched my neck and pulled the covers over me. 'I'll go to Isobel's room now,' he said. 'She's gone to the village, and after there is vespers in the chapel. Père Martin has been speaking about his plans to install you in a little love nest in town. Dame Blanche is all aflutter about that.' He meant to make me smile, but I could only see shadows.

He patted my hand. 'I'll be back. Try to sleep, please?'

I didn't answer, and a few moments later the door shut.

'Dear daughter, today I have seen the king. He has granted me exemption from the dime this year in regards to Jean because he was on the crusade, and because he fought alongside Jean-Tristan. However, he will not grant me an extension of credit, and I have had to go to the moneylenders in the city. There is one, an Italian, whom I trust.

'There is enough in the coffer to get us through this year and to buy the manor outright, which I have done. The papers will be sent along shortly. Put them in my silver chest. I have been to Bruges to see about buying part of a new dye business there, and I will tell you about it

216

when I return. However, I think we will stay near Pamplona for now, as there are rumours that France will soon be at war again. You must be careful of expenses, Elaine. I charge you with running the household and grant you the right to make whatever decisions are needed while I am absent.

'Make sure that Richard and Nurse receive their pay at the end of each week so that they may send it to their families. In addition, I want Richard to sell Isobel's two ponies. Use that money towards household expenses. I am counting on you, daughter, to do away with all unnecessary expenses. Do not be frivolous. I will try to return as soon as I finish business in Bruges.

'Affectionately, your father, François de Bourbon-Dampierre de Navarre.'

Charles read slowly, sounding the words out as he went along. I listened carefully, concentrating on each syllable.

'He said nothing about a new wife,' I said.

I heard paper being folded and a rustle as Charles tucked the missive back into his shirt. 'He'll be home soon,' he said. 'The letter is dated nearly a month ago.'

'Soon?'

'In a month, maybe less.'

'Oh, that soon.' I tried to grin, to fight the heavy sadness that weighed upon me.

'When did Elaine say I was to leave?'

'In three weeks.'

'That's cutting it a bit fine,' I said. 'If I refuse to become the priest's woman, do you think he'll make trouble for me?'

'I don't know.' Charles sounded troubled. 'Ask me . . .'

'Something you know,' I finished for him. I took a shaky breath. 'I must make peace with Elaine.'

'I'm going to return the letter.' Charles hesitated. 'There were other notes there. I had to sift through them to see which was the latest François had sent. One is addressed to François from the late

217

Queen Isabella.' He swallowed nervously. 'I took that one too. Would you like me to read it to you?'

I gave a small laugh. 'Might as well be hung for a sheep as for a . . .'

'Hush.' His voice was strained as he read.

'To François and Eleanéor de Bourbon-Dampierre. Greetings from Isabella, wife of Philip, king of France. I am writing this from Italy, after a harrowing voyage to Tunis. Alas, the crusade was a disaster, although perhaps some would not deem it so, the king's brother having negotiated a truce with the emir of Tunis just as we were leaving.

'By now, you have heard the terrible news of King Louis' death. May God rest his soul and that of his son, Jean-Tristan, dead of the flux in Tunis. This brings me to the most difficult part of my missive, the death of your own son, Jean. I am writing this to you because I have taken your daughter-in-law under my protection for the time being.

She is expecting a child, your grandchild. I hope this news eases somewhat your burden of grief. Your son fought boldly at my brother-in-law's side and died on the battlefield, unlike so many others, struck down by pestilence.

'Your new daughter-in-law will be travelling with us to Paris. If you wish, you could meet us on the road. I would like to keep her as my lady-in-waiting, though, and have her at court with me. I have also decided to find a new husband for her so that you won't be burdened financially. I know that these affairs are delicate to speak about, but I have always believed in frankness, and so I will be blunt. As long as Isobel remains with me as my lady-in-waiting, I will pay her a salary. When I find her a suitable husband, you will be exempt from paying a dowry, as her salary will go to that end.

'May God be with you, Isabella.'

Charles finished reading and folded the letter carefully. 'What do you think?' he asked.

'I don't know. For some reason, I don't think it pleased François that I was to be Isabella's lady-in-waiting.'

'At least not after he saw you,' said Charles. 'But he didn't dare ask the queen to let you go.'

I thought back to the day she'd died, and his haste to take me away. 'You'd better put the letters back in their place. The bells for vespers will ring soon.'

'Are you feeling better?' Charles asked.

I nodded and turned my face away from him. 'Leave me now,' I told him. His eyes were far too sharp. Sometimes I was afraid of what he would see.

Charles managed to put the letters back, and Elaine never noticed they'd been taken. I felt a few pangs of guilt for reading her mail, but they didn't last long.

The week went by slowly. My daily confessions with Père Martin were still the worst part of the day. Finally, I decided I had to tell him the truth.

'My sight is coming back,' I told him.

'Isobel, that isn't possible,' he said pompously. 'Cease your delusions. The blind cannot see, unless the Lord wills it.'

'Then He must have willed it,' I answered.

He didn't seem to hear me. 'Don't worry, I won't let you starve.'

'How kind,' I said between clenched teeth. Emboldened by my compliment he put his hands on my bosom.

'A man needs a woman and a woman needs a man,' he said. His voice got a bit strangled.

I pushed his hands away. 'I don't want to become anyone's mistress.'

He huffed noisily. 'I'm offering you a comfortable life,' he said. 'No one else will do the same. You're blind and a burden to this household. Lady Elaine doesn't want you under her roof. She won't hesitate to cast you into the street, and in your condition, you'd have but one option to beg. I cannot let that happen to you.'

'I'm trying to tell you that my sight is returning. In two or three weeks I'll be able to see clearly.' Right now he was nothing but a blur. A red-faced blur. But I wasn't about to say that. I slapped at his hands angrily and he drew his breath in with a hiss.

'Beware, Isobel. The Church does not like those who prophesy. It's considered black magic. If you continue, I shall have to report you as a witch.'

'I'm not prophesying, and I'm not a witch,' I sputtered.

'Don't argue. A woman needs—'

'I don't need anything but to be left alone,' I cried, thoroughly out of patience now.

Furious, he muttered a few Latin phrases, absolving me of my sins, and then Charles came to lead me back to my room.

Chapter Seventeen

'Eagle! Eagle! Why Sleepest thou? Arise! For it is dawn – and eat and drink!'
(Hildegard of Bingen, l. 1098–1179 CE)

Tempus University *Corrector's Handbook*

My sight grew steadily clearer, and two weeks later it came back in a rush. One day, I could look out my window and see the tops of the houses in the village down in the valley. I could make out people's faces, and even tell from across a room at who I looked.

Now I watched Père Martin as he strode across the courtyard from the kitchen towards the main house. His robes flapped as he walked, as it was a blustery day.

Clouds scudded across the sky, seeming to shred themselves on the trees. He glanced up and saw me. I waved, and his face was a study in surprise and outright shock. I don't think anyone but Charles believed my sight was truly returning.

He stopped and gathered his robe tighter around himself. He waved at me hesitantly.

'Good day, Père Martin,' I called cheerfully.

'You can see me?' He took a step backwards. 'Can you really see me?'

'Yes!' I smiled. 'I told you it was just temporary.'

He hastily traced a cross in the air in front of him. 'Sorcery!' he cried.

'Not at all.' I laughed at his horrified expression. His eyes were so wide he looked like an owl. 'It was the shock of the fall, but the nerve has healed. An Arab surgeon would have known.'

'Infidels!' he choked. 'Infidels and sorcery!'

'Don't be ridiculous,' I said. 'Queen Isabella, God rest her soul, favoured an Arab doctor while were in Tunis.'

'I shall write to the Holy See this afternoon. They must hear about this,' he muttered. He looked once more at my window, his face a study in confusion and fear, then he crossed himself and hurried off.

I giggled and pulled my head back in my room. Nurse was bouncing Aurore on her knee, and Aurore burbled little baby noises and tried to catch Nurse's ribbon with her chubby fist.

'Are you my little angel?' I asked my daughter, chucking her under the chin.

'Arrooo!' she agreed. A bright string of drool dripped downwards.

'She get tooth,' said Nurse, in her rusty, succinct speech. I had long ago stopped asking her if she wished to return to her husband. She had made it clear that she preferred to remain with Aurore and me. Since she didn't have the education or funds to enter a nunnery (the only choice open to her other than prostitution or drudgery), I was more than happy to have her stay.

'I can see that!' I cried. 'I can see!' The relief of getting my vision back made me giddy. I spun around, twirled my skirt out and laughed aloud. 'I have my sight back, and Père Martin is having second thoughts about me. He's starting to think that perhaps I won't be the tractable, obedient mistress he'd like.'

I laughed again, but Nurse drew her brows down in a ferocious scowl. 'Be careful,' she said. She leaned forward and caught my wrist, searching for words. Her mouth opened, but no sound came out. Frustrated, she let go of my arm and shook her head. 'H-he thinks evil thoughts,' she finally managed to stutter.

I raised my eyebrows. 'Impure thoughts? Oh.ho! And him a man of the cloth.' I smiled. 'Don't worry about him. He won't try to hurt me. The worst he does is paw my breasts.'

'Not impure.' She pointed sternly at me. 'He thinks *you* be evil.'

'That can't be true. Shall I take Aurore for a while? Now that I can see better, perhaps we can go for a walk in the village.'

'No.'

'Why not? Are you afraid I'll fall down? I can see now!' Joy bubbled within me. With the return of my sight, I could be useful again and Elaine would have no reason to cast me out.

She shook her head. 'Rain,' she said.

I looked out the window and uttered a cry of annoyance. 'You're right, the sky has darkened.' I shut the window and scratched my head. 'I have a feeling it's going to be a storm. Look at my arms, all gooseflesh.'

Nurse didn't reply, and soon Aurore fell asleep. Nurse retrieved her basket of mending, but my eyes weren't strong enough for sewing, so I wandered about the room quietly so as not to wake my napping child. The storm drew near, thunder growled in the distance and I lit a small lamp so that Nurse could see her work. There was nothing for me to do except take a nap myself, but I wasn't tired. I was in the mood for talking, but a glance at Nurse's face told me that she didn't share my good humour. I sighed and touched my hair again. It was dirty, a normal state for it to be in, as there was no shampoo. I thought that as long as it was raining, I'd go to the laundry room and get a piece of soap to wash myself.

I stripped in the laundry room then went outside and stood under the deluge, letting the rainwater cleanse me. I scrubbed my hair and skin, thankful for the late summer's sultry weather. The water ran off the slate roof in a steady stream, enabling me to rinse all the soap out of my hair. At the far corner of the stables, I noticed that Richard's family was also taking advantage of the rain to wash themselves.

Dame Blanche came naked out the laundry-room door, clutching a cake of soap. 'How are you?' she cried, over the pounding rain.

'Wonderful!' I enthused and moved over to make room. 'My eyes are almost better now. I can see you, and I can see Richard and his family over there!' I pointed.

'How amazing! It must be God's will your eyesight has returned.'

She stood with her hands clasped modestly in front of her bosom and beamed at me.

I finished washing but stayed outside, enjoying the summer shower. The water that fell was nearly as warm as bathwater and soft as dew. I opened my arms and tipped my face to the sky, for the sheer joy of feeling the rain on my skin. My hair whipped my back, and I laughed again. There was mud underfoot, but even that felt fine.

Elaine came outside then and washed in a stony silence. Dame Blanche joined me in the rain, and we linked arms and twirled each other about. She was a sprightly woman and loved to dance. At first Elaine glowered at us, but the spirit of the warm rain was infectious and she ended up joining our rain dance. I hoped she was thawing towards me. That thought made me laugh aloud again.

A flash of lightning was followed by a clap of thunder, and everyone dashed inside.

'How wonderful!' I grabbed a linen towel and rubbed myself until my skin glowed.

Elaine stared at me for a moment. 'It's true. You can see again.' Her words came out slowly, as if she was reluctant to speak to me.

'Of course!' I was amused. 'I told you it was just a temporary blindness.' I finished drying my hair and shrugged a clean tunic over my shoulders. I tied my kirtle on over it and used my towel to tie my hair in a turban. 'Can't we make peace, Elaine?' I begged. 'Please? Can you forget your anger and—'

'Why did you kiss him? Why did you try to seduce my father?' Her voice was low, but her eyes flashed in anger.

I shook my head. 'I didn't seduce anyone. I fell in love with him.'

'Père Martin wants to take care of you.'

'I don't think he wants me after all,' I said. 'I wouldn't make a good mistress for him, and he knows that. I think he just pitied my blindness. Besides, I love your father.'

Elaine stared at me for a moment before her eyes dropped. An angry blush spread over her cheeks. 'I don't believe you're capable of loving anyone,' she said. She spun on her heel and left the laundry room.

*

During the next three days, I sensed a queer tension in the household. Père Martin was gone on a short trip, and Elaine stayed out of my way. At first, I was relieved. My eyes were getting better and I took advantage of it to go to the market with Nurse and Aurore. I recognized the fruit merchant and bought some oranges from him. They were the first of the season, and I couldn't wait to give one to Nurse.

'Hello, Dame Isobel,' he said, smiling brightly at me and Aurore. 'I bet you can't guess what I have for you!'

'I can! Oranges! I'd like two please.'

When I pointed straight to the oranges, he gasped. 'How . . . how did you know?'

'My sight has returned,' I said, too pleased to notice his troubled gaze. He sold me two oranges, then stepped back, when usually he stayed beside me to chat about the weather and his trips to Spain. What was wrong? I didn't understand, and Nurse was so enthralled with her first orange she didn't notice. But I didn't like the suspicious looks the merchant cast at me.

'What is the matter?' I asked him. Aurore, sitting at my feet, gurgled happily at the orange I'd handed her.

'Go away now, witch!' His voice was loud, and he crossed himself.

At first, the people in the marketplace didn't hear, but when he repeated it, heads turned.

'My eyes got better, that's all,' I said in an attempt to soothe him.

'The blind cannot see!' he cried. 'Now leave, and don't return!' He made a sign of warding off the evil, and the people nearby backed away and muttered. I sensed the mood of the crowd turning ugly, and so did Nurse, for she pocketed her precious orange and grabbed my arm.

'We go,' she said urgently.

I snatched up Aurore in my arms and hurried from the marketplace, fleeing the angry hissing and fearful looks.

Once back at the manor, I sought Dame Blanche. Perhaps she could give me some advice. She sat with Elaine in the solar, and as I arrived, Elaine gave a stiff curtsey and excused herself, saying she couldn't stay in the same room with a witch.

Dame Blanche patted my arm gently. 'Don't heed her. When she gets angry, she says things she doesn't mean.' Her words were sure, but a frown creased her face. 'I am glad she left, for I must speak with you. Elaine is fearfully jealous and worried her father won't marry a wealthy woman. She blames you for Jean's death. I think she wants to get even.'

'Has she done something?' I asked.

'She sent a message yesterday, but she wouldn't tell me where she sent it.'

'You know who she sent it to,' I prompted.

'Yes, I think I do.' Her voice dropped to a whisper. 'She sent a letter to the Holy See.'

'That's two messages they'll be receiving, then, about me,' I said.

Dame Blanche shook her head. 'It's not a laughing matter, my child. It was only a few years ago that all the Cathari were exterminated. In some villages, there are people who point and call out "Cathari!" and that's enough to cause the suspect to be imprisoned and tried as a heretic.'

'I didn't realize that the hatred was still so strong,' I said. Worry assailed me. The people in the marketplace had whispered that I was a witch. Was that better or worse than the Cathari? I had no idea.

'Some believe that King Louis was killed by the infidel, and some say it was a heretic spy amongst the crusaders.' Dame Blanche pulled her apron over her skirt and tied it around her waist. 'I'd be careful if I were you, Isobel. Your ways are strange sometimes, and it's no ordinary thing to be healed from blindness. Perhaps people in Montpellier are more tolerant. Your parents were certainly good folk and would have been saddened to see suspicious fingers pointed at their daughter.'

'When we travelled through Italy, there were people who threw charred fish bones at us. They thought to appease the demons they believed accompanied the body of King Louis. King Louis! Can you imagine? No matter who you are, there will always be some who dislike you or even fear you.'

'I know, child.' Dame Blanche paused. 'But Elaine has done something foolish.'

'How foolish?' I asked.

'I fear that she denounced you to the Inquisition,' she said. 'She won't say if it's true, but I suspect it. Her temper has always been her biggest fault, and you angered her beyond measure. First her beloved brother, then her father, whom she adores. She feels as if you've stolen both of them from her.'

'The Inquisition?' I raised my eyebrows. 'That's a bit dramatic, isn't it? Do you think they'll even bother? They must get hundreds of complaints.'

'They've become powerful, thanks to the war against the Cathari.'

'I was in the marketplace this morning,' I said, not sure how to tell Dame Blanche of my experience. I was half-embarrassed, half-frightened about the whole event. 'I'm afraid the fruit merchant thinks I'm a witch.'

Dame Blanche gave a sharp cry. 'What happened? Tell me!'

I did, and she shook her head. To my shock, tears rolled down her cheeks. 'My poor Isobel, things are very grave. Not only Père Martin and Elaine have denounced you, but the villagers as well.'

'What should I do?'

Dame Blanche inspected her embroidery for a long moment. 'I'm afraid you must leave,' she said finally. 'Go back to your own city. You must. You'll be safe there.'

'I can't do that!' I cried, stunned. 'Leave? What will become of Aurore?'

'Your daughter will be raised as a princess, Sire Dampierre will see to that. She's related by blood and marriage to the king, and no one can take that from her.'

'I'm her mother!'

Dame Blanche saw my mutinous expression and took a hold of my arm. Her voice was pleading. She was truly worried. 'You must be gone before the Inquisition comes. Père Martin thinks your sight was recovered through sorcery. If he's gone to send a message to the Holy See, they'll look into the matter and if they speak with the villagers and Elaine . . .' Her voice trailed off and she gave a nervous cough. 'I'll help you if you need money for the journey. I have some saved, I don't need it and Elaine sees I lack nothing. Take what I offer and leave, please!'

'No!' I cried, pushing her away. 'How can you ask me to leave? How can I leave my baby?'

'Don't you understand? If you're condemned, your child will be condemned along with you and burned. The family Dampierre will lose its influence and respect. If you're not afraid for your own life, think of others.'

'It's absurd! I'm certainly not a witch!'

'Even a hint of suspicion will ruin François.' Dame Blanche shook her head sorrowfully. 'You can't pretend you don't care for him, but your love is doomed, my child. He will not be able to wed a woman questioned by the Inquisition – the king will not allow it. Not with the Cathari war so fresh in our memories.'

I stared at her. When she didn't lower her eyes, I dropped my gaze and started to tremble. King Philip would not be sympathetic to my cause. He might even agree I was a witch. After all, I'd been on that ill-fated crusade, I'd even been with his wife on the day she was killed. His wife had called me her melancholy angel. But what if Philip heard I'd been accused of witchcraft? That would make everything I'd done, all the people around me who'd died, suspicious signs. 'I'll think about it,' I whispered. I couldn't put my child's life in danger. If I were accused of sorcery or thought to be a heretic the Inquisition would kill her too. I hadn't realized that before. A cold arrow shot through my heart.

'You must leave as soon as possible so that they have no chance to catch up to you.'

'I need to see François before I can make a decision,' I said.

'It's impossible. He won't be back for another month, at least.' Dame Blanche spoke firmly.

'My hands are cold, feel them,' I said inanely. I felt as if my extremities had turned to ice.

'You poor child. Here, come sit by the fire. I'll go fetch some spiced wine and a parchment. We must write to your family and tell them you're coming.'

'I have no more family. I want to write to a lawyer.'

'A lawyer?' She looked as scandalized as if I'd said I want to write to the devil.

'Burn the heart and liver of a fish,' I murmured.

'What's that?' Dame Blanche leaned closer.

'Nothing. An incantation against demons,' I said. Then I put my face in my hands and I cried.

Charles and I left three days later, at sunrise. It was fear of any news reaching King Philip that spurred me. Suddenly I was terrified that François would try to speak to him, and that the whole debacle of Tunis would be laid at my feet. It was not so ridiculous after all. I had been everywhere that disaster struck – even leaning out my window to look at dying King Louis. Jean had gone to pay his respects, and Philip had looked up and seen me. I'd given a slight wave, and he'd nodded at me. Then Louis had died.

Afterwards, Jean had been killed. I'd been on the ship with the king and queen – and we'd survived while nearly all the other ships had sunk in the storm. And of course there had been that dreadful day when the poor queen had been killed, with me kneeling by her head, whispering in her ear. No, I would not be able to defend myself or protect Aurore.

Charles packed our meagre belongings and set about plotting our route. We'd follow the winding road that led through the mountains. Once past Navarre, we'd enter the region of France that had been devastated during the war against the Cathari. Few people lived there now, and food would likely be scarce. We had to leave before autumn set in or risk starvation.

We set off on foot, leading a donkey, and I'd bandaged my eyes again. I'd strained them in an effort to write letters, and to draw Aurore. I had no camera, of course, so I used a piece of charcoal to draw my daughter. I am no artist, and the first results landed in the fireplace. Finally I managed a decent sketch of my sleeping daughter.

Our hasty departure was also a lonely one. Richard and Dame

Blanche waved us off. Cook came and pressed another cheese into Charles' hands, and Nurse wept with great, choking sobs. Aurore cried as well, but I could hardly look at her. The pain in my chest was too sharp.

We left just after dawn. The little donkey set its hooves down delicately, Charles walked steadily, and I dragged my feet in an effort to keep moving. Behind us was the manor, and I could hear my child wailing hysterically. Each sob shattered my heart further until it was nothing but dust. Elaine hid in her room. Ahead of us, there was nothing but winding road and blue mountains fragrant with pine trees.

In my pocket was a letter to a certain Maître Houdebert. I prayed that he was still our friend, and that he would help me now that I had no one else to turn to. Perhaps he could clear my name and help me get custody of my daughter. Why hadn't I studied medieval law? I knew nothing about what could legally happen to me.

The road was clearly marked. As the days passed in numbing sameness, we trod through small stone villages and past old wooden fortresses. People in the villages asked us for news. Some took pity on us. I wrapped white linen around my eyes during the day, and kind-hearted folk offered us food and shelter. Sometimes we slept in haystacks or beneath dense hedges.

Charles kept up a lively chatter to keep my mind off my sorrow. At first, the voyage was easy. There were many villages along the way, most of the people were charitable, and we had plenty of fresh milk, cheese, and bread made from chestnut flour. When the road narrowed and grew steep, we entered the land of the Catharis, which had been scoured by war. We were alone.

Houses stood abandoned, graves dotted the hillsides, and packs of wild dogs sometimes appeared in the distance. We took to carrying staves and kept our donkey close by.

I grew more and more melancholy. The higher we climbed, the more pronounced my depression grew, until I could no longer speak. My throat ached with grief. Each step was another step away from my daughter and from François.

Ghosts accompanied me across the mountains. Round white faces would suddenly loom out of the darkness and scream silently. The child I'd killed would rouse me from my sleep, and a scream would burst out of my raw throat.

Jean rode beside me, sometimes. He never spoke. When he tipped his head down to smile at me, my undergarment slipped down his helmet and covered his eyes. I wanted to see their green sparkle, but they were hidden behind a white cloth. My eyes, too, remained hidden. The sun was bright, the stones on the road sparkled and the light stabbed my head like knives. I wrapped my linen around my eyes, took hold of the donkey's tail and shuffled along, my ghosts following me.

When I was blindfolded, I saw the child. When I wasn't, Jean appeared, and sometimes at night, there were others whom I'd never seen. They floated out of the evening sky, settled around the flickering fire and stared at me with great saucer eyes.

Charles followed my terrified glances but saw nothing, and I wouldn't frighten him with the visions that haunted me. He'd believe I was losing my mind.

Perhaps, I thought at times, this was the erasure. I was slowly being sucked into a half-world where the dead wandered. One day I'd disappear entirely, perhaps fading like mist, and the world I glimpsed would open up like a rent in space and suck me into it. My hands, when I looked at them, seemed to be fading into nothing. My fingers became transparent, the bones showing up as if on an X-ray.

Part of me realized that it was nothing more than grief playing tricks on my mind. My limits had at last been broken. Ironically, it was now I reflected on the fact that the Time Correctors had long hesitated about sending me on this mission. It had been written in large type on the top of my admission sheet: *subject to depression*. The nurses whispered about it, and my psychologist spoke to me for hours, telling me what to do when I felt the first signs. I'd been able to rise above it before. Now it submerged me.

'Aurore,' I whispered, trying to conjure her image. My whole body ached with longing for my child, adding to my misery.

'Isobel?' Charles prodded my shoulder.

Where were we? What day was it? I uncurled my body and sat up.

I pushed the linen off my eyes and blinked, trying to focus on his face. It wavered in the pale light before me, as if unattached to his head.

I blinked harder and he snapped into focus. 'What is it?' I whispered. My voice was rusty, strained with choking back screams. I shuddered as Jean surged out of the mist behind Charles. The vision was so real, so clear, I gasped, and then the blood drained from my face.

Charles turned, and incredibly, he smiled. 'François came after us!'

I dared look again. It wasn't Jean standing behind Charles, looking down at me with a face grown white with fatigue. It was François, and he grasped my arms with hands that shook. Behind him, I heard horses' hooves, and Lucien appeared too, leading three cobs by their reins.

'I've found you,' François said.

I let out the breath I'd been holding in a sigh. 'Thank God,' I said, and then I lay down again because my head spun so much I thought I would faint. I hadn't dared let myself hope that he'd come after me. But he had. My eyes filled with tears of joy.

Lucien and Charles went to fetch wood while François sat beside me. He looked at me then averted his gaze towards the flinty road where we'd been heading. 'Elaine is sorry,' he said after a while.

'I forgive her.' I found I couldn't stop smiling. Tears trickled down my cheeks, and still I couldn't stop smiling. 'I am so happy to see you, François.'

'You can truly see me?'

'You're holding two fingers up and waving them around. Stop, you look silly.' Suddenly conscious of my looks, I tried to comb my tangled hair with my fingers and winced. I was covered in grime.

'When Lucien and Charles return, will you ask them to fetch and heat water for me? I need to bathe.'

'Bathe? You look fine to me, though a bit peaked.' His jaw clenched and unclenched as his eyes devoured me. Then he pulled me into his arms and hugged me so hard my ribs nearly cracked. 'When I saw you had gone, I went mad. Elaine felt so guilty she threw herself at my feet, sobbing that she'd killed you. I nearly believed her. Dame

Blanche told me where you'd gone, and why. But don't ever leave me again, promise.'

'I won't. Please tell me, how is Aurore?' I asked. I could let myself think of my daughter again. Fresh tears coursed down my cheeks.

'She's fine and healthy and misses her mother. She'll be overjoyed to see you.' He nuzzled my neck, his arms still holding me tightly. 'I missed you, too."

'I want to start anew.' My voice was firm. 'François, I love you.'

He blushed. Green eyes sparkled behind long, black lashes. 'Dame Blanche was quite explicit about that,' he said, a chuckle at the end of the phrase. 'She worried about you. She nearly pushed me out the door to go fetch you back. And so did Elaine. I swear. She's repentant.'

'She said that the Inquisition wanted to question me. François, I don't want to put anyone in danger. I realize it's a serious charge, and I'm frightened.'

'Don't worry. The Inquisition wants to question a certain Isobel, but she fled. I think I'll wed a widow in Montpellier and bring her back to Navarre. Her name is Isault, and she's as lovely as an angel. I hear you know of a lawyer. Do you think perhaps he could draw up a marriage contract between a certain Isault and a certain François Bourbon-Dampierre?'

When his meaning became clear, I slumped with relief. 'What about Père Martin? Last I knew, he was hesitating between buying me a love nest or burning me at the stake.'

'Oh, we needn't worry about him. He's been sent to Avignon. The Church means to make a cardinal of our dear priest. As for us, we're selling the manor and moving nearer to Pamplona, where no one knows us. I'm free to wed a certain Isault. Will you be my wife, Isault?'

'I will.' I closed my eyes and concentrated, but the face that had stared at me in horror so many times was now smiling at me. Peace surrounded it in a nimbus. I knew it wasn't real, that it was simply my own mind putting this particular ghost to rest, but it made my heart swell. A warm glow surrounded me. I opened my eyes and saw François had draped his cape over my shoulders.

'We will live in Navarre and raise Aurore together,' he said.

'There will be more.' I snuggled into his embrace. 'Sons and daughters, with green eyes and dimples at the corners of their mouths.'

'My eyes, your dimples, what else could we ask for?' His voice tickled my ear.

'I could ask for nothing more, now that you've found me.' I held my hands out and looked at them. They seemed more substantial now the light had ceased to render them transparent. I had come to this world, and I would stay.

Epilogue

Ten years later . . .

The manor echoes with the shouts of three little boys chasing after their older sister.

I lean out the window to tell them to put the frog down and leave Aurore alone. She grows more beautiful each day, and François never tires of telling me she looks like her mother.

François has gone into the wool business and has entered the dye trade in Bruges, so we travel back and forth twice a year to Flanders from Navarre. When we pass through Paris, we stay with Elaine, who has married and has four children now, two girls and two boys. She and I have become friends, and our children spend summers together in the manor in Navarre.

Charles married a girl from the village and François put him in charge of the dye shop in Bruges. He's turned into a canny merchant and when we are alone together I tell him how to invest the money, what commodities will thrive, and what to avoid. He is the only person I have ever told about my past life. Loving someone means not hurting them, and the truth would only hurt my husband. He will never know I was sent back only to convince Jean to stay home. He and I are happy as we are and I make sure that our family prospers and stays out of political conflicts. My history lessons served me well, in the end. I have put my past to rest. I reinvented myself, and I believe more in my made-up story than what happened so very far in the future.

Today, the linden trees are in blossom and Aurore and I will gather the flowers and lay them to dry on clean sheets. My three boys,

235

Jean-Tristan, Thomas, and Luc, will come with us and most likely hinder more than help. Nurse will keep them in line. The boys are excited because their cousins will arrive any day now.

I'm impatient too. François is accompanying them, and I haven't seen him in a month. After I gather the linden blossoms, I will get our room ready. My heart is light. The sun is shining, the linden trees perfume the balmy air and François will soon be home.

Life is sweet, and I am more deeply in love with François each passing year. When I think of my other life somewhere in the future, it's like a bad dream that I've woken from, and I give thanks each day that the Time Senders chose me to save the crown of France.

I'm still not sure how our family will be linked with the Kingdom of France, though I know that it shall someday. We sometimes go to the court in Navarre and the queen has offered to take Aurore as a lady-in-waiting when she turns fifteen. Jean-Tristan sometimes plays with the young prince of Navarre, and he told me that the prince thought Aurore was beautiful, so perhaps she's the key that unlocks the puzzle of time and sets everything back on its track.

Somewhere in the future, a quartz-crystal book sits in the middle of an ice-blue beam of light. Written on its pages are the names of the kings and queens of France and all their descendants. Jean de Bourbon-Dampierre's name is there, and so, perhaps, is Aurore's.

Children's laughter brings me back to the present. Right now, sun is streaming through the casement windows and I hear the sound of hooves clattering in the courtyard. My beloved François is home, and I will go and greet him. The linden blossoms will wait.

The End

Author's notes on the history of the tale

For those interested in history, the crusades were a rich tapestry of events. Architecture, science, astrology, religion, stories, and trade suddenly flowed between two civilizations that had been static for many years. Good and evil came from those wars, but one thing is certain; the crusades contributed a great deal to our culture and shaped the world we know.

Real characters in the book:

King Louis IX, or Saint Louis as he is known, was born in 1214. Under his rule, the kingdom of France captured the Maine, Poitou, Normandy, and Anjou. In 1249, he took part in the Seventh Crusade, but he was captured by the Sultan of Egypt. Obliged to buy his freedom, he returned to France in 1254 and vowed to become an exemplary monarch. He built the Saint Chapel in Paris and reorganized the government, instating the fundamentals of parliament. His devotion became legendary during this time, and he gained a reputation of having 'healing hands'. In 1270 he decided to go on the ill-fated Eighth Crusade to Tunis to try and win the Emir of Tunis to his side and to construct a fort from which to attack Egypt. There, he lost his son Jean-Tristan to dysentery. He died soon after. He was canonized in 1297.

His eldest son, Philip, ordered his father's body to be dismembered and the bones boiled and cleaned in order to carry them home. His heart was packed in salt brine.

On the way back to France, Philip's wife Isabella died after falling from a horse. Philip III remarried and ruled a short time before dying from dysentery during a battle in 1285.

Their descendants:

Philip IV, the son of Philip and Isabella, was called Philip the Fair. He is considered France's first 'modern' ruler, as he opposed the pope, separated church and state, and favoured the development of judicial and administrative institutions. He made the role of the parliament and the chancellery stronger. Yet, he wasn't perfect. In need of funds, he turned against the Knights Templar, seized their wealth and had them all burned as heretics. In 1312, the last of the Templars was burned at the stake, accused of witchcraft. As he burned, he cursed Philip and his descendants. He foretold Philip's death within the year, as well as the deaths of his three sons and all their families. He prophesied that Philip's dynasty would end and that France would go to war for one hundred years.

After Philip died, his sons reigned, but they died one after the other. Their sons also died, and the only living member of Philip's family left was his daughter Isabella, married to King Edward II of England. She immediately claimed the crown of France for her son, thus starting the Hundred Years' War. The curse of the Templar had come to pass.

Nearly three hundred years later, Henry IV of Navarre was the first of the Bourbons to rule France. A Protestant, he inherited the throne in 1589, after the three sons of Henry II died without heirs. (Henry IV was married to Henry II's daughter, Marguerite). He converted to Catholicism* and managed to restore peace in

---

* 'Paris is worth a mass', he supposedly said to a friend, before kneeling to convert to Catholicism.

France, ending a bloody war between Catholics and Protestants. A popular king – dashing, handsome and romantic – he was also a shrewd diplomat. Under his reign, France prospered as he introduced silk-making, new agricultural practices, and turned the finances of France over to his minister, Sully. He was assassinated in 1610. His son, Louis XIII, is famous for being the young king depicted in *The Three Musketeers*.

La complainte | Poème de Rutebeuf

Les maux ne savent seuls venir:
Tous ce qui m'était à venir
Est advenu.
Que sont mes amis devenus
Que j'avais de si près tenus
Et tant aimés?
Je crois qu'ils sont trop clair semés:
Ils ne furent pas bien fumés,
Si m'ont failli,
Ces amis-là m'ont bien trahi,
Car, tant que Dieu m'a assailli
En maint côté,
N'en vis un seul en mon logis:
Le vent, je crois, les m'es ôtés.
L'amour est morte:
Ce sont amis que vent emporte,
Et il ventait devant ma porte:
Les emporta.'

Rutebeuf (1230–1285)
Adaptation en français moderne de la Griesche d'Hiver.

Discussion guide for
A Crown in Time

Responsibility, Duty, and Friendship

Sometimes the only thing keeping a person going is a sense of responsibility. When Isobel, the heroine, is sent back to the thirteenth century, she is wracked with guilt and seeks redemption for her act. She believes her path to redemption lies in her mission. Her sense of duty towards that mission is what makes her successful. It's not the education the Time-Senders gave her, although that helped. Mostly, Isobel discovers, what they told her is untrue. All her plans fall apart. The worst things she imagines happen. Nothing goes right. Everything is a disaster, including the harsh century she now is forced to live in. But she does not give up, and every time one plan falls through, she is resilient enough to adapt and make other plans because of her sense of duty and responsibility.

She is not a particularly strong nor brilliant heroine. All she has is her determination to carry her mission to completion. After that, she knows she will be abandoned and left to die in a century she abhors, but she will not give up. Some readers may find Isobel a passive heroine. That would be a poor interpretation of her character. In fact, she has a strength that can move mountains, and it is called a sense of duty. Instead of brilliance, I chose to feature steadfastness.

With Charles's character, I wanted to show the power of friendship. He is Isobel's helper and her beacon in the darkness. When she is depressed, he cheers her up, he offers advice and loyalty. He is sometimes the story's comic relief. He's had a dreadful childhood, but instead of turning bitter, he's developed a wry sense of humour that is at odds with his youth. Without Charles' help, it's doubtful Isobel would have survived, and without Isobel, Charles most likely would have perished. Both need each other, but it is their friendship that sustains them.

Jean's character is rather shallow. His youth, his stubbornness and his arrogance are all recognizable to modern readers. And modern readers will also recognize a certain 'affluenza' affecting him – Jean acts as if nothing can touch him, as if his title and position can protect him from harm. In that century, wealthy people – as in this century – feel protected against fate. But Jean also has his good sides. He truly loves Isobel, he is courteous, he believes in chivalry, and he also intended to marry and protect Isobel. If he had survived the Crusade, he would have come home a wealthy man and gained and important position in the court. He was counting on this – he was ambitious.

François is an enigmatic character. He has lost his son and his wife and he loved both of them. He doesn't know what to make of Isobel at first, but he takes his responsibilities seriously. He will care for and protect Isobel and his granddaughter, but he didn't plan on falling in love with Isobel. In order to fight against his feelings, he makes several trips to Paris for business, but also to put distance between himself and Isobel. He arranges a marriage between a powerful man and his daughter, but he senses his daughter's hesitation and never pushes it. He is a thoughtful person, careful of the feelings of others. He and Isobel are more compatible than Jean and Isobel, but Francois does not want to hurt his daughter, Elaine, and for that reason, he nearly sacrifices his chance at happiness with Isobel.

Questions for a reading group:

1. Isobel was in prison, then was offered a chance to go back in time and spend the rest of her life there. In what way is this an offer of freedom? Is it also a death sentence? Do you feel she deserves this?
2. Isobel accidentally killed a child. In our society, an accident like this doesn't usually end with a lifelong prison sentence. What does this say about Isobel's world? Do you think that children have become rare and precious or have laws become far more severe?
3. We learn little about Isobel's world apart the vague mention of a war and a Great Divide. There is no more fossil fuel, justice is swift and delivered by computer programs, and families are not particularly supportive of members who are incarcerated. But part of Isobel's punishment is to have an ovule removed every month. What does all this tell you? She is also isolated, or there are few people around her. Does this too seem to argue for a world which as been depopulated?
4. When Isobel arrives in the past, she is more healthy, more wealthy, and more educated than nearly anyone living at that time. But without the help of a child of ten (Charles) she would most likely have perished. Do you think you would have been able to survive in that time period?
5. She finds Jean and is unable to sway him. What other argument could she have used?
6. The people of that time were convinced their war was a holy mission. Have people changed much in the centuries that followed?

How does Isobel feel about the crusade, and how do the fighters feel? Were you surprised that families went on Crusade together?

7. Religion is an important part of the story. Isobel's lack of religion was in conflict with the fervour of the people around her, and in the end, she is accused of witchcraft. How could Isobel have avoided that? Was it inevitable?

8. The end is a happy one. Isobel finds a place in the past and seems to have reconciled herself with her life. But she only tells Charles about coming from the future. Would you have done the same? How would François have reacted to the truth?